Natasha,
Enjoy our book!

Lucky Ducky

Maddy Whitman Mystery, Book 2

Monique MacDonald and Carla Howatt

Published by By the Book Publishing, 2024

By the Book Publishing
404, 11716-100 Ave, Edmonton, AB T5K 2G3 Canada
First Edition 2024
ISBN: 978-1-7381486-5-3
Cover design by Kaylee Chiumento

Acknowledgments

We would like to acknowledge and thank Larry MacDonald and May Chouéri. You both are editors extraordinaire. We couldn't see the periods for the forest of commas. Huge gratitude also goes out to our beta readers Tanya Holm and Jennifer Mulder - we couldn't do it without you!

Monique's Dedication

To my aunt May Chouéri, thank you for always being there and taking on the huge challenge of advisor, confidante, and second mother. You get me. I love you Tanti.

Carla's Dedication

To my family and friends who put up with the long hours at my desk, the days spent holed up with Monique as we planned the outline of this novel (and the ones coming up!).

Chapter 1

"**H**ow the heck do they know where I live, Ashley? And why are they following me?" Maddy was not pleased to see a dark SUV again in front of her apartment building. She relayed her displeasure to her friend over the phone. Not only did it follow her, but it also meant that whoever the driver was, they knew where she lived. The tinted windows made it difficult to see who was behind the wheel adding to her frustration and anxiousness.

"What are you talking about, Mads? Who followed you?" asked Ashley Mueller, one of Maddy's best friends.

"That SUV I was telling you about earlier." Maddy pulled into her condominium's underground garage, parked her VW Beetle, Bugsy, and quickly took the stairs two at a time. "I've had it with these dipshidiots, who the hell do they think they are? They're going to get a piece of my mind!"

"Maddy, NO! Maddy? Maddy?"

She had hung up on Ashley and raced out the side door, making a beeline toward the SUV. She still could not make out who they were through the tinted glass, but they certainly had noticed her coming at them like a bat out of hell and took off. Maddy was hopping mad. She grabbed the nearest rental e-scooter, and followed them, rolling as fast as she could on the sidewalk as they hurried west down Jasper Avenue. She quickly caught up to them on account of the slow traffic lights. As she was about to hop off the scooter to confront them, they switched lanes, then took a couple of sharp turns, and sped down the Victoria Road hill. The scooter managed to keep up as it was now using gravity and going full-speed downhill in the shared summer lane. Ignoring the insults of pedestrians she was cutting off, Maddy veered left and followed them across the bridge over the North Saskatchewan River. Unfortunately, the scooter started slowing down as they all headed uphill, passing Hawrelak Park, and motoring toward the University area. Maddy wasn't giving up though; she knew that either a red light or the traffic circle was going to slow them down, then she would be able to catch up. She saw them about five cars ahead turning into the traffic circle. 'Great!' she thought, 'they're going to hit a light soon, and I will be all over them.'

The scooter's battery chose that very moment to die. It was not a sudden death, it was more like a slow, sputtering, agonizing, and drawn-out death. Maddy looked down to see the Dead Battery light flashing. She had just enough juice to pull the scooter up onto the traffic circle. Angry, she jumped off and gave it a kick, lost her balance, and fell flat on her behind. Adding insult to injury, people started honking at her as they drove by, enjoying the sight before them.

"Great, just great! Now I'm these morons' entertainment." Maddy growled as she got up and walked the scooter across the road from the traffic circle. She then sat on a bus bench, fuming over having lost the chance to find out who this stalker was.

How did her day go from a great start to this? It had begun with an early morning auction at the Triple-A Storage facility where she had won an exciting bidding war.

"Two hundred dollars! Do I hear two-fifty? Two-fifty? Anyone for two-fifty? That's quite the deal! This locker here could be filled with lots of hidden treasure, folks!"

A murmur ran through the crowd. People were getting bored and wanted to move on to the next storage unit. Hearing the discontent rising, the auctioneer decided to speed things up.

"Two hundred once...Two hundred twice..."

'Dang it!' Maddy thought, somewhat disappointed. She had not expected the bidding to go higher than two hundred dollars. Maddy spied in a corner what could be a bunch of paintings. There were at least ten large frames stacked on the back left behind a couple of rubber bins. These storage locker auctions could be duds or treasure troves; it was often a gamble. Even if these frames were empty, they could be worth at least a hundred dollars each. She needed to act fast before she lost this bid.

"Two-fifty!" hollered, another bidder.

The bid came from someone standing at the back of the crowd. Maddy could not make out who it was and did not recognize the male voice. She attended these types of auctions around the city and its vicinity once or twice a week to restock her inventory. It was not a bad way to earn a living; buying and selling items from confiscated or abandoned lockers could often be fun and exciting. She would not say it was a huge money-making career choice, but it paid the bills, for now. Her big plan was to eventually have a brick-and-mortar shop where she could sell and store all her purchases. It would be easier than selling them online and much more lucrative. It would also be nicer than working out of the storage locker she rented at Triple-A. One hundred times nicer, in Maddy's opinion.

"Three hundred dollars!" the auctioneer bellowed, startling her.

The latest bid came from one of the other bidders, Zane, a guy with a tattooed sleeve and spiky hair. A regular fixture at these auctions, he had come to her rescue last year when Maddy had been attacked and locked up in a storage unit just like this one. One would not say they had become friends afterward, but they were not strangers either. They were more like occasional colleagues who let each other know if something interesting might be coming up in an auction. They both liked different items and did not compete too often on bids.

They had even put their funds together once or twice over the last year, investing in lockers that might hold items they both wanted and then split them up. And yet here they were, almost a year later, and she still didn't know much about him. People tended to keep to themselves at these gatherings. Nobody was interested in revealing too much about their private lives. These auctions were not social events after all, and Maddy was fine with that.

"Three hundred! Do I hear three-fifty? Three-fifty?" The auctioneer appeared surprised by this last bid. He slowed down some, checking if perhaps there was more interest after all.

"Three hundred going once. Going twice..."

"Four hundred!" bid the male voice from the back.

"Four hundred once... Four hundred twice..."

'Double damn! It was now or never,' Maddy told herself. She had to get in on the bidding or lose those paintings. Might as well put all her money in and see if she stood a chance or if others would outbid her.

"Five hundred Dollars!" she loudly threw in.

This was the maximum she was willing to spend today. If she didn't win, so be it, there were a couple of other units' contents being auctioned off after this one anyway.

"Five hundred! Five hundred! Do I hear Five-fifty? Five-fifty...Anyone bidding five-fifty?" The auctioneer was stretching it now. He was as excited as Maddy was nervous. 'Call it already,' she willed him in her mind.

"Five hundred going once. Five hundred going twice..." He paused for dramatic effect. "This could be a unique treasure trove, folks."

'Great, just what I needed right now,' Maddy grumbled, 'an auctioneer who loves theatrics.'

"Going three times... aaand gone! Sold for five hundred dollars to the lady in the green shirt!" He wrote down the final bid and her name on the sales sheet, signed it, and handed the paper to her.

Maddy had done it. The feeling of exhilaration from winning a bid never grew old for her.

"Well done, Maddy!" Zane said, high-fiving her as he walked by. "I thought for sure that new guy was going to outbid us all."

"New guy?"

"Yeah, he's over there being interrogated by Rod."

Rod was the Triple-A Storage facility's manager and looked like he could be one of Danny DeVito's relatives. His 70-year-old aunt, Shirley, had eloped last year and taken off to Hawaii, leaving the facility and her dog, Engelbert, in Rod's not-so-qualified hands. Sadly, he had inherited Shirley's snoopiness, making everyone's business his own.

"Poor guy. Someone should go and rescue him." Maddy turned around to look at the mystery man. "Whoa..."

"What?"

"Umm... nothing," she replied. That guy was one of the sexiest men she had ever laid eyes on at the Triple-A. Things at the storage auctions were going to get much more exciting if he was going to be a regular fixture. She smiled. It would be fun to have someone new to gossip about with Ashley after an auction day. Antiques and collectibles were a cool subject and all, but variety is the spice of life. 'And,' Maddy thought, 'this variety of spice looks nice, very nice indeed.'

"Maddy? Are you going to bid on the next locker?" Zane's question brought her back from La-la land.

"What? Oh. Umm, no. I blew my budget on this one. You go on ahead without me." It was too easy to keep bidding and win locker contents. The excitement of counterbidding, that pumped-up feeling when you won a bid, those were all addictive highs. Those thrills were the

6

quickest way to lose money in this business. Sticking to her budget and making money were her goals, not losing control and going broke.

"Hope it was worth it. I'm curious to see if those frames leaning behind the bins are decent paintings." He smiled at her.

"You saw them too, hmm? I figured you had. Sorry, but I gotta run! I'll be sure to let you know." She started walking at a quick pace toward Rod and the sexy spice guy, ignoring an unusually chatty Zane. 'What has gotten into him?' she wondered. He was the kind of guy that always stood to the side and kept to himself. Maybe he had an idea of what was in the other lockers and wanted to make sure she was out of the competition. 'Bet that's what it was! Darn it, perhaps I should have been more conservative with this last bid,' she thought. By the time she finally reached Rod, the new guy had left to join the others for the next lot. 'If only Zane hadn't been Mr. Chatty Pants,' she sighed.

"Hey Rod, do you have a minute?"

"Well, hello there Ms. Maddy Whitman," Rod smiled and drew himself tall. Not an easy task when you are five foot nothing. "How can I be of service today? Want to visit Engelbert? He's in his kennel in the office."

"You locked him in his kennel? Poor Bertie."

"Poor Bertie, my eye! He's been humping anyone and anything that comes near him. I can't have him doing that. This here is an upstanding business establishment, you know?"

"Of course, it is. But didn't Shirley tell you he did that once in a while?"

"No, she didn't tell me anything at all about him other than he's an Alberta Special. Special my sweet butt! She just left and forced him on me. Said that he came with the job. And by the way, it's not once in a while, it's every damn day. You just never know who or what might trigger him. I can't deal with that dog. Might have to get a zapper or somethin'."

"You can't zap sweet little Bertie!" Maddy was horrified. "That's cruel, Rod. Try a water gun or spray bottle instead. That's more humane. He's probably just stressed out and misses Shirley."

"Yeah, hadn't thought of that." Rod took his phone out and wrote a reminder to himself. "Any specific type of water gun?"

"Nope, any kind will do the trick. You just want to distract him and make leg humping a negative experience for him."

"Got it. If it's not Engelbert that you wanted to see, then what can I help you with?"

"My locker door has been sticky and noisy lately. Think you could give it a look for me, please?"

"Sure thing. Leave me your key and I'll take a look-see while you settle up with the cashier."

"Thanks Rod, you're my hero."

Rod blushed from ear to ear as Maddy handed him her key. He was so easy to win over.

"Oh, by the way, who's the new guy you were just talking to?"

"His name's Marco something or another," Rod replied, looking slightly disappointed that she'd noticed the new bidder. "He said that he specializes in paintings and works of art. I told him that he's not likely to find a lot of valuable stuff here."

"Rod, did you fib on purpose?" Maddy gave him a knowing look which made him blush an even darker shade.

"What can I say? I want to make sure you guys don't have too much competition. I like a couple of you regulars. You don't just come here and bid; you rent lockers to store stuff too." he sheepishly smiled at her. "Plus, you take the time to chew the fat with me. This guy couldn't wait to get away."

Maddy understood where Marco was coming from. Rod could wear your ears off if you let him. She had had to make up her share of excuses to escape from him.

"Well, I better let you go so you can take a look at my locker."

"Oh yeah, right. See ya in a bit then," and off he went whistling happily away.

'What a character,' Maddy thought. 'Sweet guy but a tad too clingy.'

WITH HER AUCTION WIN paid for, Maddy went to check what treasures her new locker might hold. She hurried to that back corner and started pulling out the paintings.

"BINGO!" she cheered.

They were authentic, not prints or paint-by-number art wannabes. She took a few quick snapshots to send Ashley. Having a friend with an art history degree would come in handy today. While waiting to hear back from her, she carefully transferred the paintings over to her locker. Rod was already there with the door raised open, busy making a big production of oiling it. Only he could make a simple task look like brain surgery.

"Found some good stuff in that locker, eh Maddy?" he asked without looking up.

"I sure hope they turn out to have been worth it," she replied while moving them to the side wall, away from any potential oil spills.

Her phone buzzed. She pulled it out of her back pocket to take a look. Ashley had texted back telling her to bring the paintings home with her. That sounded promising. At least it wasn't a 'Nope, discard them.' Now to go move the rest of the stuff. Maddy hoped the bins would also contain artwork.

"How's it coming along, Rod?" she asked as she scooted by him.

"I'm almost done here." He pointed to the door frame with his chin. "It needed a lotta lubrication. I don't think Aunt Shirley's former handyman kept this place running properly."

"You're truly the best, Rod, definitely the right man for the job," Maddy said as she walked in the direction of the other locker.

"Do you need a hand moving some of them bins over?"

"Nah, that's okay. I don't want to trouble you. There are only six bins anyway. It shouldn't take me too long."

10

"It's no trouble, I'll go grab a trolley from the office and meet you at the locker in five. It'll be faster that way."

Sometimes there were added benefits to 'chewing the fat' with Rod.

This morning had been going great for Maddy, then that dark SUV with tinted windows pulled out behind her from the Triple-A Storage parking lot. She at once noticed the luxury SUV. It had an emblem that only used to be found on sports cars' hoods. Now family-sized vehicles had them too. The world's obsession with owning the best or the most expensive make in existence was getting out of control as far as Maddy was concerned. 'What's up with people?' she thought as she took the ramp onto the Yellowhead Freeway toward her downtown Edmonton condo. Eventually, she forgot all about the show-off SUV and started to sing along to the tunes blaring on the radio. Several songs later she did an automatic shoulder check and looked in the rearview mirror before changing lanes. It appeared that the same SUV was still following her.

"What kind of Oilers' playoff penalty nonsense is this?" Maddy blurted out. She wondered if it could really be following her. That or they too could be heading downtown.

She took advantage of the yellow light at the next intersection and sped through it. She looked in her rearview mirror again and her heart leaped in alarm when she saw the SUV blowing through the red light. She slowed down, it slowed down right behind her. She changed lanes and passed two cars, then changed back into the first lane. So did the SUV. This was getting increasingly suspicious.

Taking the next exit off the freeway, she decided it was time to confirm once and for all if it was tailing her. The vehicle followed her, again. While trying to figure out what to do next, she noticed a Costco coming up at the corner and did a quick turn into its parking lot. Maddy drove down a couple of aisles, then pulled into the perfect hiding spot between an Escalade and a large Ford pickup truck.

She turned down the radio, her eyes darted around the parking lot looking for the SUV. The vehicle was nowhere in sight but how could she be certain it wasn't out there, waiting for her?

After sitting in her car for five minutes she began to doubt her sanity. There was no logical reason for anyone to follow her. That was simply ridiculous. Laughing at her paranoia, she threw her car into reverse and backed out of the stall. All the stress brought on by last year's terrifying experience with a kidnapped woman and a demon mask had unquestionably affected her. She looked back on her morning thus far and realized that some of the elements had been similar to the day she had won a storage unit that contained some serial killer's trophies inside. That is probably what triggered her reaction to the SUV traveling behind her. Today's event was a coincidence, nothing more.

'Yup, you need to get a grip on yourself. No one is following you and life is back to normal so chill out,' she told herself as she drove home. She turned the radio back on and tuned into the local news channel. Her life was going great, her business was growing, and she had wonderful friends around her. It was time to focus on the positive and stop looking for trouble.

That's when the SUV reappeared, parked in front of her building.

Maddy couldn't believe how quickly her morning had changed. Now here she was, sitting on a bus bench staring at that e-scooter

'I should have listened to Ashley and not followed them,' she told herself. 'I'd be sitting on my couch right this moment enjoying a nice, cold drink and listening to a podcast instead of waiting for a stupid bus, sitting on a stupid bench!' Maddy closed her eyes and tried to visualize a positive end to her day. She had started taking meditation classes, but visualizing calmness was not her strength. Her peaceful place often included a glass of wine and food which made her hungry and distracted her from staying calm.

"Your chariot has arrived, Ms. Whitman."

Maddy looked up and saw Ashley waving cutely and calling her over from her car's open window.

"How did you find me?"

"We downloaded that GPS tracker on each other's phones after our last escapade, remember?"

"Oh yeah! Smartest thing we've ever done," Maddy said as she jumped into Ashley's car.

Ashley drove Maddy home and told her in no uncertain terms to stop chasing cars. A promise they both knew would be hard to keep.

Maddy swiped her fob on her condo apartment's front entrance sensor and waited to hear the click before pulling the door open. As she walked into the foyer, a large, dark SUV slowly drove by.

Chapter 2

Maddy sat comfortably on her couch, feet tucked underneath her. An evening at home with her best friend, sipping on a glass of Merlot after an exciting day was simple perfection. Ashley was sitting across from her, researching the paintings and tapping rapidly on her laptop. As Maddy watched her, Ashley's brows came together slowly, and a look of consternation grew on her face.

"What? Did you find any of the paintings? Don't just sit there frowning!"

"Patience Mads, patience. I want to make sure I have the right information. You don't want me to lead you astray, do you?"

"Yeah, yeah, yeah, just tell me if I can retire or not."

"At least one of these might be worth something," Ashley scrolled a bit more. "I don't think it'll be retirement-level worthy though."

"If it can help pay next month's rent then that would be a worthwhile consolation prize."

Ashley worked on her laptop a while longer as Maddy watched her attentively. Whenever she wanted to ask a question, Ashley lifted a finger for her to wait. Finally, her friend spoke.

"Just sent off an email to an acquaintance who's more knowledgeable in this area than me," she told Maddy. "I think the largest painting might be worth something fairly substantial, but I would prefer to run it by him first."

Her laptop dinged within minutes. Ashley looked down and clicked a couple of times.

"It must be your lucky day, Miss Mads. He happens to be in town this week, we're going to meet, and I might even be able to bring him here to see the painting in person."

"Excellent, I knew you'd be the right lady to talk to!" Maddy said happily. "You're simply the best!"

"Better than all the rest!" Ashley raised her wine glass in a toast.

They chatted for a while, discussing their work, Maddy's lack of a social life, and Ashley's busy one. Eventually, the topic turned toward Maddy's long-lost step-grandfather, Rudy 'PopPop' Carmichael, whom she had been getting re-acquainted with.

"How are things going with you and PopPop?"

"Pretty good. I mean, it's kinda weird having someone you were told was dead years ago suddenly come back into your life."

"Like he had risen from the dead?"

"Exactly, but it's been nice to reconnect. He's still pretty angry that my stepfather lied about his death. It couldn't have been easy hearing that your son wanted you out of his life so badly that he was willing to write you off that way," Maddy said.

"What a jerk! So many years wasted. You could have had much-needed family support if your grandfather had been around."

"I know! But I had you and Rick." Maddy smiled thinking of their other best friend. "You know how grateful I am for you both. Anyway, that's all behind us now. We've been catching up on lost time. I have to admit, it's nice to get to know him from an adult's perspective. He's a hoot!"

"You were just a kid the last time you saw him, right? That would have been a few years before we met in high school."

"Yeah, I was around ten years old." Maddy bit her lip. "He was here one day, then dead the other."

"And your parents just told you he died? No explanations? No funeral or anything?" Family members turning on each other was something Ashley despised more than anything.

"Pretty much, I didn't think it was odd at the time. I mean, first of all, I was young, and second, that's just how my family rolled." Maddy shrugged. "All that's in the past though. We're enjoying each other's company now; it's all that matters."

"I'm glad to hear that, hon. If anyone understands family angst it's me. I think it's good for you to have a positive connection with someone from your family, even if it is with a long-thought-dead step-grandfather."

ASHLEY HAD BEEN GONE half an hour when Maddy finally decided to stop being lazy and clean up. She picked up their empty glasses, walked over to the kitchen sink, rinsed them, and placed them on the counter to wash in the morning. With a smile on her face, she reflected on their conversation. Sometimes she lost sight of how important her friendships had been for her over the years.

She shut the lights off in the living room and was heading to bed when her cell phone rang. She just wanted to get some sleep and hoped that whoever was on the other end would make it a quick call.

"Hello?"

"Hi, Maddy? It's Zane, from the storage auctions?"

"Hey Zane, you do realize I know who you are, right?" Maddy laughed. "It's not like I know a whole lot of Zanes."

"Yeah, I guess," he laughed along. "Anyway, I found something today and I thought maybe you could give me a hand with it."

"I will if I can, what is it?"

"I was going through a big box in one of the storage units from the other day, remember the one just west of town in the industrial area?"

"Uh-huh..."

"Lots of garbage, for the most part. I'd been hoping to find some old comics or even a valuable book or something but no such luck."

"Uh-huh..."

"Then I found a puzzle," he said, expecting some kind of reaction from her.

There was silence on both ends of the phone.

"Uh-Huh?" Maddy tried to spur him on. She really wanted to go to bed.

"Which is where you come in."

"You want to know if there's a market for puzzles?" she asked, confused as to why he was calling her about it this late in the evening.

"No," it was Zane's turn to sound confused as to why she would think that. "I'm wondering if you could help me figure it out."

"Oh! I see! What kind of puzzle is it?"

"It's paper."

"No, sheesh," Maddy laughed. "I mean is it a jigsaw puzzle or what?" she clarified.

"I don't know what it's called. There are questions that you need to answer."

"I see. Like a riddle then."

"Maybe. I'm not sure."

"Do you know who the puzzle belonged to?"

"Nope."

"So, you want me to help you answer questions in a puzzle, which might be a riddle, and belonged to an unknown person from an unknown origin?"

"Pretty much."

"Heck yeah! My life is boring at the moment. Count me in," she answered, suddenly awake. "What do I need to do?"

Zane laughed again.

"There are seven clues, and at the bottom, it says 'The answer will point the way to a year's supply.'"

"What the heck? A year's supply? That could be worthwhile. Okay, what's the first clue?"

"There's a bunch of numbers and then a bad poem that goes:

'My first name is the starting post.

and goes from coast to coast.

Because if you want to play

This letter is the way.'

"How many numbers and what are they?" she asked.

"It's two long strings separated by a dash; 53.547968858129664 - 113.52468458835229."

She put her phone on speaker and had him repeat it so she could tap it into her notes app.

"What do you think?" Zane asked after a long pause.

"Just a sec, I'm thinking,"

"Take all the time you need."

The numbers looked very familiar. After thinking about it some more, she started to laugh.

"We're such dopes." She flipped onto another app as she spoke to Zane. "We're not very good treasure hunters if we can't even recognize latitude and longitude directions!"

"Of course! Sheesh..." Zane said. She could imagine him smacking his hand on his forehead.

"It looks like it's a strip mall of some kind," Maddy frowned as she looked closer and zoomed the picture on her phone. "But I'm not sure where to go from here."

"What kind of stores are there?"

"There's a drug store, pizza place, coffee shop, post office, dentist. You know the usual."

"Hmmm, maybe the rhyme hints at something?" Zane suggested."

They both re-read the clue.

"I think we can take the first line at face value; the answer is probably the first letter. Now what goes from 'coast to coast'?"

"But don't the last two lines have anything to add to it, as a clue I mean?" Zane wondered aloud.

"Not sure they add much. 'Because if you want to play, this letter is the way.' Doesn't that just mean we're working on the first clue? The first letter of the word?"

"Maybe, but I'm going to go check out Google Maps. I feel like I'm doing this blind. I'll do the street view so I can see the stores."

"Well, you have fun with that. I was getting ready to call it a day and I'm starting to fade here," Maddy said, closing the app she was using. "I'll take a look at this again tomorrow if you haven't figured it out by then."

"Sure, leave me all alone," Zane teased. "I called you because I'm not good at these types of things; I thought you would help me!"

"Goodbye, Zane."

Maddy laughed at the pouty sound in his voice. This was a whole new side of him she was seeing, a more relaxed and fun Zane rather than Mr. All Business. She kind of liked it.

"Sleep well, Maddy."

Chapter 3

Saturday mornings were meant for something other than vacuuming your apartment. Yet, here she was, doing exactly that. Maddy was out of breath from her exertions when she heard her phone ring. Somehow, while vacuuming laps around her living room, she had misplaced her cell. Thankfully, the caller was phoning again instead of leaving a voicemail. Following the sound of the ringtone, she imagined how much easier it must have been to find your phone back in the days when everyone had landlines attached to a base with limited movement. It did not take too long to find her cell; it had been left lying face down on the kitchen counter.

"Hello!" she answered, too tired to even check who the caller was.

"Good morning hon!" Ashley greeted her. "You sound out of breath. Are you busy?"

"No, not really. I was vacuuming and now am just finishing up my weekend house cleaning, but that's it, why?" she replied, picking up the vacuum and tucking it away in the closet.

"Perfect. I'm sitting here with Jon, the friend I told you about. The one who's an art dealer. He wants to see your painting if that's okay."

"Oh! Like, right now?"

"Yes, why? Is there a problem with that?"

"Umm, no, it's fine; I just need to make myself presentable for company."

"You're always presentable!"

"I'm wearing my Minions pajamas bottom."

"Oh, then yes, we'll take our time getting there."

Maddy quickly put away all the cleaning supplies in her bathroom, changed clothes, and ran a brush through her hair. She didn't think of herself as vain but there was a limit to how casual she was willing to look when meeting a stranger.

Twenty minutes later, her doorbell rang. 'So much for taking their time,' she thought. Looking through the peephole to make sure it was Ashley, her breath caught in her throat; Jon was quite attractive. 'That's two drop-dead gorgeous men in one week!' Maddy thought. Either she had won the jackpot in the running-into-good-looking-men lotto, or she was so out of the loop that all men were starting to look hot. This guy's thick brown hair, piercing blue eyes, and square jaw were only the beginning. She took in the cleft chin and his long, dark eyelashes. Suddenly, she wished she had taken a moment to put on her makeup and spritz some perfume. She patted down her hair, making sure nothing was sticking out, smelled her breath, straightened her T-shirt, and opened the door.

"Hiiii!" she said in a high and, even to her ears, overly excited-sounding voice. "Come in! Come in!"

"Hi hon," Ashley said, giving her a 'what's-up-with-you' look. "Sorry, we're interrupting your Saturday cleaning."

"Oh, no problem at all. My place wasn't even that messy to start with," Maddy said too cheerfully.

"Maddy, I'd like to introduce you to my friend Jon. We met in Europe when I took that university art course my first year after high school."

"Oh yeah, that was the first time you went there." Maddy extended her hand out for him to shake. "Hi, Jon."

He shook her hand and held on to it for what appeared to Maddy to be a bit longer than necessary.

"Good morning Maddy, it's a true pleasure to finally meet you. Ashley used to speak about you constantly." Jon smiled.

"Oh, well. Ha! Ha! I hope you didn't believe half of what she told you," Maddy giggled.

Now Ashley was really giving her an odd look, eyes widening, sending a 'Cool it sister' message. Maddy gave her a 'What?' look right back.

Jon smiled awkwardly as though he wasn't quite certain what else he should be saying. Maddy groaned inwardly, wondering when she would ever grow up and become more confident around men.

"I was telling Jon about those three paintings. I showed him the pictures I took, and he wanted to see the larger one in person to confirm if it's the one he thinks it is," Ashley explained.

"I want to ensure that it is not simply an excellent reproduction," Jon added. "It's difficult to see certain details via a cellular phone's photograph. These other two are not rare pieces, but could still fetch a fair price, even if they turn out to be reproductions," Jon said decisively. "They could interest some collectors of Canadian art who can't afford an original. "

"Oh, alright. I'll take them to local galleries then. I might even take my grandfather along; it would be a good excuse to get together with him. We didn't see each other much for years." She stopped herself. She was rambling on again. It was time to act like a grown woman. "Let me go and grab the larger one," Maddy said as she headed to her bedroom.

She brought the painting in question to the living room and propped it up against the coffee table. The three of them stood there, gazing at it. Jon then leaned in to inspect it more closely. He pulled out his phone and took a picture of its upper left corner where an Egyptian cat was sitting on a ledge, eating a dead mouse. He then did a Google lens search. After several minutes of scrolling, he held his phone up next to the painting. He seemed to be comparing something on his phone with the painting. As they waited, Maddy gazed over him toward Ashley and found her looking back at her, frowning, and shaking her head, as though saying, 'What's gotten into you girl?' Maddy shrugged and raised her eyebrows.

Five whole minutes went by before Jon finally straightened up and sighed.

"What? What's wrong?" Maddy blurted out. "Why the sigh?"

"It's an original painting by Billy Forest," he said. "That's the good news. It's worth around ten to twenty."

Maddy went quiet for a moment, looking quizzically between Jon and Ashley.

"Ten to twenty?" she finally asked.

"Yes, ten to twenty," Jon repeated.

"That's ten to twenty thousand dollars, Maddy," Ashley clarified.

Maddy's face lit up.

"But, please, do not get too excited," Jon continued. "This is where the sigh comes in."

"What do you mean?" Maddy's excitement faded just as quickly as it had appeared.

"It says in this article that it's been reported stolen."

ONCE JON LEFT, MADDY filled two mugs with coffee and handed one to Ashley. They stood in front of the painting, drinking in silence. Ashley finally spoke up, her eyes still glued to the painting.

"Tell me Mads. What was all that weirdness about with Jon when we first got here?"

"He's hot," Maddy replied matter-of-factly, raising her cup to her lips. They stood there for another minute, staring at the painting, then at each other.

"You're going to have to report this, you know?" Ashley remarked.

"His being hot?"

"Maddy..."

"Yeah, I know. I'll go to the station first thing Monday morning."

"How long has it been?"

"Me being around a hot guy?"

"No." Ashley sighed. "How long has it been since you've had to talk to the police?"

Maddy laughed. "A few weeks at least."

In the auction-buying business, especially with goods stored in lockers, you often had to make sure you weren't selling items that may have been stolen. Anything that seemed valuable had to be researched. If it was stolen, then you had to contact the police. If you were honest that is. Maddy chose to be honest. In her experience, it never paid to be sketchy.

"I don't suppose you want to see if Kyle's on shift today?" Maddy asked. She already knew that there was no way in hell Ashley would agree to reach out to their detective friend Kyle.

"Not a chance, I don't want to give him the wrong idea. We're on good and very clear terms right now."

"Yeah, I suppose," Maddy grinned, remembering how hard Ashley had worked to fend off Kyle and his major crush.

"I'll go tomorrow," she finally said. "Right now, I just want to order some pizza."

"Has there ever been a time when you didn't want to order some pizza?

"Nope."

Chapter 4

An incessant knocking on her front door had rudely awakened Maddy. "Who on earth could it be at six in the morning?" she moaned while rolling out of bed. The knocking was getting louder and more urgent.

"I'm coming! I'm coming! Hold your horses. Do you even know what time it is?" She looked through the peephole and saw her upstairs neighbor, Azibo Abebe, getting ready to knock on the door one more time.

"Azibo, what's the emergency?" she said, quickly unlocking the door before other neighbors decided to check out what all the racket was about. "Why are you banging on my door this early?"

"Sorry Maddy, but I'm losing it." Azibo was madly gesturing, as he invited himself into her apartment. "Damn geese have nested on our roof again and their honking is driving me insane. They started at five this morning!" He walked to the window, opened it and looked up through the mosquito screen.

"I didn't hear any honking. I was sleeping. You're the one who woke me up." She walked to the window and looked out. "There's nothing there. Can we please close the window? It's still kinda chilly out there."

He took a step back and let her shut the window. Maddy shivered and grabbed a throw off the armchair, then turned to look at him, hoping he would leave.

"I apologize; I don't know what to do." He turned around and looked toward the kitchen. "Is that coffee I'm smelling? I sure could use a cup. There's no way I'll be able to stay awake at work." Azibo owned a security company and worked various shifts. Maddy had the impression that today was going to be an early one.

"I'm not sure if the coffee is ready. I have it set for six-thirty. I think it's in the bean-grinding mode right now. Sorry."

"Don't worry about it. I'll grab a cup on the way to work. Look, I need your help. We need to get rid of them or do something to get them to stop this cacophony."

"Caco what?"

"Cacophony. You know, horrendous noise?"

"Oh. Okay, but I don't understand why you think I can help. Do you want to add my name to a letter to the condominium board or something?"

"No, I hadn't thought of that. That's a good idea, but it would take forever for them to act. Anyway, you're more easily accessible and I was told that you knew how to deal with Canada Geese."

"What? Who told you that?" Maddy rolled her eyes at the building's active rumor mill.

"Old Mrs. Nakamura. She said you had some issues with geese last year."

"It was one goose, not geese, and it was delivered to my door, in a box, dead. I'm not the condo's resident Canada Goose expert." Maddy wasn't surprised that it came from one of their building's most notorious resident gossips. She had milked information out of sweet but nosy Mrs. Nakamura herself.

"Oh. She didn't tell me that. It must have been terrifying. You should have called me. If you want, I can set up a security camera system for you. This way you can see who comes and goes to your door and have video recordings of all the delivery people too. You would be surprised how it deters people from doing stupid things."

"That won't be necessary, thanks. I'm sure it was a one-off situation. I don't expect any more dead animal deliveries anytime soon." Maddy needed to get back to bed and try to get at least another hour of sleep.

"Look, Azibo, I'm sorry but I can't help you here. Why don't you write to the board like I suggested? Maybe they can do something about it," she walked to the front door and opened it, hoping he would get the hint and go home. This time he got it, but as he was leaving, he repeated once more his offer to set up a security camera system.

"Just in case, Maddy, you never know these days. All these delivery people coming in and out, and nobody watching where they go once in the building."

"Tell you what," Maddy said, "I promise to think about it," and with that she closed the door behind him.

Maddy crawled back into her bed hoping to get a bit more shuteye. She had no such luck. All she did was toss and turn until her alarm went off. At least she knew a hot cup of coffee would be waiting for her before she had to go to the station with the stolen painting.

"UP TO NO GOOD AGAIN, Ms. Whitman?" asked the officer sitting behind the police station's reception desk. Maddy gave him a side-eye look and ignored him as she finished signing the visitor log. He buzzed her in and handed her a visitor's pass.

"Just doing my job, Officer Kowalchuk," she remarked as she passed him. "Unlike a certain officer, I know."

They both knew she was referring to his delayed handling of a murder weapon, less than a year ago. The result of this played a role in slowing down the search for a murderer and saving a kidnapped woman. This all led to Maddy almost getting shot.

"How about letting bygones be bygones, eh? After all, everything turned out okay."

"Let bygones be bygones?!" Maddy stopped dead in her tracks. "You have some nerve, you irresponsible, jack..."

"Maddy!" Kyle interrupted. "So glad you stopped by to see me!" Taking her by the elbow, he quickly guided her away from the desk. "You can't keep getting into arguments with Kowalchuk every time you stop by the station."

"I don't."

"Yeah, you most certainly do."

"I most certainly do not!" she huffed. Then, calming down a bit she sheepishly had to admit it. "Okay, maybe I do. But you have to agree that he had it coming after what happened at the funeral home. Asking me to let bygones be bygones. That dipshidiot jackass!"

"That jackass, as you call him, has paid his dues, Maddy. He had to take disciplinary leave without pay, remember? And it's not like he was the kidnapper or killed anyone. He was slow to process something. He could have gotten away with just a reprimand, you know?"

"Hmph. That slow process is part of the reason I still have nightmares. He should have been kicked off the force."

Maddy sure could hold a grudge. Not that Kyle could blame her. What she had experienced could have caused PTSD in anyone. But he still felt that Kowalchuk had unfairly and wrongly become the one person she laid the blame on for everything she believed had gone wrong with that investigation.

Kyle led her into his office and pulled up a chair for her. "Anyway, you mentioned you thought you might have purchased a stolen painting?"

"Yes. And by the way, thank you for seeing me on such short notice." She sat down and pulled out the painting from a large black garbage bag. "It's a painting by Billy Forest and worth quite a bit of money."

"How much?"

"An art buyer told me it could be worth ten to twenty thousand dollars."

Kyle whistled. "For that thing?"

"Yeah. Beauty's in the eye of the beholder, right?"

"No kidding." He laughed. "Who told you this painting was stolen?"

"Ashley's friend, Jon."

"Jon?"

"Yeah, he deals in valuable artwork. She messaged him and he happened to be in town, so he came over to look at it." Maddy noticed a look of relief on his face. "They're just friends, in case you were wondering."

"I see, and I wasn't." Kyle tried not to look too interested.

"He recognized it, then searched on some website or other. That's when he found out it had been stolen."

"You did the right thing to bring it here. If you had tried to sell it and someone else realized it was stolen, you would have been hard up trying to prove your innocence."

"I figured as much. Dealing with stolen property isn't what I do. I would never put my professional reputation at risk. Anyhow, I thought you would know what to do or how to reach the owner."

"I don't personally look after this kind of stuff, but I'll contact the Property and Exhibit Unit. That's their domain. With a bit of luck, it will turn out that the owner lives in the Edmonton area. That would make it easier to return it to them and would avoid our having to do an international search. That would involve so much red tape." He picked up the painting and gave it a closer look. "Man, this thing is ugly. Anyway, I've had to deal with Interpol on exactly two occasions. Trust me, it's not fun. Unfortunately, they have the only international-level database with certified police information on any stolen or missing works of art or 'objets d'art' as people in the art world, like Ashley and her friend, Jon, would call them."

"I see." Maddy's eyes had started to glaze over.

He put the painting down and looked at her. She had a far-off look.

"Hello." He waved his hand in front of her face.

"Sorry, I missed that."

"I'm boring you, aren't I?"

"Yup. I know I should be interested in all of this information and details, especially because of the stuff I find and all, but that part of it doesn't fascinate me. I prefer the stories behind them, their history, you know?"

"Still the romantic, eh?" He smiled. "Not that I blame you, romance can be nice."

"Don't get me wrong, I also like money. The more, the better."

They both laughed.

"I'll take the painting down to Property and Exhibit, they're on the main floor. Let me walk with you to the lobby, P and E is on the way there."

As they walked down the stairs, Maddy stopped and looked at him, "How come you haven't asked me about Ashley?"

"Why? Was I supposed to?"

"You kinda always bring her up."

"Ashley made it very clear, the last time we spoke, that she only wanted to be friends. I must respect that. I'll be here when she changes her mind. Until then, I need to see other people and distract myself. It's how it has to be."

"I don't buy it, Kyle."

"I don't care whether you buy it or not, Maddy. It's the truth." Kyle started down the stairs again. "It doesn't mean that I've stopped caring about her. I can't. I love her. But I also can't waste my life. What if she never changes her mind? I'll end up a lonely, miserable, old man with lots of what-ifs."

"What do you mean by 'can't waste' your life? Either you're waiting for her or you're not waiting and you're seeing other people. Which one is it, Kyle?" Maddy asked. He increased his pace down the stairs. She hurried down behind him trying hard to catch up. He waited for her at the first-floor landing and opened the door, letting Maddy exit the staircase and enter the hallway ahead of him. They walked a few steps before he stopped and turned to look at her.

"Look, I've been dating someone, okay? Please don't tell Ash. I don't know whether it'll become serious or not. For now, we're only having fun. I need that in my life. Work can't be all I do with my time," he said almost apologetically. "Anyway, this is where I have to leave you. I'll let you know what P and E says." He hugged her and disappeared through a set of double doors marked 'Do Not Enter'.

'Sorry, Kyle,' Maddy thought. 'I'm definitely telling Ashley about your love life. Maybe it will knock some sense into her.'

IT WAS NINE O'CLOCK when Maddy left the station. On her way to pick up PopPop she remembered that she had left one of the paintings at home. They planned to go to a few art galleries together and she wanted to show them all the paintings. She called PopPop as she stepped out of the elevator on her floor.

"Hey sweetheart, is everything okay?" asked Rudy Carmichael, her grandfather.

"Yeah, I'm just running a bit late. I forgot one of the paintings."

"Oh, don't worry about it, take your time and drive safely. Alright?"

"I always do PopPop. You don't have to worry about me... What the hell?" Maddy slowed down as she approached her apartment door, her wide-open apartment door.

"What's wrong? Maddy?"

"I've got to go," she whispered into her phone and hung up, not wanting to alert anyone who might be in her home. She quietly walked in and grabbed her emergency baseball bat kept by the front door. She entered the living room and looked around. It had been turned upside down. The sofa cushions were tossed aside, and books and papers were pulled off the shelves and strewed everywhere. She turned toward the kitchen. There wasn't anyone in that area, but all the cupboards and drawers had been left open, the one that held dishtowels had been emptied and the towels were spread out on the counter. Her gaze went to her bedroom. No sound was coming from that direction, but the door was open, and she could see through it that the dresser drawers were barely hanging on. She at once texted Kyle, 'Someone's broken into my place,' turned her phone to silent mode, and slipped it back into her pocket.

She inched her way toward her bedroom. Something moved, and she stopped dead in her tracks. Was the intruder still in her bedroom? She was going to show them who they were messing with. She ran into her room with the bat over her head ready to strike a home run. Going straight to the moving curtains, she swung as hard as she could, lost her balance, got tangled in the fabric, and landed hard on the floor. Letting out a scream, she scrambled to get up. She thrashed in the curtains until they and the rod fell, almost hitting her on the head. She jumped out of the way and turned quickly around to see if anyone was behind her. The room was empty.

The window was slid open, and a warm breeze was blowing through it. This appeared to have been the cause of the curtains billowing. Maddy hoped that meant that whoever had broken in was gone. She got up and inspected the damage to her bedroom. It had been ransacked. All her clothes had been pulled out of the closet and thrown pell-mell all over the floor. The mattress had been lifted and dropped back down askew. Her underwear drawer had even been emptied.

"My underwear for god's sake!" she yelled angrily. She picked up the rod with curtains still attached and leaned them against the wall, then bent down to pick up the baseball bat. Before she stood up, with her head upside down, she spied through her legs a pair of men's runners still attached to their owner. She quickly stood up and turned around in one swift movement swinging the bat as hard as she could.

"IT'S ME! WHAT THE HELL?" Kyle had barely had the time to lean toward his right as the bat swooshed past his head and grazed his shoulder, knocking him onto the bed.

"Kyle? You scared the living daylights out of me!" Maddy cried out.

"I scared the living daylights out of you? You scared the hell out of me!" he yelled as he got up. "What were you thinking?"

"I was thinking that some crazy person was still in my apartment, that's what!" She sat down on the edge of the bed, shaking. "Why didn't you say you were here?"

"I didn't want to give the intruder a heads up in case they were still in here."

Kyle sat next to her and put his arm around her just as the mattress toppled over and they both landed in a tangle on the floor.

"You okay kiddo?" Kyle asked as he gave her a hand to get up.

"Yeah, I am now. Just shaken up a bit. What are you doing here?"

"You texted me that someone had broken in. I was going by on my way to an investigation site when I got your message. Obviously, you didn't get my reply."

"What reply?"

"The one that said, 'Get out, now!'" He shook his head.

"I put my phone on 'Silent' so as not to reveal myself to the intruder."

"Maddy, will you never learn?"

"Someone broke into MY home!" she sobbed.

"Okay, okay, I know how upsetting this can be," he walked her out of the bedroom, set the pillows back on the couch, and sat down with her. There was a knock at her door. Rudy's head popped in.

"Maddy, are you home? Are you okay?"

"I'm here PopPop. I'm fine. Kyle's with me."

"What happened here?" Rudy looked around. "It looks like a tornado came through your place! Do you need help tidying up?"

"I think, Rudy, that you two should leave things as they are until Maddy can file a police report. I'll message someone to come." Kyle got up and went out into the building's hallway.

"What are you doing here, PopPop?"

"You left me no choice, after the way you hung up the phone," he hugged her.

"Thank you. I love you so much."

"I love you too, Madsy."

"Alright," Kyle said as he walked back into Maddy's apartment. "Someone will be by very soon to take your statement. Do a walkthrough and check if anything is missing. Make a list of items and give it to the constable." He turned to Rudy.

"Are you going to stay with her? I need to go to do an investigation."

"Yes, yes, I'm not leaving her."

"I'll be fine, Kyle, thank you for everything." Maddy stood up and hugged him. Kyle winced. "I hurt your shoulder, didn't I? I'm so sorry."

"Nothing's broken, slugger. Just a bad bruise. I'll check on you later with the info on that painting, okay?"

"Oh, yeah, the painting. I almost forgot about it!"

She walked Kyle to the door and quickly went to look for the painting. It was still there, behind her laundry room door which was more the size of a closet than an actual room. It was the only storage space she had available to put the paintings. That is probably why the intruder had missed it if that is what they had broken in for. She and Rudy did an inventory. Not a single thing had been stolen, not even her jewelry. The police constable came, took Maddy's report, and checked her front door locks for any signs of break-and-enter. There were none. She asked Maddy if she was certain she had locked her door. Maddy hesitated. She wasn't sure. She'd been carrying that painting. She remembered pulling the door shut behind her.

"Oh damn, I didn't lock it because my hands were full," she said. "I was going to put the painting down and use my keys to lock the door, but I didn't. I pulled the door hard with my foot. I remember now, being glad that it had closed because of the wind pressure from the open windows." Maddy smacked her head with her hand. "I'm the one who left the windows open."

"It would appear that the intruder had easy access entering your apartment then. Count yourself lucky your door wasn't damaged," the constable said. "That's an expensive repair."

"That's one way of looking at it," Rudy grumbled.

"I'll enter your report as a 'Break and Enter' in the system, but without any witnesses," the constable added. "Or anything stolen. I don't expect much to come out of it, unfortunately, unless there's another similar break-in in the neighborhood."

"Aren't you going to dust for fingerprints or anything?" Maddy asked.

"We only dust for fingerprints if anything is stolen or if your door is broken or damaged to get entry into your home," she replied. "Here's my card. If you do notice anything missing, don't hesitate to give me a call. And please, always lock your door. You were lucky this time."

After the constable left, Maddy and Rudy did a quick tidying up.

"Are you sure you still want to go out?" Rudy asked.

"Yeah, I need a change of scenery. Anyway, nothing was stolen. I think they probably broke into the wrong apartment. I never keep any valuables or store stuff worth much here." She picked up the forgotten painting. "Plus, I need to sell these babies."

"Alright then, but lunch is on me," Rudy said, taking the painting from her. "Let's get this baby on the road!"

Chapter 5

"This place makes the juiciest burgers ever!" Rudy exclaimed, wiping his mouth for the tenth time. "I can't believe I've never heard of it before."

They had finished conducting their art reconnaissance outing. She thought maybe she could chat with some of the owners, put feelers out, and ask if they knew the artists of the other paintings she had purchased. Perhaps they might even be interested in buying a couple for their gallery.

Their first stop was not as successful as she had hoped. They sold Canadian art, the gallery owner had explained, but only by Indigenous artists. Maddy did not come out empty-handed though. The owner knew of one of the artists and was able to give her an approximate value for that painting. Not only that, but he also offered to buy it from her for his personal collection if she couldn't find a buyer, at a reduced price, of course. She thanked him and told him she would get back to him if she couldn't find another buyer. Because he knew who the artist was, and he wanted to buy it, she figured that it was probably going to sell for more than what he offered. Maddy might not know much about art yet, but she was no fool.

Their second gallery stop gave them the names of the other artists, but they weren't interested in buying them or putting them on consignment. The third gallery owner purchased the painting the first gallery wanted and another without haggling. Maddy only had to provide the auction sale slip, which she knew to bring with her.

She still had more paintings to try and sell, but their growling stomachs demanded a lunch break, and the smell of grilling burgers was in the air. It was hard to resist the aroma wafting over from Woodshed Burgers which was up the block from the last gallery they had visited. PopPop did not need any convincing.

"It's not my favorite burger spot for nothing," Maddy told him, slurping the last bit of Strawberry Sunshine shake from her cup.

"I'm glad the last gallery showed some interest in two of your paintings," Rudy said between bites.

"Yeah, lunch with you and two sales on the same day." She smiled. "You're my lucky charm."

"I wish we hadn't lost so much precious time being apart, you know Maddy?" he sighed.

"It wasn't your fault, PopPop." She reached for his hand. "If my jerk of a stepfather hadn't lied to the both of us, it would never have happened. But we're making up for lost time now, right?"

"You betcha, sweetie pie!" Rudy smiled at her. "How he turned out the way he did, I'll never understand."

Maddy could see how much spending time together meant to him. And it meant the world to her too.

"We have so much to catch up on," Rudy added. "Like, what's your favorite color for starters?"

"My favorite color?" She laughed. "Lime green. Yours?"

"Purple."

"Purple? Like the 'Flying Purple People Eater' or Prince's 'Purple Rain'?" She winked at him.

"Haha! More like Prince. It's not just any purple, it has to be royal purple. That's an elegant color."

"But of course, only royal will do." This was fun. Maddy liked having a grandfather around again. Their friendly ribbing was interrupted by her cell phone vibrating. It was a text from Zane about that puzzle hunt he was obsessed with.

"Sorry about that PopPop. It's my friend, Zane. He found this puzzle, and has his mind set on figuring it out and winning the prize."

"A puzzle?" He straightened up in his seat. "I love puzzles!"

"He's asking for help with one of the clues. It's the first one. He's been stuck on it since last night."

"Read it to me, please. I might be able to help. I'm pretty good at that sort of thing."

"Why am I not surprised?" She brought up Zane's text. There's no guarantee that there's an actual treasure. Okay, here goes:

'- 53.547968858129664, -113.52468458835229

My first name is the starting post.

and goes from coast to coast.

Because if you want to play

This letter is the way.'

She looked up to find Rudy concentrating with his eyes closed.

"We figured the first hint was a location, like the latitude and longitude."

"That makes sense. Did you look it up?"

"Zane said that it was a strip mall with various shops."

"Can you pull it up on your phone?" he asked eagerly.

"Sure." Maddy typed the location on the map app, and the strip mall came up. "Here you go," she handed him her cell.

"'My first name is the start, and it plays an important part...'" he repeated the first half of the clue, concentrating on each word. Rudy started scrolling around the strip mall photo. "There's a smoke shop called Pipes, a Rexall drugstore, a Child First daycare, and the Post Office."

"Yeah, we looked at it last night and nothing jumped out at us," Maddy explained. "It makes no..."

"Aha!" he interrupted. "I got it!" There was quite a satisfied grin on his face.

"What is it? Tell me, tell me." It was Maddy's turn to sit up in her chair. His excitement was contagious.

"The hint says it right there. It's staring us right in the face."

"PopPop, please don't make me beg."

"Okay, okay." He laughed. "'Because if you want to play this letter is the way.'"

Maddy looked confused.

"Letter... Where do you mail letters?" Rudy asked, raising an eyebrow.

"Oh! I get it now." She looked at the phone. "So, the clue to the puzzle is at the post office. But where?"

"Not sure." He furrowed his brow. "The name could be part of the answer, or perhaps the first letter, being 'the start'. Maybe it starts with 'C'?"

"C?"

"Yes, Canada Post starts with 'C' and 'Starting post.' Easy as pie."

"PopPop, you are brilliant. I'm going to call Zane right now and tell him." She dialed his number.

Rudy sat back, quite pleased with himself, as he listened to Maddy explain his reasoning to her friend.

"It's SO obvious now that we have the answer, isn't it?" she asked Zane.

"Your grandfather is a genius! Tell him to be expecting us to reach out again for his help." Rudy's smile stretched from ear to ear, as he overheard Zane's comment.

"He heard you. I think he's as excited about this treasure hunt as you are. Hey, I have to let you go, there's another call coming in."

Maddy hung up and looked to see who was calling her. It was Kyle.

"Sorry PopPop, I have to take this call. It's my friend Kyle from the police station."

"The police station? Is it about the break-in?"

"Maybe, or it could be about one of my paintings. He's just looking into it for me. It seems to have been stolen from someone."

"Oh, well, of course, it's important. You must take it. You sure live an exciting life sweetheart."

"Too exciting sometimes," she said before answering. "Hi, Kyle."

"Hi Maddy, I heard back from the Property and Exhibit Unit."

"Great, and did they find out anything about the owner? Was it truly stolen?"

"They did, and it was," Kyle replied. "Stolen, that is, from an art collector right here in Edmonton. There was a string of art thefts in the city a year ago. It was one of the works taken from an upscale neighborhood."

"So where do we go from here? Do I need to come down to the station to meet him or do the police deal with the owner going forward?" Maddy asked.

"A bit of both," Kyle replied.

"What do you mean?"

"The owner has to come down to the station, show his I.D., and sign a release form. Then we give him his painting. You don't have to come to the station."

"Okay, I don't follow. Where do I come into this?"

"There's a $2,000 reward for the return of the painting."

"A reward! Why didn't you start with that tidbit instead of your long story?" Maddy looked up at Rudy, excitement written all over her face.

"This was way more fun." Kyle laughed. "You're always doing this to me, so it's kind of payback."

"What do I need to do to get the reward?" she eagerly asked.

"I'll give you his name and number. He already has your name. All you have to do is call him and make arrangements to meet with him."

"Perfect. Thank you so much, Kyle. This money couldn't have come at a better time."

Maddy pulled out a pen and wrote the name and number on a napkin.

"Let me repeat that." She repeated the phone number, then the name. "That's George Biskoff, one 'K' and two 'F's'. Got it. Thank you so much, Kyle! Talk to you soon."

"PopPop, can you believe it? There was a $2,000 reward!" Maddy's face was lit up like a Christmas tree.

Rudy leaned forward, "Did you say 'George Biskoff'?"

"Yeah, do you know him?"

"It's possible. I knew a George Biskoff in college. He was my best friend. We lost touch after he went to British Columbia, to get his MBA."

"You seem to have bad luck keeping in touch with people."

"That's because there was no social media back then. We both moved around at the same time and never had each other's new addresses."

"I guess that's one of the good things about social media. I better call him right away and go get my reward before he changes his mind."

"Are you sure that you're up to more running around after this morning's events?"

"What events?" Maddy gave him an innocent, wide-eyed look.

"You know very well what events."

"Nothing was taken, PopPop. Whoever broke into my place saw that I had nothing worth stealing. Heck, even my cheap jewelry didn't appeal to them. I'm quite certain they're not coming back. I feel pretty safe. I was just momentarily shaken up, that's all."

"That's my Madsy! Great attitude," Rudy smiled and tried to fist-bump her, failing miserably. "Hey, would it be okay if I tagged along with you when you go get your reward? I'd love to see my old buddy again."

"Of course, you can. It will be fun to see you two guys reunite."

Chapter 6

"How did George sound when you spoke with him? Does he remember me? Was he happy that I was coming along?" Rudy was as anxious as a teenager getting ready for his first date.

"PopPop, I told you twice already," Maddy answered, trying to concentrate on the road. She did not like taking Whitemud Drive but this freeway was the fastest way to get to George's place by car. "He was very excited and grateful that I'd found his painting."

"But what did he say about seeing me? It's been so long. He remembered me, right?"

"Yes, George remembers you. You're pretty hard to forget," Maddy teased. "He can't wait to see you. Said that you used to be the absolute best of friends and that he misses you very very much. He also said that he couldn't wait to give you a great big bear hug."

"George used to give the tightest of bear hugs. Didn't matter who you were. He hugged you, and hugged you hard."

"Thanks for the warning."

Rudy remained quiet for the rest of the drive, deep in thought. It took another twenty minutes to finally arrive at their destination. It was one of those large stone houses people might call a mansion. The house was quite beautiful but too big, in Maddy's opinion, for only one person to be living in. She could get lost for days in such a place. They slowly pulled up onto a U-shaped driveway that curved in front of the entryway. Maddy was not sure where to park so they just left the car at the door. Rudy almost jumped out of the car. She had never seen him move so fast and picked up the pace to catch up. He had rung the doorbell and was straightening up his coat and smoothing his hair when she reached him. A man in a conservative suit opened the door. He looked to be in his forties, too young to be George.

"Good afternoon, may I help you?" he asked them.

"You're not George. Where's George?" demanded Rudy, trying to look over the man's shoulders.

"Pardon me?"

"Forgive my grandfather's exuberance," Maddy said, trying to show that they did have a semblance of manners. "We're here to see George Biskoff. I'm Maddy Whitman, and this excited gentleman is Rudy Carmichael. Mr. Biskoff is expecting us."

"Of course, my apologies. Please do come in." He stepped aside to let them enter. "My name is Bradley. I'm Mr. Biskoff's assistant. If you don't mind following me, he's waiting for you in his study." He escorted them through a wide hallway lined with a multitude of paintings on the walls, so much so that it could easily be mistaken for an art gallery. At the far end of it, he stopped in front of an ornate oak paneled door and turned to Maddy.

"Might I please have your car keys, Miss? I need to park your vehicle in the underground garage."

"Oh, okay. Here you go." She pulled her keys out of her pocket and handed them to him, feeling oddly embarrassed. 'Of course,' she thought to herself, 'such a house would have underground parking.'

"Thank you. If you don't mind waiting here for a moment while I let Mr. Biskoff know that you've arrived." He knocked on the door before opening it, and disappeared inside, closing the door behind him.

"WOW! PopPop, you didn't tell me your friend was loaded."

"I had no idea. He wasn't when I met him in college. He's obviously done well for himself over the years." Rudy said, admiring the painting in front of him.

The door opened again, and Bradley gestured for them to enter.

"Mr. Biskoff is ready to see you now."

"Enough with the formalities, Bradley!" a voice roared joyously behind him. "This is one of my dearest, long-lost friends who's finally coming back into my life!" George rushed toward them. "Rudy! You big lug, come here. Come here, come here! Let me give you a hug."

"George! You son of a gun! Look at you, you haven't changed a bit," exclaimed Rudy, arms wide open, more than happy to give as good a hug as he was about to get.

Both men hugged and patted each other on the back. George then stepped back and smiled at Maddy.

"And you, young lady, must be his beautiful granddaughter. I would like to hug you, but Bradley here has informed me that I must ask permission first. Therefore, may I hug you?"

"Of course, but gently, please. I bruise easily," she quickly added after seeing the tight grip the old men had given each other.

George laughed and gave her a gentle yet still-strong hug. Rudy was right. That man certainly liked bear hugs.

"Please, come, sit down." He waved them toward two oversized couches on either side of a huge glass wall, framing an incredible view of an uninhabited bend in the North Saskatchewan River. George smiled at seeing them admire the view. He then turned and nodded to Bradley, who took his cue and quietly left the room.

"You have such a beautiful home, and this view is unbelievable," gushed Maddy.

"It's not as beautiful as the one my last house had. My wife got that one in the divorce," George lamented.

"You married Stella? And then divorced her? But she was wonderful! You were made for each other." Rudy was shocked by this friend's revelation.

"Yes, and no. I did marry Stella." He looked at Maddy and clarified. "She was my college sweetheart, the love of my life, and first wife." He then turned to Rudy. "She died of cancer when she was only 26. We learned she had it when we were trying to have kids and couldn't."

"What a great loss." Rudy frowned. "She was such a sweet woman."

"That she was," George answered wistfully. "Then I married an older woman, Giovanna. Feisty Italian gal."

"I know the type," Maddy commented, thinking of Tasha, Rick's wife. She was one feisty lady.

Both men quizzically looked at her.

"Sorry, thinking out loud. Ignore me. Please, George, do continue."

"It was both our second go around at marriage. She already had two kids, so we never had any. She left me four years later to go back to her first husband. She was quite rich. I sued her and got a mighty nice settlement."

"But she kept the house? Being rich and all?" Maddy's curiosity was piqued. She was a sucker for all heart-related matters.

"No, that was my third wife."

"Third wife? Good old George, you always liked the ladies but never had much luck with them." Ruddy gave him a sympathetic look. Then looked at Maddy and explained, "George always looked like Ricardo Montalban. The ladies loved that."

"Ricardo who?"

"A famous, suave-looking actor back in the day. Never mind, you're too young to know about him. Anyway, George here was a good-looking guy, and the ladies couldn't resist him. Unfortunately, he didn't pick the nicest ones, until Stella came along, that is. She was one of a kind. He had no luck with any others before her."

"No luck whatsoever. That's never changed," George sighed. "My third wife was Jennifer. She fooled around on me so many times that my head's still spinning today. I bet she even had an affair with good old Bradley here," he said, waving his finger toward his assistant who had re-entered the room, carrying a tray of tea and pastries. Bradley just raised an eyebrow at George.

"Okay, maybe before she brought him to work for me. Afterward, not sure," he added with a sly grin.

Bradley closed his eyes and slightly shook his head. It appeared not to be the first time he had heard this accusation. "I will be in my office doing some paperwork for the foundation. If you need me for anything else, sir, or when your guests are ready to leave, please buzz me, and I will bring their car around."

"Thank you, Bradley," George replied.

Once his assistant had left the room, George continued his story.

"Bradley is extremely loyal. I can trust him with anything. My ex-wife, not so much. If anything did happen, it would be because she had made herself impossible to resist." He poured each of them a cup of tea. "Bradley is helping me with a foundation I started, I would like to build a children's art gallery. I believe the earlier you expose children to art, the more they'll grow to appreciate it as adults. It's my legacy, my way of giving to children since I never did have any of my own." He placed the teapot back down on the tray. "Please help yourselves to cream and sugar, and some pastries too, they're quite tasty."

"You shouldn't have troubled yourself on our account, George," Rudy remarked, putting a couple of lemon squares on his plate.

"I slaved over a hot stove for ya old buddy," George replied dramatically.

They both laughed like it was the wittiest remark anyone had ever come up with. Rudy looked at Maddy, who stood there like a mom dealing with two 12-year-old boys, and explained that it was an old inside joke from when they were roommates. She was not sure it would have been funny even back then and told them so. Both men just shrugged and laughed even harder.

"We both had a serious aversion to cooking back in our bachelor days." He gave George a conspiratorial look.

She just nodded. They were enjoying their reunion. It was as if they had only been apart for days, not decades. She wondered if her friendship with Ashley and Rick would have survived such a long separation. Of course, it would. She knew one hundred percent it would. She looked up at George and saw that he and PopPop were still laughing at their inside joke. This made her like George even more. PopPop needed a friend like George in his life. Everyone needed a George.

"That foundation is such a generous thing for you to set up," Maddy said.

"Bah, it's nothing. It's my way to contribute to society," he replied. "It's the least I can do while using up oxygen on this planet."

Maddy was not trying to butter him up, she was honestly impressed. So many people with money only want to make more money, not help others. This giant of a man appeared to have a teddy bear's heart. 'Kind of like PopPop's,' she thought. These men were remarkably similar. She had a feeling that this reunion would lead to all sorts of fun shenanigans for these two. Well, she hoped they would be fun. She had read about seniors getting in so much trouble for not behaving their age. Somehow, she feared this would be them. 'Lucky me.' She laughed at the thought.

"You're a good man, George." Rudy was proud of his friend. Not wanting to embarrass him more, he brought the subject back to his ex. "So, it was Jennifer who got your old house?"

"Yes. She left me for a younger man, Evan, or Fabio, or some other fancy-named guy. Jennifer is 30 years younger than me and an energetic beauty, if you know what I mean, wink-wink-nudge-nudge." He winked at Rudy. They both guffawed again.

"Unfortunately, I just couldn't keep up with her. She got bored and left me."

"Those young ones usually do after a while." Rudy agreed. "What? Why are you looking at me like that, Maddy? There's more to me than being your PopPop, you know?"

"Apparently," she replied, praying that he wouldn't get into those details in front of her.

George bent over in laughter and slapped his knees, "Your grandfather was quite the Romeo in his time. The ladies couldn't resist him. I'm sure that's still the case!"

'Oh, no, no, no don't go there,' she mentally repeated over and over. There were things Maddy preferred not to know or imagine. Geriatric sex was one of them. She redirected the conversation back to Jennifer.

"I guess your ex-wife had a good lawyer."

"The best my money could buy," George laughed again. "She took almost half of my art collection, plus a darn good alimony." He got up to stretch his legs. George looked a bit stiff and achy. "You know, I still love her. After her lover left her, we struck up a friendship again. Nothing romantic, mind you. Although, I wouldn't have minded. She's slowly giving me back my art collection. Piece by piece."

"That sounds very nice, but what's in it for her? Why would she do that now?" Rudy asked.

"She's bored. So, she started this game, you see." He walked to his desk and took out what looked like a letter. "Jennifer holds one collection at a time for ransom."

"For ransom?" Maddy was finding this friendship with his ex to be a bit quirky. Curiosity got the better of her. She needed to know more about these two. Was there hope or was she using poor old George?

"It's only fair that I give her money for them. After all, she did get them as part of the divorce settlement," he explained. "I would prefer she got their market value from me than from another collector. They were part of my prized collection, and I miss them something bad. Especially the collection she's ransoming now. It's my favorite one."

"Why not just sell them all back to you then? Why play games?" Maddy didn't understand.

"He did say that Jennifer was bored," Rudy pointed out. "I bet you're bored too, George, am I right?"

"Nothing escapes you, Rudy. Still sharp as a tack. You should have gone to business school with me. We would have conquered the world together, I tell ya. Maybe it's not too late. Let's talk more later." George sat back down. "Anyway, Jennifer and I both love treasure hunts. We even took part in an around-the-world one where we traveled from country to country, collecting clues and such. It seemed pretty natural to have some fun together now that we were on speaking terms again."

"Maddy and one of her friends, Zeke, or Zach, or something like that, are on a treasure hunt these days too."

"It's not quite the same thing, PopPop. I'm pretty sure Zane's prize isn't worth as much as this art collection. George, I have to say, forgiving her is very big of you." Maddy was impressed by his attitude. "When it comes to exes, I'm certainly not as forgiving."

"Bah! Life's too short to stay angry just for the principle of it. And it's certainly too short not to have fun when you can. Right, Rudy?"

"Right, George. You haven't changed. Boy, am I glad that we've found each other again."

"Me too, old friend, me too. Here's one of the ransom notes she wrote me." George handed it to Rudy. "Every week, she sends me one. It gives me hints at the location where I can find the next piece. I go there, drop off an envelope with the money, and pick up a package that contains the artwork."

"But what if someone intercepts the letter and finds it instead of you?" Maddy asked.

"The hints only make sense to us. Nobody else would get them. Read it to her, Rudy."

Rudy pulled his reading glasses out of his pocket and placed them on his nose. He cleared his throat and began reading.

'To find your sweet baby,

You will have to duck.

Perhaps under the willow tree?

The same as where you proposed to me.

If you are not there at the time we wed,

Then your precious will lose its head.'

"I see what you mean," Rudy agreed, folding his glasses and replacing them in his pocket. "Only the two of you would know the location of that tree and the time you were married."

"If they are all as specific as this one, then, yeah, I guess that it would be hard for anyone else to figure it out," Maddy conceded.

"And they are. I love her play on words too. She's got one great sense of humor. All this flirting and mentions of places that matter to both of us are encouraging. Perhaps she'll fall back in love with me." George looked so hopeful.

"You never know." Maddy had never met this Jennifer, but she doubted that love had anything to do with this game. It was likely all about the money. But who was she to burst his bubble? "Love acts in mysterious ways" she added, not wanting to hurt his feelings.

"How many more collections of yours does she have?" asked Rudy.

"Three more large collections. This one has 12 pieces. I already got two from it back."

"You have quite an extensive collection. I recognized a Monet and one of Picasso's sketches," Rudy observed. "Maddy has started buying and selling paintings, amongst other things," he added proudly. "Maybe you could teach her a thing or two about art. It might help her figure out if the pieces she purchases are worth anything."

"PopPop, that's not exactly what I do, and besides, I wouldn't want to bother George."

"It wouldn't be a bother! You found my stolen Forest after all. It's the least I can do."

"That's so kind of you." That was so nice of him. She could use all the help she could get in the art field. Maddy hated to always be bothering Ashley. This way, perhaps, she could alternate between the two. Ashley was a terribly busy woman but never refused to help her. This would give her friend a break.

"Please tell me, Maddy. Is the painting in good condition?" George asked. "I'm worried that it could have been damaged. Being stored in a locker is terrible for paintings."

"I'm not knowledgeable about such things. It looked alright to me," Maddy honestly replied. "Ashley and her friend Jon didn't comment on its condition. I presume it means it's okay."

"That's a relief," George said. He then smiled and his face lit up. "Would you like to see the two pieces I have from the collection Jennifer's holding for ransom right now?"

"I would love to!" Maddy exclaimed.

"Who's the artist?" Rudy wanted to know.

"Spencer," George replied.

"Mitchell Spencer?" Rudy whistled in admiration.

"The one and only. This collection cost me a bundle. They're very rare and hard to come by. Nobody wants to part with theirs," George explained.

"Were they part of his earlier works or his less modern period?" asked Rudy.

"Earlier work. That's why they're so special to me." George smiled.

"You've heard about him, PopPop?" Maddy had never heard of this artist before.

"You bet I have. I love art! Mitchell Spencer was a huge deal when we were in college. He was way ahead of his time. Kind of like a Canadian Andy Warhol, if you like." Rudy turned to George. "Now I'm excited to see them!"

Maddy made a mental note to research this artist. She had so much to learn about artwork. Especially since as of late she was finding more of it in the lockers she was buying.

"These are exquisite. The colors are so bright. Their shape is so well-defined and smooth. They look almost too delicate to touch," George described them like a proud papa.

"Now, you've made me very curious about them. Please, show us. They sound incredibly beautiful," Maddy was thrilled to see such unique pieces of art. She couldn't wait to tell Ashley about them. She was certain that she had heard about Mitchell Spencer and would be extremely jealous. For once Maddy would have seen some art that Ashley hadn't. This added to her giddiness.

"Alright, give me a minute. They're in the side room here. Oh, and here's your reward for finding my painting. Thanks again, my dear." George took an envelope out of his pocket and handed it to her. He then walked over to a door next to a mahogany bookshelf. He punched in a code on the numbered lock. They heard a click. He opened the door and entered the other room.

"If they're part of the collection I think they are, you're in for a treat," Rudy whispered to Maddy. "You're going to love them."

After two or three minutes, George reappeared wheeling an elaborate box on a high trolley.

"It's temperature and humidity controlled," he explained. "You can't take any risks with these rare pieces." He pulled out a pair of white cotton gloves and solemnly slipped them on. "If you want to touch them, I have another pair for you." He handed Maddy a pair of identical gloves.

She carefully put them on. The anticipation was killing her.

With a flourish, he opened the case as Rudy and Maddy looked in, expectantly.

Rudy, who had been holding his breath this whole time, exhaled with an "Oh, it is them!"

Maddy, stepping closer to get a better look, was taken aback by what was sitting on the velvet lining, staring blankly back at her.

"Are those... Umm... Are they... rubber duckies?"

Chapter 7

The two men froze; their faces were two identical masks of shock.

"What did you say?" they asked in unison.

"Umm... I asked if they were... Umm... rubber duckies?" By now Maddy had realized her faux pas and tried to downplay it with a small giggle.

"They most assuredly are not rubber duckies!" George exclaimed indignantly. "They're one of the most famous series that Mitchell Spencer has ever created."

"Of course they are, I'm so sorry. I don't often come across valuable modern art in my line of work," Maddy said sheepishly, cheeks blushing.

Rudy tried to move past his granddaughter's mistake by engaging George in more conversation about the ducks.

"What are they made out of George?" The two men were soon deep in conversation and wandered away from Maddy to sit on the couch.

"Spencer used paper mâché, shaped and sculpted them, then painted the ducks and dipped them in an acrylic plastic mixture to give them that shine and lustrous look..."

Maddy quietly followed, sitting opposite them in one of the overstuffed leather chairs. She looked around the room. It was quite opulent. She appreciated the deep mahogany floor-to-ceiling bookcases filled with gilded hardcover books. There was a beautiful desk against one wall. Old furniture was her thing, Maddy could have sworn it was an authentic antique desk from the late 1800s. It had a distinctive design with pedestal legs and a hutch-style ornate top. The cupboard-like doors were open, and she could see a multitude of drawers and cubby holes. She would have to ask Ashley what style this was or try to take a picture without anyone noticing, and then do an Internet search. Her eyes wandered to the large windows in the room, bordered by thick, heavy curtains and held back by tassels. Maddy was in awe. She had only seen such extravagant rooms in movies and TV shows.

She heard someone call her name. Maddy turned to see that the two men were looking at her expectantly.

"Oh, I'm sorry, I was just admiring your desk," Maddy said. "It's exquisite."

"You have good taste, my dear. It's a Wooton desk." George beamed as he looked at the desk. Pride was as plain on his face as if he were introducing his genius child. "This particular one dates back to 1879. One year before William Wooton stopped making them."

"George was telling me that he has only retrieved two of the ducks to date," Rudy told his granddaughter.

"So, you have lots of fun ahead of you." Maddy smiled at their host.

"Well, I'm afraid that isn't quite accurate my dear." George frowned and looked disappointed.

"Unfortunately, George requires a medical procedure on his hip and he's unable to pick up the next duck," Rudy explained to Maddy.

"Why don't you just tell your ex that you're having surgery and can't? Maybe she'd be willing to postpone the pick-up date."

George looked uncomfortable; his eyes lowered to the hardwood floors.

"Jennifer is considerably younger than me. I'd rather not highlight our age difference at this point."

Realization dawned on Maddy. George truly did hold out hope of a reconciliation with his much younger ex-wife. If she found out he was having hip surgery, it might remind her of why she did not want to be married to an old guy. By telling her he risked setting himself back in his playful courting, if not completely out of the game. Maddy had a tough time on the dating scene. She imagined being a senior and trying to date would be even worse. Especially, if they wanted to date outside of their age group. A much older guy would have to be something else for Maddy to consider wanting to date him. Money would not even come into the equation for her. But she knew a few women her age who would not have a problem with this if it meant bagging a rich sugar daddy. She felt for George. Jennifer sounded more and more like a gold-digger.

"Oh, I see. That's unfortunate."

Silence fell over the group and Maddy noticed both men looking at her expectantly. Her eyes darted from one man to the other.

"Why are you both looking at... Oh no!" She realized what they wanted. They sure didn't take long to get started on their shenanigans.

"Why not Maddy?" Rudy asked imploringly. "All you would have to do is go and pick up the duck and bring it back here. Once or twice."

"Once or twice?"

"It really would depend on how fast I heal," George explained.

"Why can't you get your manservant...What's his name, to do it?" Maddy waved her hand in the direction of the door. "

Neither man answered her. Eventually, George spoke up.

"Bradley's my assistant, not manservant. And, when you get to be my age, Maddy, the only thing that doesn't start to give way easily is your pride."

She looked at him, softening as she realized he was sharing a very vulnerable part of himself with her. Feeling his age, he was putting up a front, trying not to admit the obvious. To ask a younger, more virile man for help would be a blow to his pride.

"Please, Maddy?" PopPop begged.

Sighing deeply, she answered, "Yes."

Long before the word had even reached their ears, her gut told her she would regret it.

Chapter 8

Finally, the much anticipated first ransom money-ducky exchange night had arrived. Maddy decided to dress all in black for the occasion. 'That's what all undercover agents do,' she told herself, trying to find an excuse to dress up as the ones in those detective shows did. She might as well fully play the part and have fun while doing this. The thirteen-block drive down Jasper Avenue in Bugsy to Ashley's uptown condominium apartment building did not take long to navigate. The Pearl was one of Edmonton's tallest apartment towers. Ashley was waiting on the sidewalk, waving enthusiastically at Maddy when she pulled up to the curb.

"I can't believe that I'm going to see a Mitchell Spencer Duck, and actually touch it!" Ashley gushed like a teenager with a crush before she had even closed the car door. "I never, in my wildest dreams, thought I would get this opportunity! Do you know how rare this is? They're all in private collections. You can't even find a single one in an art gallery or museum! And you got to see two of them?" She was vibrating with excitement. "What are you waiting for? Let's go! Let's go!"

"I'm waiting for you to put your seatbelt on," Maddy replied, then matter-of-factly popped her gum.

"Oh, right, sorry." Ashley buckled herself in. "Okay, Go!"

"Alright, alright. Calm down, I'm going." As she pulled Bugsy out onto the road, Maddy gave Ashley an identical look to the one she had received when Maddy had gushed over Jon. She had not the foggiest idea why everyone was so taken by these ducks. Never again would she make the mistake of saying this in front of George or PopPop, even though she still thought they looked like rubber duckies. All they needed was an 'S', 'M', or 'L' on their underside and they could be mistaken for those Lucky Duckies in the game of chance at the fairs. Between the Billy Forest painting and these duckies, she questioned people's taste in art. It appeared she would have to do that research on modern art after all if she ever wanted to understand their weird attraction.

"Did the police ever find the owner of the locker George's painting was found in?" Ashley asked.

"No. Turns out the person had given the Triple-A a fake name and paid in cash," Maddy answered.

"It's not surprising. If you had stolen goods in your locker, would you fill up forms with your real name?"

"Nope, I wouldn't."

"So, back to Spencer's Duck. Where exactly are we going to get this rare little beauty?" Ashley asked.

"You know that park you and I went to last spring? The one where we had lunch in the small restaurant by the lake? It was the day you broke up with what's his name, Dan? No, not Dan. Dominic?"

"His name was Dave, and yes, I recall. It was Hawrelak Park."

"There's a willow tree on the river side of the park. George proposed to his ex-wife there. They were married at sunset so that's the time when it will be placed there for us to find it. Not before."

"And how did he figure this out? From a clue she left him?"

"Yup, apparently it is like a hidden treasure courtship for them. She leaves a clue, he picks up the ducks, and leaves payment."

"It sounds more like a business transaction than a courtship."

"That's what I thought too. In my opinion, it's George's wishful thinking."

They crossed the river and approximately ten minutes later they pulled into Hawrelak Park. After finding the pond and the river, they pulled into a parking stall and cut the engine. They looked toward the waterfront and sure enough, there was a large willow tree that had a park bench near it. Maddy had been worried about how she would know they had the right tree but there was no mistaking it. It was the only one with a park bench, just like George had described. Ashley looked at the sky and then at her watch.

"We have a couple of minutes left."

"Yeah, I don't know if she's dropping it off right at that time or what, but I don't want to risk going early and running into her or missing it altogether," Maddy said.

They sat in the car, watching people wander about, most riding their bicycles, and others jogging or walking by on the trails. She could not see anyone carrying a duck or a box that might have one in it. Of course, George had told her not to try and catch Jennifer in the act of leaving it. He wanted to play by the rules and did not want her to know someone else was picking the duck up for him. They were to leave the money in the black zippered cloth envelope he had provided, take the duck, and bring it back to him. Maddy wondered if this was how rich people entertained themselves, needing to do eccentric things instead of going out to the movies. Then again, she was not rich, and she could be accused of doing eccentric things. This outing was a case in point.

At the exact minute when the sun was setting, according to her weather app, Maddy reached for the black pouch and stepped out of the car.

"Alrighty, let's do this thing," she told Ashley. Although she had rolled her eyes when Ashley had first started pleading to be her plus one on this outing, she was secretly glad to have her along. It was not that she was worried about her safety, it was about the memorable experience they would have together. How many friends were able to say they had done an art ransoming and swap at sundown? In Edmonton's river valley at that. This was going to be one more 'Remember when...' story for their rocking chair days.

They casually walked across the park and toward the willow tree. As they approached, Maddy looked around it while gesturing to Ashley to look for the duck further away.

Ashley scrambled down the slope, toward the river until she was close to the bank. She spotted it and shouted to Maddy that she had found it.

'No wonder George had wanted me to do this exchange,' Maddy thought. 'It would have been quite the challenge with his leg issues.' She walked toward the beginning of the slope and looked down at where Ashley was standing.

"Okay, don't open it or anything. Just grab it and we'll leave the envelope in its place." Maddy tossed the envelope down to her and continued to be on the lookout for any potential trouble. She then saw a bearded man, who was walking by, stop and look down at Ashley. He hesitated, then started to go down. He slipped and fell, making a lot of noise as he slid, almost taking Ashley with him, and landed near the edge of the river. She yelled at Ashley to look out and run when two other guys came up from behind and startled Maddy. They came and stood right next to her. Then one winked at her as he called out to the guy below.

"Hey Fred, you need to stop falling head over heels for the pretty ladies!"

Fred flipped his friends the bird and scrambled back up the slope, never looking back at Ashley, and gave Maddy as wide a berth as possible. He caught up to his friends and punched one hard on the arm. She could hear his two friends laughing all the way to their car. Ashley made it up without any incident, laughing at the scene that had just unfolded before her.

Once back inside Bugsy, Maddy let out a sigh of relief. "That was easy. Although for a minute there, I thought that guy was coming after you." She was not sure what she had expected to happen, but her adrenaline had been pumping like mad.

"He kind of was," Ashley said, giving her a knowing smile. "You realize you would make a pretty lousy cat burglar right?" she teased.

"Yeah, I know. I don't do well with this cloak-and-dagger stuff. I prefer the detective style of action."

"Yes, please don't remind me. I still have PTSD from that funeral home experience," she reminded Maddy. We barely made it out alive before it was demolished. Now that's the type of excitement that I prefer to avoid."

"Enough walks down memory lane for now." Maddy turned to Ashley. "Go ahead, open the box."

"Squee! I can't believe this!" Ashley opened her purse, pulled out a pair of white cotton gloves, similar to the ones George had given Maddy to wear, and quickly slipped them on.

"Do you always carry white museum gloves in your purse, Ash?"

"Yes, I do. Any other silly questions? No? Good. Now let me enjoy this moment." She placed her gloved hands on the box, closed her eyes, inhaled deeply, then slowly lifted the lid.

"Oooh, look at that!" Ashley whispered. Maddy leaned over to take a peek. Maybe it would look different than the other ones she had seen at George's home. Perhaps this one would not look so much like a rubber ducky. No. It was almost identical except for the lipstick on its beak.

"Like seriously, are you and PopPop playing a joke on me or something?" Maddy asked.

"What? How? Maddy, why would you say that?"

"What's so great about this duck? Please do tell me."

"Maddy, if you don't appreciate modern art, that's okay, not everyone does. But trust me, this is an amazing piece."

Maddy turned the key in the ignition and put the car into drive.

"The whole world was going crazy," she muttered to herself as Ashley continued to coo over the contents of the box on her lap.

THAT NIGHT, AFTER SAFELY delivering the red-lipped duck to George's house, Maddy video-called her grandfather.

"Hi PopPop, how was your day?"

"Fine, fine. More importantly, did you get the package to George? No one followed you or saw you, right?" PopPop was acting as though she had survived a clandestine undercover project, and spies were eavesdropping on their conversation.

"Which package are you referring to?" she teased. "There are so many secret packages I'm supposed to pick up that I lose track quite easily."

"Funny girl, you know which package I'm talking about. Did you get the duck or not?"

"If you are referring to the Mitchell Spencer Duck, yes, I got it for George and left it at his house with Bradley."

"Good, good."

"So, what did you do today?" Maddy was tired of this whole duck story and wanted to talk about something else.

"I went to the library to see their presentation on penguin biology, then I had coffee with an old friend. Afterward, I was feeling a bit tuckered, so I had an afternoon siesta. The rest of the day I spent reading the newspaper. A real newspaper, not those online versions. Overall, a nice but uneventful day. Did you know that penguins mate for life?"

"As a matter of fact, I did," laughed Maddy.

"And did you know that a group of penguins is called a raft when they are in the water, but when they are on land, they're called a waddle? And you won't believe this. Penguins poop every twenty minutes! I go to the bathroom often enough as it is. I can't imagine having to go every twenty minutes, Ha! Ha! Ha!" Rudy belly laughed. "How about you, my sweet Madsy?"

"I'm not sure my bathroom schedule is something I would like to discuss at this time."

"No, no, I'm not asking you about your pooping schedule! Other than the duck caper, I mean, what else did you do today?"

They continued to talk about their day and made plans to see another presentation at the library together the following week. Maddy mentioned she had an auction she was attending the next day and invited him to come along. She was not sure if there were going to be any interesting lots for her to bid on, she explained, but that was part of her work. She attended more auctions where she did not do any bidding at all than those in which she did.

"That sounds like a lot of fun! I would love to see what you do for a living," Rudy responded more enthusiastically than Maddy thought he would. She was not entirely sure what he expected to see but she hoped he would not be too disappointed.

"Sounds good, I'll send you a text with the time and place. How does that sound?"

"Perfect, can't wait to meet you there."

THE FOLLOWING DAY MADDY pulled into the parking lot of the storage yard and approached the front office to register for the auction. She walked up a couple of rickety wooden steps that took her to the front door. As she was reaching for the handle, the door flew open, sending her stumbling backward and down the steps.

"Oh my, my apologies. Are you alright?" A baritone voice spoke above her.

"I'm fine, just my pride." She began to rise when she heard laughter behind her.

"Maddy my dear, are you falling for the guys again?" Rudy guffawed.

"Haha..." Maddy stopped midway through brushing her jeans off. "Oh!" She had looked up and met the eyes of the man who had flung open the door. It was the same man she had bid against for the paintings. He looked down at her and extended his hand to help her up.

"Have we met before? I never forget a pretty face, and yours is unforgettable," he said, one side of his mouth rising in a smile.

"Yes and no, the auction, the one... the one before this one," she stuttered. Rudy's head jerked to the side, and he stared at his granddaughter.

"Yes, that is the one. I saw you there. You won the bid on the locker I had my eye on." He smiled at her again. "My name is Marcus Hammond."

"Nice to meet you, Marcus," Maddy responded, staring into his deep brown eyes.

"And your name is?"

"Oh, sorry! My name is Maddy, Maddy Whitman." She felt color slowly rise in her cheeks.

"How did that unit work out for you?" Marcus asked.

"Unit?"

"The one you outbid me on.

"Oh, yes. It was good, really good. There were several great pieces of art in there. One piece, in fact..." Maddy began to talk rapidly.

"Hey honey, you said you needed to register before bidding. We better hurry up and do it or we'll miss things." Rudy interrupted her, putting his hand on the small of her back and nudging her forward, toward the office.

"Maybe I'll see you during the auction?" Marcus warmly smiled at her.

"Yes, of course," Maddy grinned widely in his direction before entering the office.

Once inside, she swung around to confront her grandfather.

"What was that all about? You were borderline rude!"

"I don't know much about your line of work, Maddy, but I don't think it's a good idea to be telling strangers everything about your business. You don't know anything about this guy," Rudy told her. "I mean, except that you have the hots for him."

Maddy's jaw went slack, her eyes widening in surprise.

"You have to stop looking at me like that. I may be old, but I'm not blind or stupid." He chuckled.

Shaking her head, Maddy walked up to the counter with her credit card and driver's license to register and obtain her bidding number. As she did, PopPop's words echoed in her mind. He was right; she shouldn't go spouting off information like that, especially when there was a considerable sum of money involved. She didn't know anything about Marcus Hammond except that he had silken blond hair, mesmerizing dark brown eyes, and shoulders twice the width of hers.

The auction was uneventful as far as auctions went. Maddy did not find anything she felt could make a reasonable amount of money when resold. The majority of units were either full of outright garbage or were crammed with old rusty tools and musty moth-eaten furniture that people had stored and long forgotten about. Most of it would probably be taken straight to the junkyard by whoever won the bids. Zane had not even bid. It had been a wise move on his part.

"There you go PopPop. You had a true-to-life experience of what my work is usually all about. Standing around and walking away with nothing most of the time." She rested her hand on his shoulder and smiled at him as they walked toward the parking lot.

"Why hello there," Maddy heard Marcus' velvety smooth voice behind them. "I didn't have much luck, did you?"

"No, I'm afraid I didn't either."

"I'm looking for original paintings or artwork of any kind," Marcus said. Sharing information was not out of the ordinary between regular auction bidders. Exchanging what they were in search of often paid off in case someone saw something and then told them about it. Marcus probably wanted to know if she knew of any lockers with artwork coming up for auction.

"Isn't it a bit of an odd place to be looking for art?" Rudy's eyebrows rose as he questioned him.

"You would be surprised what one can come across," Marcus answered him without taking his eyes off Maddy. "If you hear of anything, whether at an auction or through any other channels, please let me know." He handed her a glossy black business card.

"Of course, it'd be my pleasure," Maddy replied with a flirty smile.

He walked away winking at Maddy. She looked down at the card and saw it held only his name and an email address in gold embossed lettering. Nothing else. There was no business name, not even a phone number.

"I don't like that guy Mads," Rudy told her. " And I don't trust him either."

"Hmmm."

"Don't be telling him about any art or artwork you may be hearing about... from anywhere." He looked at her quite seriously.

"Oh, don't worry PopPop, I won't. It was all innocent flirting. I need to have fun from time to time." She looked back down at the business card. "He's a bit intriguing though, isn't he?"

"I know much too well about innocent flirting and what it can lead to. I'm quite experienced in that department, remember what George told you?"

"I'd rather not."

Chapter 9

When Tasha called, Maddy had just finished her breakfast and was in the middle of paying her end-of-the-month bills. They chatted about the girls and how work had kept Rick busy lately.

"People are repairing their cars or getting used vehicles instead of buying new ones nowadays," Maddy observed. "It's more affordable and better for the environment."

"I know. And it's not that I'm complaining about the extra money that comes with extra work," Tasha said. "But life is a lot less fun when that man of mine isn't here, and when he is, he's tired."

"Aww, that's so sweet," Maddy jokingly made a gagging sound. She aspired for a love like theirs. It did not surprise her that they missed each other. Those two were long-time-married peas in a pod.

"Speaking of sweet stuff, bella, how's your love life been lately?"

"Same as the last time you brought it up. Non-existent. And I'm getting tired of it. It has gotten so bad that I'm finding every man that crosses my path attractive."

"Oh really? Do tell me about these attractive men you are crossing paths with. Are any potential soulmates among them? Or are we talking about friends with benefits?"

"Ha! No benefits yet. One was a guy who bid against me for the paintings. I noticed him right away and he is a brown-eyed golden-haired Adonis."

"Ooh, sounds promising!"

"He's swoon-worthy for sure, but I'm now hesitant. It was all a bit odd. He was acting like PopPop didn't exist and I didn't like that. Plus, PopPop didn't like him. That could be problematic."

"Che peccato, that's disappointing. I liked the idea of a golden Adonis for you." Tasha sighed.

"Yeah, and then Ash brought over her friend Jon, an art dealer, a darker version of the Adonis but with blue eyes and a smooth British accent. He's the one who said the painting was valuable."

"And what was wrong with him? Does Ash have her eyes on him?"

"Nah, I don't think so. If she had been interested, she'd have pursued things before now. They've known each other for years, from back when she was in England."

"Well then?"

"Well then what?"

"Well then, what are you waiting for? When are you going to ask him out?"

"Oh Tash," Maddy whined. "I'd prefer to be asked out."

"Che cosa! For shame! What kind of attitude is that? You're a strong, independent woman and business owner! Why should the guy be the one to have to do it, hmm?"

"Don't start with that again, you know how much I detest asking men out!" She got up and started pacing.

"Of course you do. Everyone hates doing the asking. You're just making excuses. Do you think guys love it? Imagine putting yourself out there, risking rejection time after time. If you're interested in this guy, call him up and ask him for coffee. If it makes you feel better, tell him you want to thank him for his advice."

Maddy stopped, mid-pace.

"Hmm... Well, I guess I could do that," she mused.

"Of course you can! Now let me know how it goes, Amica. Ciao bella!"

Maddy tossed her phone on her couch. Tasha didn't waste any time and Maddy knew that within the hour she would be expected to let Tasha know if he accepted her invitation and all the juicy details of their conversation. No one should mess around with that Italian girl. Unfortunately, the idea of calling up a guy she was interested in out of the blue, even with an excuse, turned her into a nervous wreck. She needed to build up the nerve to do it. A walk should help. She filled her water bottle up, grabbed her keys, and decided to walk down the trails along the river. It was a lovely morning out; most people were at work and the trails were quiet. She walked down the stairs at Ezio Faraone Park and headed west. She then crossed the street at the Glenora Club. That's when the feeling that she was being followed started. She stopped and quickly turned around. All she saw was a car waiting to turn right onto River Road. The driver must have only been looking at her walk by, nothing sinister. She started jogging. It was high time she got into shape.

Every summer she said the same thing, but this year she meant it. She was able to keep a good pace until she was across from Victoria Park where she petered out, then bent over, dizzy and exhausted. She drained her water bottle in one shot and at once felt nauseous. 'Stupid move, when will you ever learn?' Maddy scolded herself. Seeing the skating Oval across the street, she decided to use the facilities to cool down a bit and to refill her water bottle. One of these winters she needed to drag her friends down here to go skating. She'd seen pictures of it all lit up in a multitude of colors, creating a shimmering kaleidoscope on the ice surface. It would be so cool to swish on the ice surface down by the river amongst the trees. She texted Ashley and Tasha separately, telling them to note this potential activity.

'What are you doing texting me from Victoria Park instead of asking that Adonis out on a date?' Tasha texted back.

'Damn,' Maddy thought, ignoring the text for now. She splashed a little water on her face and filled her bottle. Feeling much better, she decided to walk through the park and stop by the truck stand advertising BC Fresh Fruit in the parking lot. That's when she felt eyes on her once more. This time she slowly turned around and saw the same car, idling next to the truck. It had to be a coincidence. They probably also wanted to buy some fruit. She paid for her cherries and decided that she should probably do a loop instead of turning back. Maybe she could grab a scooter near the golf course, ride it home, and not push herself any harder today. She walked along the edge of the road toward the golf course, nibbling on cherries, while enjoying the sunshine.

The lunch rush hadn't yet begun, and it was still quiet on the road. She saw four golf carts in the distance. They were probably dedicated retirees enjoying a morning of golf. Maybe she should learn how to play golf. It looked like a relaxing game. You drove around in those fun carts and got exercise and fresh air. She thought that maybe golf was more her type of exercise, slow and easy. She could also wear cute outfits. Ashley golfed. Maddy would get her to give her a few pointers and such. She decided to call Ashley to see if she'd be interested in helping her learn how to golf, and, of course, to check if it would be okay with her to ask Jon out. When it came to men, it was always better to ask a friend about dating someone they knew rather than being that person who stepped on their toes.

"Hi Ash, did you get my text about skating at the Victoria Oval next winter?"

"Hi Mads, yes I did but I was in the middle of a call with a potential client. Sorry, I forgot to text back. Great idea! It would be fun, then we could all go for a nice mug of hot chocolate or something. We should make sure Tasha and Rick bring the girls along. We don't get to see them much anymore."

"Yeah, teenagers. Go figure, eh?" Maddy laughed at the idea that she was now one of those people saying this kind of stuff about teens. "Hey, I wanted to ask you something."

"Go for it."

"I was wondering if... damn it, it's that car again!" This time she knew for sure it was following her; it was driving slowly alongside her.

"What car?"

"A car is driving alongside me, Ash! I've had enough of this!"

"Can you see who it is?"

"No, the windows are tinted, exactly like the van's the other day. Bet it's the same person. I'm stopping this dipshidiocy this minute!"

"Maddy, please don't do anything stupid. Where are you?"

"I've just entered the Victoria Golf Course parking lot."

"Listen, go to the clubhouse and call an Uber, okay?"

"Fine, you're right. I'm going now. Bye."

As she hung up, a man wearing a balaclava jumped out of the moving car and grabbed Maddy. She screamed and kicked as the figure dragged her closer and closer to the car. Maddy dropped her bag of cherries and dug her hand into her pocket, pulling her keys out. She quickly had one between her knuckles and stabbed the perpetrator repeatedly anywhere she could. He let go of her. She took advantage of this momentary break, picked up her phone, and ran as fast as she could across the golf course toward the clubhouse. She could hear him running behind her. She swerved onto the golf course, hoping one of those seniors she had seen might be there and come to her rescue, but he was on her before she could get further away and slammed her face down onto the ground.

"Where's the Forest painting?" he demanded.

"What?" Maddy asked, unsure of what she had heard.

"The Billy Forest painting, bitch! Where is it?"

"I gave it to the police! Who the hell are you?"

"Damn you! Tell nobody about this, it never happened, got it? Or else your precious grandfather gets it." He got off her and ran toward the road, leaving Maddy behind, head still facing down. When she thought he was far enough from her, she sat up and checked that she wasn't hurt. The threat to PopPop was something Maddy wasn't going to take lightly. The guy had wanted the painting, but she no longer had it. That was probably the end of that. There was no need to tell anyone and worry them for nothing.

MADDY HAD CALLED ASHLEY back and asked for Jon's phone number. She also double-checked with her friend to see if she did not mind her asking him out for coffee.

"Oh, not at all, go ahead and ask. Jon's a nice enough guy, but as far as I'm concerned, all that good-looking going on in one man is a bit too much for me," Ashley reassured her.

"Too much?"

"Yeah, you know, he attracts all the spotlight and attention. It's hard on a girl's ego."

She did have a point, Maddy thought after hanging up. Dating a man who was as good-looking as Jon could lead to all kinds of insecurities, even in a woman as gorgeous as Ashley. Did she want to open herself up to something like that? 'Basta! Don't even!' she could hear her Italian friend scolding her. Tasha was right. Maddy was looking for any excuse not to contact him. She was borrowing trouble for a relationship that wasn't even a coffee date yet.

"Hi Jon, it's Maddy. Maddy Whitman, Ashley's friend."

"Well hello there Maddy," Jon answered. He sounded pleased that she was calling.

"I have some news to share about the painting and was wondering if I could buy you a coffee, as a thank you for your expertise, and perhaps let you know what happened. If you're interested that is. But you don't have to, of course, if you are busy, I would completely understand." The words rushed out of her mouth all nervously. Why was she so nervous? He was just a man. A gorgeous one, but still, just a man.

"That would be lovely," he answered, seemingly amused by her rushed delivery. "Are you busy tonight? Say around 5:30?"

"That sounds good. How about we meet at Good Java? Are you familiar with it?" He wanted to meet her tonight. She was so relieved.

"Absolutely, see you then."

Maddy stood for a minute looking at the phone in her hand, very proud of herself. She had done it. 'No problemo' as her sixteen-year-old self would have said.

She fired off a text to Tasha to update her on the Jon front. In response, her friend sent a GIF of a stick woman, bumping and grinding away.

MADDY WAS FIVE MINUTES early for her date with Jon. She wanted to arrive before him so they could avoid the uncomfortable moment of deciding who was paying for their drinks. When she entered the coffee shop, she found him sitting at a table tucked in a quiet corner of the café. He had beaten her to it.

"I'm so pleased you came, Maddy," Jon stood up and stepped forward to greet her. "What may I get you?" he asked, pointing to the menu board above the counter.

"Oh, you don't have to pay for mine," she said, shifting from foot to foot.

"It's my absolute pleasure."

"Alright, if you insist. I'll have a decaf café latté with one pump of sugar-free caramel syrup, please."

"Perfect. If you don't mind staying at our table, I shall go and order our drinks. This way we will not lose it." He tilted his chin toward the table he had just gotten up from.

Maddy placed her purse on the seat of one of the four chairs and sat down at another. She rubbed her hands together, not sure what to do with them. Should she place them in her lap or clasp them on the table? 'This is ridiculous,' she told herself. 'For god's sake. It's only coffee. That's all it is.'

To distract herself, she looked around the café, noticing one young couple making out over their Americanos, and a group of older women crocheting while sipping their teas. The café seemed to be having its last rush of the day, that witching hour when people cut off their caffeine intake; something she had started doing herself if she wanted a good night's sleep.

"Here you are. I didn't enquire on what size of latté you preferred; therefore, I purchased a medium one," Jon said, setting the to-go cup down in front of her. "I wasn't certain how long you wanted to stay, not wanting to be presumptuous I had them put our drinks in takeaway cups."

"That's quite fine. Medium works for me," she responded with a smile. "But I was supposed to buy you coffee as a thank you for your expertise with the put."

"Oh well, next time. I appreciate you humoring the gentleman in me."

They talked for a while about the work he had in town, and she begged him to tell her stories of Ashley from when he met her years ago.

"A gentleman never shares stories about his lady friends. You are likely to have better stories than I anyway. You knew her when she was even younger," he protested. "I think you should be the one sharing stories. Tell me, was Ashley an ugly duckling growing up? The one who turned into the swan by secondary school? Let me guess, teeth straightening braces? Thick lensed glasses?"

Maddy shifted a bit uncomfortably. It served her right to bring up the topic, but she didn't want to share Ashley's story with him; it was Ashley's story to tell.

"Okay, you're probably right," she conceded. "I should be respectful of stories that aren't mine to tell."

A comfortable silence fell over the table as they each drank their coffee. Jon kept looking at Maddy expectingly. She was wondering why until she remembered that she was supposedly there to tell him about the painting.

"By the way, you were right about the Billy Forest painting; it had been stolen," she began. "The police located the owner and returned it to him."

"I'm so sorry you paid for something that you had to turn over to the police," Jon said sympathetically.

"Oh, no, it's quite alright. The owner had a reward for its return," Maddy said.

"That's excellent! So, the reward paid for the storage unit?"

"It did, and then some."

"I'm so glad to hear that there was a positive outcome for you and that it was returned to its rightful owner." He gently blew on his coffee before taking another sip. Maddy felt shivers go down her spine as his breath reached her cheek.

"Thank you," she said, trying hard to stay focused on the conversation. "That painting paid for the unit and made me a nice profit. I also sold the two others Ashley had shown you. Now the rest of the paintings are gravy."

"You had more than the three paintings? And Ashley looked at all of them? There weren't any other important pieces that stood out amongst the rest in her opinion, were there?"

"Yes, Ashley took a look at all the paintings, although she did tell me that contemporary art was more your specialty than hers. We didn't want to bother asking you to look at all of the paintings, only the ones she wasn't 100% sure about," her heart began to beat a bit faster. "Did you want to come up and take a look at the rest of them?"

"Why Ms. Whitman, are you inviting me up to see your etchings?" He leaned forward, a conspiratorial grin on his face.

"Ha, ha, I guess technically, I am." Now that they had spent time together, she realized how easy and pleasant he was to talk to.

"Well then, since the coffee is takeaway, let's go to your place and take a look at those etchings, shall we?"

They quickly left the café and crossed the road to her apartment, which was located on the opposite corner from where they had met. They quietly rode the elevator up to her floor, avoiding any eye contact with each other. She was beginning to feel nervous again. Was he coming up thinking she was using the paintings as an excuse to get him alone? Or was he serious about seeing them? Had she misread the situation? Was she ready for what might come out of this invitation? Her brain was spinning with questions and a multitude of possible scenarios. She was starting to doubt what she might be getting herself into. The elevator seemed to be taking forever to arrive at her floor. When the doors finally opened, she had to control her rush to get out of there. Maddy unlocked her apartment door and let him in ahead of her. Jon then turned around and stretched his arm above Maddy's shoulder to close the door behind them.

"Umm, the paintings are in here." By this point, she had decided it was best to play it cool and assume this was a visit to see the paintings. She didn't want him to think she was desperate. Maddy did have some self-respect after all. It wasn't until she was in the process of opening the door to the room where she had stored them that it dawned on her that 'in here' was her bedroom. 'Oh, subtle Maddy,' she thought, 'real subtle. Now what will he think of your motives? Etchings, my patootie.'

Luckily, that morning she had tidied up and made her bed, there was no need to worry about being embarrassed by a messy room. No sexy bra or granny panties were lying around on the floor.

The paintings were leaning against the wall by the closet, and she invited him to look at them. There were seven paintings left, and Jon flipped through them quickly.

"Ashley was spot on; while several of these are pretty, they are by no means worth much," Jon said decisively. "These other two here might get five to seven hundred dollars each, at most."

"We thought as much, at this point, I'll be happy to get something out of them for being pretty."

"Do you often find pieces of art in the storage units you bid on?" he asked.

"No, not really. I find some strange things but not usually a lot of art."

"What is the strangest thing you have ever found in one?" He leaned up against her bedroom wall, smiling at her.

"Probably a serial killer's trophies," she answered without hesitation.

"Pardon me?" his eyes widened.

Maddy burst out laughing at the expression on his face. "It's a long story but let's just say it was a shock and I hope to never find anything similar again!"

"You're an interesting woman, Maddy Whitman." They both laughed and their eyes locked. Maddy's breath caught in her throat.

"Well, I hate to cut this short, but I have to get back to my hotel. I have an online business meeting to attend and it's UK time," Jon said quietly.

"Oh yes, of course," Maddy answered trying hard not to sound too disappointed. She didn't want him to think she had expected him to stay.

"I had a lovely time this evening. I hope we can do it again?"

"Yes, I would like that very much," Maddy answered.

"Alright then, as you North Americans say, it's a date." He slowly pushed himself up from his leaning position. "Let's agree to make plans for a longer visit when I have more... time?" He smiled seductively.

"That would be nice."

They walked to the front door and as they parted, he added that if he came across any clients looking for pretty artwork, he would send them her way. He then turned around, reached for her hand, and lightly brushed his lips over it.

Maddy closed the door and pressed her back up against it. She knew it was just as well he had left, but part of her was more than slightly disappointed.

"Boy, oh boy," she murmured.

She was still standing there, staring into space, when her phone rang. She roused herself enough to reach for her purse and pull out her cell. It was Zane. 'What does he want?' she wondered.

"Yeah?" she answered.

"Um, hello, Maddy?"

"Yes, it's me, sorry. What can I do for you?" Maddy sat up and shook herself out of her dream daze.

"I just wanted to chat about the next clue. Is this a bad time? I can call back later if I'm bothering you."

"No, no, it's fine. Go ahead. Whatcha got?"

"It's another poem, and it goes like this:"

'Like points on a compass,

I'm located on the left side.

Flashing blades try to pass

This is where royalty will abide.

Cold as winter,

water's sister.'

Maddy felt the words go in one ear and out the other without stopping. She was having trouble paying attention to what Zane was saying, her mind wandering back to Jon.

"Would you be able to text the clue to me so I can think about it?" she asked. "I'm a bit distracted right now and can't give it my full attention."

"Nothing serious I hope?" Zane sounded concerned." Are you sure? Maybe I can help?"

"Trust me, Zane, this is something that I would prefer to deal with all on my own."

Chapter 10

"Let me tell you, these Sunday brunch potlucks are da bomb! I love tasting all these new recipes," Rick stretched with the satisfaction of having a happy and full belly.

"Nobody says da bomb anymore, Daaad," teased Sophia, Rick, and Tasha's oldest twin by two minutes.

He ignored her and continued. "That German chocolate cake you baked, Ash, is fan-tas-tic! One to bake again, I tell ya," he said while cutting himself a third slice.

"Better watch your waistline, amore, or you will end up looking like a pudgy porco ready for the slaughter," teased Tasha.

"Ewww, Mom! Why must you be so gross?" moaned Chloe, twin number two.

"What's gross about what I just said?" Tasha looked at everyone else.

Both Ashley and Maddy looked down at their plates. It looked like one of their mother-daughters' head-butting debates was about to start.

"A pig ready for slaughter isn't anything pleasant to think about," said Chloe. "Especially after eating Pork Adobo."

"Which was also delicious. My compliments to the chef." Rick tried to lighten the mood and turned to Maddy, "It had the right amount of garlic for this Middle Eastern palate," he said with an approving nod.

"You girls are just too sensitive," Tasha scolded them.

"And your eggs Frittata were excellent, habibti." Rick blew his wife a kiss. "Not soggy. Perfectly fluffy."

Maddy was taking in the scene around the table. She loved her quirky chosen family. Rick and Ashley had been her friends since high school, and Tasha fit right in when Rick started dating her during their college years. When their twin daughters came along, they chose Ashley and Maddy as godparents. It felt natural and right to Maddy. It filled the empty spot in her heart that had been aching since she had left her dysfunctional home at sixteen and moved in with Rick's big-hearted Lebanese family.

"Now you're just trying to deflect the situation, Rick," Tasha was having none of that.

"I think the girls helped to do that first, with their Grooosss comment," piped Ashley, obviously holding back a laugh. "You know, Rick eating like a pig and all?" She grinned. Somehow, he always managed to sidestep Tasha's concern over his diet.

Tasha gave her a 'don't you get involved' look that wiped the smile off Ashley's face and brought silence to the table. Tasha gave the mom's eye to everyone looking at her; she then grabbed the knife and cut herself a second piece of cake.

"Well, you miserable bunch." She laughed. "What's good for the gander is good for the goose who laid the golden eggs. Anyone else want more cake?"

Rick got up, walked over to his wife, bent down, and gave her a big smooch. "I love you, my golden egg layer you."

"Oh gross! Get a room," grumbled Chloe.

"And on that stomach-churning note, we have to run," added Sophia, pushing her chair away from the table.

"Where are you two going now?" Maddy wanted to know. "We've barely seen you both since you became teenagers."

"Going to meet your boyfriends?" teased Ashley.

"They better not be," scowled Rick. "If I find out that you girls have boyfriends, that's it. Grounded for life. Halas! That's it!"

"Rick, cut them some slack," Maddy came to her goddaughters' defense. "They're teenagers, smart, and well-behaved."

"Yeah, and maybe we're not into boys, you know? It is the 21st century, after all, Dad," Chloe teased her father.

"You're not helping your case, girls," Tasha said, as she got up to clear the table. "Help me put the dirty dishes away, then you can go. Just be home by 4:30."

"And none of that 'Dad' stuff! It's Baba. You're going to use Arabic whether you like it or not young ladies," Rick added.

"Bye, aunties! See you later BABA!" chimed the girls as each kissed everyone and then made their escape through the kitchen.

"Aren't you going to ask where they're going?" Rick wasn't pleased with his apparent loss of control.

"They told us this morning. They're going to the library to do a group project. Remember?" Tasha replied.

"Oh yeah, right," Rick nodded. "So, Ashley, changing the subject once more, have you heard from Kyle lately?"

"No, I haven't," she sent a frosty look at him, daring him to say more.

"Shouldn't you be calling him or something?" Rick ignored her warning. "He's a cool guy." He had hit it off with Kyle and badly wanted some more testosterone in their little group.

"No, I should not," Ashley wasn't impressed with Rick using her to distract from his fumble. "And you know why, so drop it."

"Come on Ash..."

"Rick, I said NO. I can't anyway; I've started seeing someone."

"You what?" That was news to Maddy. "You started seeing someone and didn't think to tell your best friends? I'm insulted. I'm hurt. I'm... I'm..."

"Oh, stop it, Maddy. You are not," Ashley grimaced. "I just started seeing this guy, Garry, last week. We're not serious but we did decide to be monogamous. It's safer these days. We're having fun, going to dinner, movies, and stuff."

Rick and Maddy began talking over each other.

"Garry? As in Gerald or just Garry?"

"How old is he?"

"What does he do for a living?"

"Have you slept with him?"

"What's the catch? There's always a catch with these nice guys who aren't married."

"Whoa, whoa, whoa!" Ashley laughed. "That's a lot of questions. Some are also way too personal for me to answer."

"You can't just dismiss us like that," Maddy said.

"I certainly can, and am," Ashley replied, folding her arms for added emphasis.

"Well then, I have some news about Kyle myself," Maddy left them hanging.

Ashley sat up in her chair, curious but unwilling to encourage her. Rick, on the other hand, was worse than an old busybody grandpa.

"You have news about the good detective? What are you waiting for? Share, habibti, share!"

"He has also been seeing someone," Maddy replied, looking straight at Ashley.

"And?" Rick prompted her to continue.

"And that's it. They're also having fun. He doesn't know if it will become serious or not, but he's not dismissing the possibility. He doesn't want to be alone anymore."

Ashley lowered her eyes and stared at her plate. Maddy wondered if the news about Kyle had hurt her, and she was trying not to show it. Maddy felt bad if she upset her friend, but she needed to get her act together and realize that she and Kyle were meant for each other.

"Maddy..." Tasha had also noticed Ashley's face.

Maddy shot back with a 'What?' look.

"Ashley, anything new in the art world?" Tasha felt it was time to save her friend and change the subject.

"Thank you for asking, Tash," Ashley said. "Not for me, but Maddy came across some cool art on her last storage unit auction. One turned out to be stolen!" That quickly changed the subject.

"WOW!" exclaimed Tasha as she picked the cake up and took it into the kitchen.

"Stolen?" Rick was easily distracted. "Tell us more." He reached for a bottle of Arak, his favorite Lebanese liqueur. It was good for the digestion after a big meal, or so he claimed.

"Yeah, and I got a generous reward for returning it to the owner too," Maddy added. "Please pour me some of that aniseed deliciousness, won't you?"

"Niiice," Rick looked impressed. "Sometimes your finds can end up being worth more than others, eh?" He poured everyone a glass of Arak, then passed around a bowl of ice and a jug of water for each one to adjust their drinks to their liking.

"And get this. PopPop knew the guy. They used to be best friends in college and then lost track of each other when George, George Biskoff the painting's owner, left to study somewhere else," Maddy took a sip of Arak. "Mmm, this is so yummy. Anyway, this George guy is well-to-do now, with money from a divorce, investments, and such, and is quite the art collector. He's also the friendliest, quirkiest guy. No wonder he and my grandfather got along."

"I would love to see his paintings if they're anything like his Spencers!" Ashley leaned forward.

"Did you recognize any paintings at his place? Is he looking for more? Maybe you could introduce us? I did help with the duck rescue after all. And you know how I'm always looking for new clients."

"Recognized any paintings?" Maddy laughed. "Remember, Ash, it's me you're asking. I don't know enough about art to recognize any painters. That's what I have you for. But PopPop did mention that he recognized a Picasso and a Monet."

"Really? That's exciting." Ashley was impressed. "There aren't many Monet's in Edmonton, outside of the art gallery."

"Monet?" asked Tasha as she came back into the dining room.

"Yeah, PopPop has a friend who is an avid art collector. He even started a foundation to build a special children's art gallery."

"Okay, Maddy, please you must introduce us," Ashley was visibly excited. "I have so many ideas for something like that. It would be such an incredible opportunity."

"This guy, who you tell us, is a big art collector and he's the one who collects the rubber duckies you told me about?" Rick asked incredulously.

"Oh. My. God." Ashley's mouth dropped. "Please, please don't call Mitchell Spencer's Ducks rubber duckies!"

"Yup. He owns a bunch of these rubber duckies," Maddy was enjoying herself. It was fun when the attention was on someone else instead of her.

"Oh my god, I'm going to die!" Ashley's friends had never seen her get so excited over anything. "You HAVE to stop calling them that. They are 'Spencer Ducks.'" She turned to Rick and Tasha, adding, "They're all in private collections. You can't just go to a gallery and look at one. It's quite rare to be able to see one."

"Okay, okay, I promise to refer to them as 'The Ducks' from now on." Maddy laughed.

"And they're not made of rubber," Ashley corrected her. "That's a common mistake non-collectors make."

"I know. Both George and PopPop made sure to point that out."

"Can I help you ransom the next one, please?" It was obvious that Ashley wanted to see as many of them as she possibly could.

"Ransom?" Rick and Tasha exclaimed at the same time.

Maddy explained about George and Jennifer's divorce, their little ransom game, and how she had already delivered one envelope full of money.

"Why is it that rich people are always so eccentric?" asked Rick. "They can't do things normally; everything seems to have to be that much more exciting or riskier. What gives with that?"

"I wouldn't call it eccentric," Tasha said. "It's more like they can afford to do things out of the box. Just for fun. Kind of like what we sometimes do when we go on vacations or a concert."

"You call us going to Disneyland with the twins, eccentric?"

"Well, maybe not Disneyland, but when we went camping in a tipi. It was different, not the usual camping trip, kind of outside the box," Tasha reasoned.

"And you guys certainly did not spend thousands of dollars on that tipi experience. Anyway," Maddy said, "I'm going to do another exchange. If you want to come with me,

Ash, you're welcome. Then you can go with me to George's house to deliver them. It's the least I can do for all the help you've given me with his painting and 'The ducks.'"

"YAY! Let me know when and I will drop everything."

"Even a date with Garry?" Rick snickered.

"Shut up, Rick," all three threw back.

Chapter 11

"Mornings arrive much too quickly these days, especially Monday mornings," grumbled Maddy as she rose out of bed, slipped her fuzzy bunny slippers on, and stumbled toward the bathroom to prepare for the long day ahead.

She had been putting off office work that needed attention lately. Instead, she had been chasing ducks and Englishmen. There was sorting, filing, and researching her latest auction purchases that needed to be done. A Tiffany studio-style lamp, for example, was in her locker office at the Triple-A storage and could be worth something. It was probably not an authentic Tiffany, but she could get between one to two thousand dollars for it if it turned out to be vintage or antique. She hoped it would have a date stamp or maker's mark somewhere on it.

After getting dressed, she poured herself a cup of coffee. How she ever survived without a coffee machine that ground her coffee and had a pot ready for her when she woke up, she didn't know. She never wanted to go back to that time ever again. It was one of the little luxuries she allowed herself. The rest of her money was being squirreled away for the day when she would have enough to rent a brick-and-mortar shop. She dreamed of having a place to display all the treasures she found at auctions, to have a space in the back for a proper office, and maybe even storage. Nobody could accuse her then of not being a real professional, like that Paris Andrews woman kept voicing every time she did business with her.

If Paris wasn't a top and consistent client of hers, she would have dumped her months ago. Unfortunately, or fortunately, depending on how the mood struck her, Paris bought a lot of Maddy's auction finds for a good price. 'One day,' Maddy thought. 'One day I won't need her as a client. I'll have many other well-off clients and be able to tell her to put her snobby attitude up her...'

Her cell phone rang, and Maddy turned her thoughts to her grandfather. She knew it was him by his 'Stayin' Alive' ringtone. He had chosen it for himself, thinking that 1970s song's title suited him. Plus, he had informed her, he used to love dancing to the Bee Gees at the local discos back in the day. It was hard for Maddy to imagine PopPop doing disco moves, but his personality certainly did fit the bill.

"Good morning sweet PopPop of mine. How you doin'?" Maddy teased.

"I'm doing well, sweetheart. George, on the other hand, is quite depressed. He received some very disappointing news this morning."

"Oh, no! Is it his health? Did something happen to his hip again?"

"No, nothing like that. I fear that for him, it's much worse."

"Did someone die?"

"He could have dealt with that, but no, nobody died. He received a text from Jennifer. She's tired of playing games with him. She wants the duck exchanges to be over and done with. Those were her exact words, 'Over and done with'. George is heartbroken."

"Oh. What does this mean, then? Is she keeping the rest of the ducks?"

"Thankfully, not. She wants to exchange them all at once for the whole lot of cash they're worth."

"Guess the flirtation is over. Poor George. He had such high hopes of reigniting their romance. I feel bad for him."

"Yes, he's taking it very hard. He doesn't want to deal with it or chance seeing her," Rudy sounded upset for his friend. "That's why I called. Could you come by his place after work today to arrange the final duck trade for him?"

"Of course. I have a lot to do but as soon as I have everything done, I'll text you and let you know when I'm on my way."

"I appreciate it, Maddy. So does George. You're the best granddaughter. I love you."

"I love you too PopPop. Talk to you later." Maddy put her cell phone in her jeans' back pocket, grabbed her laptop and purse, and left her apartment. On the way down the stairs to the garage, she thought about poor, heartbroken George. 'Guess it's best for him that Jennifer finally just ripped the band-aid off,' she thought. 'But why now? What prompted her? Another boyfriend?' She guessed they would probably never find out her reasons. Maybe it was best that way. George didn't need his feelings hurt even more than they already were.

She opened the door to the underground garage and quickly surveyed her surroundings. Nobody seemed to be hiding in any shadows. Management had finally repaired the broken light fixtures, and Bugsy was parked under a bright new LED one. Maddy had learned her lesson to always be aware of where you're walking when alone. She wasn't about to make herself an easy target ever again. 'No sirree Bob!" she said out loud.

'Speaking of Bob,' she thought. 'I better stop at Bernard's Antiques and drop off that teapot he said he'd take off my hands,' Maddy made a mental note to go there after she visited her storage office at the Triple-A's.

It was an unusually cool day, and Maddy was disappointed she wouldn't be able to drive around with Bugsy's top down. Summers were not long enough in Edmonton to fully enjoy a convertible, but she still liked to feel the wind blow through her hair as often as possible. That wasn't going to happen today. She turned her cell phone recorder on before driving out of the garage so she could make a list of all the things she needed to deal with at her office as she drove over. First on her list was the Tiffany-style lamp: Google picture search, compare it to her lamp, research possible value on various auction sites, examine the lamp, and note any damage or discolorations, etc. Then there was the vinyl record collection she had found in one of the bins from last Friday's auction in Lacombe. Who would have thought that a storage locker in small-town Alberta would hold such a treasure trove of LPs from the 1940s through to the mid-1960s? Some were small records, 33 shellac EP's or LP's. Those could be worth something if they weren't scratched. She will have to bring those home after sorting them to look at them in better lighting, and she had to grab that teapot for Bob. Bob was a quirky man, anywhere between five to ten years younger than her grandfather. He owned a shop called Bernard's Antiques and Collectibles not too far from her place. He was very generous with his time and enjoyed teaching Maddy a thing or two about his business so she could at least be able to tell if she had found something of potential value. His lessons on coins had proved invaluable.

Her list was finished when she pulled up to the Triple-A's gate. She punched in the code, and it slowly swung open, squeaking every inch of the way. Maddy didn't know why Rod, the manager, hadn't fixed it since he had taken over from his aunt Shirley. The racket it made announced everyone's comings and goings. There was no possibility of a stealth arrival. 'That's probably why he hasn't repaired it yet' Maddy guessed. As though summoned by her thoughts, Rod appeared at his office's door.

"Hey there, Maddy! How are ya? Found any graphic novels lately?" Rod was a serious collector, always on the lookout for rare or unique graphic novels.

"Rod, I swear, you'd be the first one I'd tell if I came across any comics."

"They're NOT comics, Maddy! How many times do I have to explain the difference to ya?" Rod said, sighing dramatically.

"Oh Rod, it's way too easy to tease you. I know the difference. I'm just trying to get a rise out of you, that's all." Maddy couldn't help herself; it was fun to get him going.

Graphic novels were the only subject Rod was sensitive about. She liked how he became animated whenever he spoke about them.

"Funny, real funny. You got me good," Rod blushed.

"Where's Bertie?"

"I had to lock Engelbert in the back office. He's humping everybody again."

"Did you try the spray water bottle?"

"Yeah, he jumped around, trying to catch the water. Dumb dog!"

"Darn, I was so sure that might work. And I'd say he's not too dumb, he did outsmart you." Maddy tried not to laugh.

"You're quite the stand-up comic these days, aren't ya?"

"I try my best. But seriously, you should take him to a vet to get him checked out. Maybe they can recommend something."

"Maybe you can take him off my hands. That would help."

"Sorry Rod, my building doesn't allow dogs," Maddy was ever so grateful right now that her condo bylaws were extremely strict regarding pets.

"Anyway, I better get to my locker and do some much overdue work."

"If you need any help moving things around, just holler. I don't mind giving you a hand or whatever you might need. Or I could even keep you company, you know?"

"Thanks, I'm good. I need to concentrate." Maddy needed to get away from him or he would tag along all morning. "I better go. I'll stop by the office to give Bertie a belly rub."

"You'd be doing it at your own risk," he smirked. "I won't be responsible for his behavior."

Maddy parked her car and walked to her storage locker. She unlocked it, rolled up the door, and turned the light on. Setting down her laptop on her work desk, she looked around, surveying all the items she had stored. She was more than a little behind now. It was time to get cracking and sell a few items. Her mortgage payment was coming up and she needed funds.

Two hours had gone by and she had gone through most of her backlogged items. It was time to figure out what the Tiffany lamp was worth. She picked it up and put it on the desk to examine it. Thankfully, it did have a marking on the bottom. She sat down and started her research.

A knock on the storage unit's door frame startled her. She looked up to see Zane, standing there smiling at her.

"I walked by an hour ago and noticed you were deep in concentration. I didn't want to disturb you."

"Oh, hi Zane. Yeah, I've been at this for almost two hours now. I don't mind the break. How are you?"

"Not bad, I was here for the auction of those smaller lockers down row 34. I thought I might bump into you there, then saw Rod who told me you had lots to do."

"I do, I don't even have any room to bid on anything else right now," Maddy gestured at all the items piled on top of each other. "I need to sell a lot of this stuff to make room for more inventory. I read online that there's going to be a large auction at a storage facility in St. Paul."

"Hey, let me know when and I'll join you. Some of the stuff that people store and forget about in these farming communities are vintage Canadiana."

"That's what I'm hoping to find." She was getting excited just thinking about what could be in those lockers. "I'll be sure to tell you. Maybe we could rent a van and go together?"

"Sounds good. Have you had any luck with your treasure trove?" Zane asked, surveying her unit.

"Some things are worth more than others." She smiled. "This lamp is worth roughly $700. Not what I was hoping for, but it will pay some of my bills."

"Not bad for a Tiffany wannabe."

"Yeah, that's what I thought too...Hey, what smells so good?" Maddy sniffed in his direction. "I smell fries. Do you have fries in that bag of yours? Please, please tell me you have French fries."

"As a matter of fact, I have two servings of fries, burgers, and Saskatoon milkshakes," Zane smiled.

"Two of each?" Maddy smiled back. "Like, one of each for me too?"

Zane nodded and handed her one of the bags. "I went to grab some lunch and figured you might be hungry, seeing as how hard you've been working and all."

"Oh my God Zane, I could kiss you right now!"

"That won't be necessary." Zane looked down at his feet, shrugged, and added, "I owe you for helping me with the puzzle."

"Speaking of puzzles..." Maddy looked at him expectantly.

"Yes, speaking of puzzles, did you have a chance to look at the clue I gave you?" he asked.

"Yes, and I have some ideas. I thought we could brainstorm a bit, but not before we eat, and then I'll have to get back to work."

Zane unpacked their lunch while Maddy moved her paperwork and laptop out of the way.

"Oh yum! This is so good Zane, thanks again,"

"No problem, it's the least I can do for your help with this puzzle thingy,"

Maddy reached for her phone and opened the text containing the next clue Zane had sent her.

'Like points on a compass,
I'm located on the left side.
Flashing blades try to pass
This is where royalty will abide.
Cold as winter,
water's sister.'

"So first off, I was thinking it's referencing the direction west because that's the left side of a compass. I'm afraid that's as far as I got. The 'flashing blades try to pass' part hung me up."

"Well, I was wondering if it maybe is somewhere in West Edmonton Mall. Or is that too literal with the west clue?"

"No, I don't think so, but it can't be just West Edmonton Mall because of the rest of the clues."

They sat chewing their burger and popping fries in their mouths when suddenly Zane started to laugh.

"What kind of Albertans are we? Or even Canadians at that?"

"Huh?"

"It's the ice rink at West Edmonton Mall. That explains the flashing blades trying to pass and the ice is water's sister."

"And, royalty resides in a palace," Maddy laughed as she chimed in. "Of course! West Edmonton Mall's skating rink is called the Ice Palace."

They set their food down and high-fived each other.

"I can't believe I missed the hockey reference!" Zane exclaimed. "I'm glad none of my teammates are here to witness this. They'd never let me live it down."

"You play hockey?"

"Yeah. Why do you look so surprised?"

"You don't fit the stereotype, that's all."

"Stereotype? Because of the hair?"

"Well, umm, yeah."

"Shame on you! Here I thought you were an open-minded woman."

"I am! It's just that I can't see you wearing a helmet with your spikey hair."

"I don't wear my hair this way when I play hockey." Zane laughed.

"I... I feel so stupid now."

"Nah, don't. I think it's pretty funny. I've been playing since I was a kid. Now I'm in a beer league. I love it. It helps me burn off steam," Zane said. "Anyway, enough about me. Let's get back to this puzzle. We're doing pretty good. So far we've got Canada Post and West Edmonton Mall Ice Palace." Zane grinned in self-satisfaction.

"Remind me how many clues there are in total and what do we do once we have them all figured out?" Maddy asked.

"There are seven in total, so five more to go. Once we have them all figured out, we need to sit down and look at all the clues together as a whole. On the paper, under the list of clues along the bottom, it says 'The answer will point the way to a year's supply.'"

"A year's supply? A year's supply of what? Gas or even groceries? That would be a substantial prize considering today's prices," Maddy said.

"For sure. And if we figure it out and win anything, we'll split the prize right down the middle, fifty-fifty."

"Now you're talking my language, Mr. Hockey Player. Text me the next clue then and I'll get working on it tonight," she told him. Maddy had a little incentive now.

"Will do. Although I'm warning you, they're getting harder and harder. The next one's clue is:

'My name says it all
and it shows my drive
As I reach forward, I strive.
My mission is to create a community
Without which there would be disunity.
Some say I'm a saint
With my yeast and beans'"

"Gee, that doesn't sound random at all!" She stared at Zane.

ZANE LEFT; HIS MIND filled with all the possible riches ahead. Maddy continued to work for another hour or so, then wrapped the lamp and teapot in packing paper. Placing the lamp carefully into Bugsy's front trunk, she wedged it between her emergency blanket and an empty gas can. She set the teapot on the passenger seat and drove to the front office to check on Engelbert. Satisfied that little Bertie was healthy and not too unhappy in the back office, she rubbed his belly goodbye. Thankfully, no unwelcomed humping had occurred. Then off she went to Bernard's to see Bob.

Maddy easily found a parking spot close to the shop, right in front of a handmade jeans boutique she always wanted to visit. She had to remind herself that PopPop and George were likely waiting impatiently for her. Disappointed to not have time to do any window shopping, she walked right past the boutique and into Bob's shop. The little bell above the door jingled as she walked in. She expected Bob to pop his head from behind the backroom curtains. Instead, it was Niko, his son, who walked through them.

"Hey there Maddy! How have you been keeping?" he asked with a huge smile on his face.

"I'm not doing too bad, how about you?" Maddy said, returning his smile.

"I've been pretty busy, that's for sure. Certainly, busier than usual." He cleared the glass countertop and retrieved a white cotton cloth from the shelf below.

Maddy did not often see Niko around the shop. He was usually upstairs repairing something or another for his dad. Bob was training him to take over the business as he wanted an early retirement.

"Where's your dad? I'm supposed to meet him this afternoon."

"Dad's away for a few months. He told me you were coming with a teapot he wanted to buy." Niko said, spreading the cloth out onto the counter. "Why don't you place it here and I'll take a look at it. He told me exactly what to look for."

"I hope Bob's alright. He's not sick or anything, is he?" Maddy said, placing the teapot on the cloth.

"Oh no, nothing like that." He picked up the teapot and started to examine it. "Believe it or not, an old friend of his won a three-month stay at some timeshare in Hawaii and invited him along." He turned the teapot upside down and pulled out a large magnifying glass to look at the writing stamped on the bottom. "Looks like the real deal to me. No cracks, no fissures. Do you want cash or an e-transfer?"

"An e-transfer's fine. I'll email you a receipt when I get home," Maddy replied. "Hawaii, you say? What is it with Hawaii? Everyone I know is moving there."

"He's most definitely not moving there. He can't afford it. But he's going to live the easy life for as long as he can."

"I'm surprised he's going to leave you in charge for that long."

Niko raised an eyebrow at her while entering the money transfer.

"No offense," she quickly added. "You know how picky he is. What I meant is, I'm surprised he trusted you with the shop, all alone."

"You're not making things better, Maddy. Better stop while you're ahead." He laughed.

"You know what I mean, Niko! Oh, crap, you're making fun of me, aren't you?"

"Perhaps. Don't worry, I'm just kidding. Dad's very protective of the shop, I know. I took a couple of week-long courses on valuation and pricing at Christie's, in New York, over the winter. That put him a bit more at ease."

"WOW, New York? Maybe I should look into taking one of those." Maddy was impressed. Niko sure matured and became more responsible over the last year.

"You should! I learned about some stuff even Dad didn't know about. It's been good for business too." He put the teapot aside. "Have you come across any paintings lately? I've heard rumors that someone's found a stolen Billy Forest and a few others in a storage locker. Was that you?"

"Holy! News travels fast in this town." Maddy wondered how Niko heard about her recent purchases this fast.

"So, it was you! Very cool. I want to expand into paintings. Not a lot, but the occasional one to hang in the shop and perhaps catch the eye of potential buyers."

"Really? That's great. I can send you some pictures of what I have. You can let me know if any would be of interest to you."

"That would be awesome! It's always a pleasure doing business with you Maddy."

"Thanks, Niko," Maddy replied, walking toward the door.

"And please tell your friends about Bernard's Antiques and Collectibles!"

Maddy turned around as she was stepping out, "You know Niko, you're starting to sound just like Bob."

"What can I say? The apple doesn't fall far from the tree."

She waved goodbye and walked back to her car thinking that the day was getting better and better. She found out some of her purchases were valuable and got a free lunch courtesy of Zane. There was the possibility of solving a puzzle and winning a prize. She sold the teapot and added Niko as a potential art buyer. Yes, this day was a good one, and it was going to finish on a high note. Even though George's heart was broken, it meant that her rubber ducky trading escapades were ending. She gave Ashley a quick call on her way there to give her a heads-up that the final delivery was probably going to take place the next day. She then called her grandfather to let him know she was leaving the Westmount area, and on her way to see him and George.

When she pulled up onto George's driveway, she saw Bradley, standing on the landing, waiting for her.

"Thank goodness you are finally here, Miss Whitman. Mr. Biskoff is at his wit's end. Your grandfather has been trying to cheer him up all day, to no avail."

"Bradley, please call me Maddy. I'm uncomfortable calling you by your first name if you don't call me by mine. Please?"

"I'm afraid it will have to be Miss Whitman. May I have your car keys, please?" he said as he ushered her inside. "Mr. Biskoff expected to see you sooner. Was there traffic?"

"Here you go. I'm sorry," she said. His comment had made Maddy feel guilty for not getting there sooner. "There's a lot of construction going on around town. That's what caused my delay."

"It's always faster to take Groat Road when possible. Saves me about 10 or 15 minutes."

"I don't like the twists and turns on that road. People drive like race car drivers on it. Is George feeling that bad?"

"I haven't seen him this depressed since the divorce. He can't sit still and says he can't live without her. Miss Whitman, it's quite heartbreaking to watch."

"I'll see what I can do," she said as he opened the study door and announced her arrival.

"Finally!" Rudy stood up from his armchair and rushed toward her. He hugged her and whispered in her ear, "I've tried everything to cheer him up. Nothing's working."

"Let me try something. I have an idea," she whispered back.

"George, PopPop here tells me that Jennifer is getting bored with the duck exchange?"

"How's that going to help?" Rudy asked, lowering his voice.

"Yes, she sent me a text saying she wanted to be done with them and trade the rest all at once. I think she's bored with me. What will I do now? How can I get her back?"

"Listen, George, Jennifer might just be bored with the ducks, not with you or the games." Maddy looked at Rudy, encouraging him to get in on the conversation.

"That's true, George. She didn't say she didn't want to see you." Rudy added.

"What do you mean?" He looked from one to the other.

"You told me that she had paintings too, isn't that correct?" Maddy asked.

"Yes, several actually but..."

"Did she mention them at all?"

"No. I don't understand what you are getting at?"

"Me neither," Rudy said.

"Well, she wanted to play this game with the ducks and all the artwork, no?"

"Yes," both men replied.

"And, she didn't say bring all the paintings too now, did she?"

Understanding slowly crept onto Rudy and George's faces.

"That's right! Jennifer didn't say that in her text, George," Rudy chimed in.

George stopped pacing and sat down on an armchair. He looked up at Maddy and smiled.

"You are brilliant. Rudy, your granddaughter is a genius! Jennifer is only bored of the duck exchange, not me. There are still the paintings to exchange! Once we trade the ducks, we can start a different game for the paintings, one at a time."

"Exactly." Maddy walked over and sat on the other armchair. She felt bad about possibly giving him false hope. But it wasn't a lie, not really. Jennifer's text didn't mention the paintings after all. For the time being, at least, she had cheered him up. "Now, what's the plan for the duck trade?"

"Here, read her text. It describes exactly where to drop the money envelope off." George pulled out his phone and scrolled down to Jennifer's last text before handing his cell over to Maddy.

"Government House's upper park? Is that behind the old Provincial Museum building on 102nd Avenue?" she asked.

"Yes, that's the place. To be honest, I have no idea why she chose it. We never went there together; it has no meaning for us. And she didn't even bother trying to make up a clue or anything." George was perplexed.

"Maybe she's doing something nearby before or after. It could be a matter of convenience," Maddy reasoned. "It says here that she wants to meet tomorrow evening, around eight. I'll bring Ashley with me again. That is if you don't mind, George? She's a big fan of Mitchell Spencer's work. And, she has great ideas for your children's art foundation that you might find interesting. Ashley has a master's degree in art history from the Royal College of Art and is well-connected."

"Sure, sure. I owe you, Maddy. Anyway, I could always use help with the foundation, especially from someone that knowledgeable."

"Alright, that settles it. Tomorrow evening it is, then," Maddy shook George's hand. He let go of her and pulled her into one of his bear hugs, a gentle one. Maddy hugged him back. He was so much like PopPop.

"I'll have Bradley drop off the envelope with the money around seven tomorrow evening. This way you don't have to worry about having such a large sum of money lying around."

"That makes good sense, George. I don't like the idea of Maddy walking around town with that much money on her," Rudy said.

"You both know that I am a grown woman, right? I can handle myself and large sums of money. But that's okay, seven works for me."

Maddy was secretly relieved. Not that she couldn't manage it. The responsibility of carrying that much money on her all day while doing other things is what disconcerted her. She certainly couldn't leave it in her apartment.

"Do you need a ride home, PopPop?"

"No, thank you, sweetheart. I'm spending the night here. We have so much catching up to do. Drive safely and text me when you get home, okay?"

"Sure thing. You two behave now, you hear? I don't want you getting into trouble like you used to.

"Got it!" Rudy and George saluted her.

Bradley appeared out of nowhere with her keys. 'How did he know that I was leaving?' she thought and wondered if he had been eavesdropping on them. If there was something she didn't like, it was people listening in on private conversations.

"Thank you for helping to calm him down," he said as he went with her to the mansion's front entrance.

"How did you know I calmed him down?" Maddy asked him. "And how did you know that I was ready to leave?"

"I didn't," he replied hesitantly. "I noticed he was not agitated and in a pleasant mood when I walked in." He straightened himself and continued, "As for knowing you were ready to leave, I also had no idea. It was time for Mr. Biskoff's medication. I was coming in to remind him to take his painkillers. I saw you standing there, appearing to be saying your goodbyes. Your keys were in my pocket, and I had the chauffeur bring your car around. Does that answer your questions, or do you have more you would like to ask me?" He straightened himself up some more.

"No, that's all for now," she replied. "Thank you."

Chapter 12

"Did you call your car insurance company?" Ashley asked.

"Why would I call them?" Maddy could not understand her friend's anxious behavior since she had picked her up.

"Because you need to increase your insurance! What if we get in an accident and the ducks get damaged? They're irreplaceable!"

"First of all, we're not going to get into a car accident. Second, they will not get damaged. Ash, I've carried valuable items in my car before. I'm not irresponsible. I have enough insurance on it as it is."

"I don't know about that. These are unique, each a one-of-a-kind piece."

"Listen, even if, God forbid, we get into a crash of some sort, it's unlikely that all of them would get damaged. My insurance is plenty enough to cover one or two damaged duckies."

"If you say so. But..."

"I do say so. No ifs, ands, or buts. Now stop being so nervous. What is with you tonight?"

"I don't think you fully understand what we will be handling here. It's like having a carload of Andy Warhol's. Having so many of these in one place is rare. It's a huge responsibility."

"Ashley, I have a good idea of what we are handling. I'm more concerned about the cash that's in that backpack on the seat behind us."

"And that's another thing. Why all that cash? Why couldn't George get a bank draft or something like that?"

"Because Jennifer, his ex-wife, insists on cash-only transactions. No traces that way. No taxes to pay," Maddy explained.

"It does kind of make sense from that perspective. Those two are odd ducks, no pun intended."

"Ha! You're funny. Yes, they are an odd pair, that's for sure. Whatever turns their crank, I guess."

"Oh, there's the entrance to Government House. Turn left here."

"I know where it is Ashley. It's behind the old museum."

"The parking lot is almost deserted. Why don't you park closer to the sidewalk, away from those two cars and nearer to the hedges? That's where she said the case with the ducks would be, right?"

"Yup, that's the spot." Maddy pulled up to the closest parking spot and turned the engine off. "Let me check the text George forwarded to me; I think it said it would be under the hedge to the right of the old carriage house." Maddy took out her phone to look. "Yes, it's on the right-hand side, where the sidewalk starts to curve away."

"Why don't I get behind the wheel while you go do the exchange? This way, you can hold the case on your lap while I drive. You know that I drive safer than you. How does that sound?"

"You do not drive more safely! But I'm not going to argue with you right now. Whatever makes you feel less anxious, we'll go with it, okay? Roll down the windows so you can hear me in case it's down the hill and I need help like last time." She got out of the car and walked around to Ashley's side. Ashley opened the door and climbed out, letting Maddy reach for the money-filled backpack on the seat behind her.

Maddy slipped the pack on and walked toward the exchange location. Spotting the case, she turned around and gave Ashley a thumbs-up. Squatting down to examine the case more closely, she popped the locks open to confirm that the ducks were there. Satisfied that they were, she locked them back in. While in the process, she heard something rustling above her head and looked up just in time to see a large object coming down at her. Without thinking, Maddy lunged forward knocking down whoever was trying to brain her. Scrambling to her knees, she grabbed the case, crawled backward, and got up as quickly as she could.

"Start the car! Ashley! Start the car!"

Ashley, having seen Maddy disappear into the hedges and then come back out running like a mad woman, did not hesitate to start Bugsy up. She put the car in reverse, backed it out of their parking spot, and had it facing the exit's direction just as her friend grabbed the door handle. Maddy handed Ashley the case, tossed the backpack behind her seat, and locked the door. One hand grabbed the seatbelt, the other reached for the duck case. She hollered to Ashley to hit the gas pedal. Before you knew it, the car was screeched out of the parking lot.

Ten minutes later they were on Whitemud Drive, heading toward George's house.

"What the hell happened Maddy?" Ashley was still gripping the steering wheel, white-knuckled.

"Someone was hiding in an opening behind the hedges. I don't know if it was Jennifer, but whoever it was, they tried to knock me over the head!"

"What? Why? With what?"

"I don't know why or with what. All I know is it was something bigger than my head, dark, and coming at me," Maddy was shaking. "I have no idea what came over me, but I just dove at them."

"That was quick thinking, girlfriend. You might have saved your skin back there." Ashley was starting to relax a bit. "Grab my water bottle. It's on the floor. You need something to drink to calm down. This is insane."

Maddy sipped on Ashley's water and took a deep breath.

"George is going to have some serious explaining to do! This was supposed to be a simple exchange." She looked at Ashley.

"It appears to me that Jennifer wanted the money and the ducks. What a biatch!"

"Yeah, a major one at that." Maddy rolled down the window to let a bit of air in. "Okay, you need to take the second exit after this one. Then it's another 15 minutes or so to George's place."

Chapter 13

A shley slowly pulled the car up to the front of George's house and whistled in admiration.

"Oh my, this is one beautiful home." She leaned forward to better look at the mansion through the windshield. "And it's huge!"

"Don't you think it's a little too big for someone who lives on their own?" Maddy asked her, still fuming over the exchange. "I mean other than his manservant, Bradley, there's nobody else living here."

"I thought you said Bradley was his assistant?"

"Manservant, assistant, six of one, half a dozen of the other. He does almost everything except cook and clean for him, or take care of the grounds, and the car."

"I presume he has a housekeeper, chauffeur, and gardener for those things," Ashley said. "One person couldn't look after all of this by themselves." She gestured at the property.

"Yes, he has staff to look after all those other things," Maddy replied as she stepped out of the car. "But these people aren't family. I would be so lonely in a big place like this. I'd probably want to move you, Rick, and his whole family here, including Mama Leila."

"Thoughtful of you, but you might want to rethink Mama Leila these days."

They both stepped out of the car.

"He most likely needs a big mansion for his art collection," Ashley mused. "The loneliness you mention could also explain why he agreed to play these art cloak and dagger games with his ex-wife."

"It's a possibility, I guess," Maddy replied.

"Is that Bradley at the top of the steps? He is extremely cute," Ashley whispered. "I thought you said he dressed in suits."

"Yeah, that's him. I'm surprised to see him in dusty jeans. Anyway, better get your keys out and hand them to him."

"My keys? Why?"

"He's going to want to park your car in the underground garage."

"Fancy, fancy."

"Good evening, Miss Whitman, and Miss?" Bradley asked, looking admiringly at Ashley.

"Good evening, I'm Ashley Mueller, Maddy's friend." Ashley presented her hand to him.

"It's a pleasure to meet you, Miss Mueller. Please excuse my appearance. I was working on my motorcycle. May I have your car keys?"

"Of course, and please call me Ashley."

"Thank you, Ashley."

Maddy stared intently at both. 'Ashley, not Miss Mueller?' she thought. 'What was up with that?' Maddy was not sure what she was witnessing here or how to feel about it, watever 'it' was.

"Please follow me. Mr. Biskoff and Mr. Carmichael are waiting for you in the study," he said as he led them down the hallway. "May I bring you something to drink?"

"We can use something strong, Bradley, please. It was quite the evening." Maddy replied.

"I gather things didn't go as well as you expected?" He opened the study door and introduced them. As Ashley walked past him, he asked her if they would prefer Scotch on the rocks or Port.

Maddy raised an eyebrow and answered for both, "I believe George has some Scotch right here. Straight up will do for us, please, and thank you."

"I can take care of things from here, Bradley," George said. "Thank you, I appreciate you making yourself available on your evening off. I will ring you when it's time to bring their car around."

Bradley nodded to his boss. He then smiled at Ashley before leaving the room. George gingerly stood up, favoring one leg. "The surgery went well but I'm still not 100 percent."

"Ashley, what a pleasure to see you again," Rudy walked over and hugged her. "George, this is Maddy's best friend, Ashley."

"It's so nice to see you again, Rudy," Ashley replied. She then walked over to George to shake his hand. "And a pleasure to meet you, sir."

"She's one smart cookie, just like my Madsy here." Rudy looked at his granddaughter and smiled proudly. He then noticed that she was looking disheveled and not too happy. "Maddy, what's wrong? What happened to you?"

"What happened to me? What happened to me? I was attacked, that's what happened to me! I was lucky not to get injured, and that Ashley was there with me," Maddy then turned to George "That Jennifer of yours is a madwoman, do you hear me? A. Mad. Woman."

"MY Jennifer?" George was aghast.

"Maddy, you said you weren't sure it was Jennifer," Ashley corrected.

"I can't be sure because I didn't hang around long enough for introductions once I tackled them."

"Tackled?" Rudy quickly made his way to his granddaughter and hugged her. "Are you hurt? Here, sit down," he walked her to the leather couch.

"PopPop, I'm okay. Shaken up but all right," she took his hand in hers. "I bent down to collect the case with the ducks, and before you could say 'Quack', I saw a huge object coming down at me. I tackled the legs in front of me and took off with the case."

"She looked pretty scared, I can attest to that," added Ashley.

"My Jennifer would never attack anyone. She is a gentle soul!" cried out George.

"Well, your gentle soul tried to knock me out. Here are your precious rubber duckies and the backpack with the money. I didn't even think of dropping it off. I was too busy running for my life."

Nobody dared to correct her about the ducks. They were all too shocked to say anything. Ashley took both items from Maddy and handed them to George. She then walked to a table where a crystal decanter and glasses sat. She opened the decanter and sniffed. Satisfied that it was Scotch, she poured everyone a glass.

"Thank you, Ash, I do need this drink," Maddy took a huge sip.

"We all do," Ashley replied. "Take it easy with that. You must keep your wits about you."

"Right. Anyway, George, I'm done with any more exchanges between you and Jennifer. I'm sorry but this is not what I signed up for. I'm tired of being attacked for handling your art."

"She's right, George." Rudy patted Maddy's hand and looked at his friend. "This was supposed to be an easy exchange, not something that would put her in harm's way."

"Maddy, you sound like you were attacked more than once. What are you keeping from me?" asked Ashley suspiciously.

"Nothing. Never mind, I'm just rattled."

"I didn't want anyone to get hurt!" George said. "Nobody was supposed to get hurt. This makes no sense whatsoever." He sat down opposite them. "I will give her a call tomorrow morning and find out what happened. Maybe she was followed? Perhaps she sent someone else because she knew I couldn't make it? And that person was greedy?"

"Well, whatever the reason, you can count me out. I'll take my fee and be on my way."

"I'm so very sorry, Maddy. I understand. This isn't how it usually plays out." George opened the case to look at the ducks. Ashley quietly moved closer behind him to peek over his shoulder. Things did not work out how they had planned but she wasn't going to let that stop her from seeing Spencer's Ducks.

"There's an empty space!" Ashley exclaimed.

"There's a missing duck!" George said, looking up at them.

"What do you mean 'there's a missing duck'?" Maddy walked over to look at the case. "She kept one? But why?"

Rudy stood up and joined the group gathered around the case. "Well, George," he said. "I believe you'd better add that to your list of questions for Jennifer when you call. And I think you better call her tonight."

Chapter 14

Maddy woke up to the smell of fresh roasted Columbian coffee. 'Ah,' she thought, 'that wonderful, brain-defogging elixir of life.' She would probably need a double shot to deal with the inevitable call she was expecting from George and her grandfather with information about Jennifer.

An hour later, the phone call that interrupted her while posting items online did not come from George but from Ashley. She was meeting a client in Old Beverly and was craving Ukrainian food.

"I'm not too far from that amazing Ukrainian restaurant. Do you want me to pick you up something? I could swing by, and we could have lunch together."

"Are you thinking a quick lunch or a long lunch?" Maddy asked.

"I'm pretty open this afternoon so an extended lunch would be nice. If you've recovered from yesterday, that is?"

"Yeah, it's all good. An extended lunch sounds about perfect right now," Maddy added. "Could you get me a half portion of The Real Deal, number 8, please?" She started to drool at the thought of their juicy Kielbasa sausage.

"Excellent, see you in an hour or so."

She had barely hung up when her long-expected call came through.

"Maddy, George here."

"Hey George, how are things this morning? Did you get answers from Jennifer?"

"That's why I'm calling you. I can't reach her! I've tried all night. I texted her, I called her cell, and her home landline. Nothing, nada. She didn't answer."

"Does she always answer your calls? After what happened yesterday, maybe she's trying to avoid you?" Maddy was still not impressed with Jennifer.

"No, she's never avoided me in the past. I would at least have received a text telling me she'd get back to me."

"What if she's afraid that I might press charges?" Maddy was not convinced of George's ex's innocence.

"No way. I told you, my Jennie doesn't have a violent nature," George was insistent. "And she would want the money. There's no way she would walk away from it."

"Well, she certainly is in a predicament, isn't she? Either she comes forward, claims the money, and explains herself, or disappears, avoiding the repercussions of her actions, and leaves empty-handed." Maddy had not realized how much she had been affected by yesterday's attack. She was not usually so grumpy. "I'm sorry George, it sounds like you're worried."

"I'm very worried. All of this makes zero sense." He sighed. "Rudy and I are going to drive by our place to check in on her. I mean her place, it used to be ours." He sighed again. "If she's not there, the staff will be. Maybe they can help me find her."

"All right, keep me updated, okay?"

"I will, and Maddy?"

"Yes, George?"

"I'm truly sorry about yesterday. Please think of a way that I can make it up to you."

"It's in the past now. No harm, no foul. I'm not hurt. Call me later." She really could not blame him; he had not known that someone would be lurking in the hedges. The more she thought about it, the more she wondered if it could have been someone other than Jennifer. She was starting to recall a bit more from yesterday evening. Those legs she tackled seemed too thick to be a woman's.

"UNCLE ED'S PEROGIES and kielbasa are the tastiest you can get this side of Mundare," Maddy exclaimed. She and Ashley were enjoying their respective Real Deal specials on Maddy's condo's rooftop patio. It was such a beautiful day that they thought a picnic surrounded by flower planters and views of the city would be perfect and they were right. "Thank you for treating me. You didn't have to, Ash."

"I know, but I felt bad after what you went through yesterday."

"Like I told George, I'm okay. I was a bit shaken up yesterday, but I didn't get hurt. That's what counts, right?"

"A bit shaken up?" Ashley was not buying any of this. "You were fit to be tied! You were biting people's heads off left and right."

"I was not! I was slightly upset, that's all," Maddy wanted to leave that memory far behind. "Speaking of yesterday at George's. What was that all about between you and Bradley? Hmm?"

"I have no idea what you're talking about, none whatsoever." Ashley looked indignant.

"Really? Sweet smiles, call me Ashley... A little more and you might have handed him your number."

"And who says I didn't?" Ashley grinned.

"You did not!" Maddy's jaw dropped. "Did you?"

"No, I didn't. Give me some credit here. I might be flirty but I'm not easy. And besides," Ashley added, "I'm seeing Garry, remember?"

"It's Kyle that you should be seeing, not Garry."

"Maddy, come on, really? Can't you just let it be with me and Ky... Look out!" Ashley grabbed Maddy by the shoulders and almost smacked her face into her two remaining cabbage rolls.

"Are you trying to finish the job, Ash?" Maddy sat back up and wiped sour cream off her face. "Why'd you do that?"

"Did you not see those two geese fly right over our heads?"

"Obviously not! I was too busy snorting cabbage rolls." Maddy looked around. "Where did they land?"

"They're right there." She pointed to a large planter with low ornamental grass. "Aw, look, they have three wee little goslings."

"Aw, they're so cute! I forgive you for face-planting me in traditional Ukrainian fare." They both laughed. "No wonder my neighbor is so upset, they've nested right above his apartment."

"That must be loud. I don't think I could live with all that racket."

"Let me tell you, he certainly can't. I hope the condo board doesn't hurt them." Maddy liked the idea of having wildlife on her rooftop; it added a touch of nature to downtown living.

"They can't hurt them. That would be illegal. They cannot move them until the goslings are a bit older, I think. Let me check." Ashley pulled out her cell phone to find out the rules regarding wildlife within city limits. "They have a wildlife helpline... Hmm, there's info on how to stop them from nesting. Oh, wait, here's something. Oh dear."

"That didn't sound good."

"It's not. Let me read it to you 'Canada Geese are protected under the Migratory Bird Act, and it is illegal to tamper with a nest once it's made.' I guess your neighbor is out of luck."

"Does it say anything about when the nest can be removed?" Maddy was hoping the site said never.

"Apparently," Ashley read on, "'The incubation of the eggs is about one month, so once those nests and eggs are there - they're there for a month and you can't do anything.' Oh boy."

"What about after they are hatched? These goslings aren't newly born."

"They're supposed to go to the nearest waterway," Ashley answered.

"But those little guys can't fly yet. How are they going to get there? We need to help them."

" We? There is no 'We', not when these wee goslings have big-ass cobra chicken parents hanging around. Are you nuts?" Ashley was not going to have any part in that scenario.

"Okay, you might have a point. But what if we put a camera and kept watch for when the geese leave? Then we can grab the babies and take them to water?"

"Mads, are you listening to yourself right now? If the parents even get a whiff of us coming near these goslings, we're as good as dead. They will divebomb us until we bleed to death!"

"Now, you're exaggerating."

"Am not! And did you stop and think about where we, no, YOU, would take them? The North Saskatchewan river? Paul Kane Park? Hawrelak Park?"

"I don't know, somewhere with water..." Maddy was starting to see Ashley's point.

"This article says they start flying at ten weeks. By the looks of them compared to these pictures, I'm guessing they're almost ready. It shouldn't be long." Ashley sensed that Maddy needed a bit more convincing. "Also, do you really want to separate those babies from their parents? They're bonded forever! That would just be cruel."

"Okay, you're right," Maddy's maternal instinct seemed to kick in. "There's nothing we, sorry, I, can do."

"Well, I'm relieved you've come to your senses." Ashley relaxed a bit. "Wait, you have come to your senses, right? Please, tell me that you're not going to come on your own and try something stupid, like move the whole family?"

"No Ashley, I'm not going to do anything about it on my own."

Maddy's answer did not put Ashley's mind at ease.

LATER THAT AFTERNOON, Maddy was busy listing a few more items when her phone rang. It was Zane and he wanted to talk to her about their latest clue.

"I think I have a general idea, but not specific enough," he explained. He repeated the clue for her:

'My name says it all
and it shows my drive
as reaching forward I strive.
My mission is to create community
Without which there would be disunity.
Some say I'm a Saint
With my yeast and beans.'

"Could it have something to do with beer? Because of the yeast?" he asked.

"Or a bakery," Maddy pointed out. "It's not just beer that has yeast my friend, or do you have a one-track mind?"

"Oh, good point." Zane's voice sounded dejected. "I thought I was being so clever."

"No, no it was a good guess. We can at least narrow it down to having something to do with beer or a bakery."

"Do you think the line 'Some say I'm a Saint' could refer to St. Albert?"

"Possibly," Maddy agreed. Let's start with that premise."

"Now, let's do a scroll through the different names of bakeries there." Maddy did a Google search on her laptop and began naming businesses listed. "Wild Earth, Breadlove."

After a few minutes, Zane declared it could not be a bakery as none of them fit with the rest of the clues.

"What about a coffee shop that sells bakery items?" he asked. They both began scrolling again.

"Starbucks, Tim Hortons, Tealicious." There was silence on the phone line as they both considered the different coffee shops and tried to make them fit with the clue. Finally, Zane had had enough.

"I give up! There are lots of Tim Hortons and they serve bakery items and coffee but there is nothing special about that, or maybe it doesn't matter?"

"But how does the name 'say it all'? Or how does it show 'my drive' or how it 'creates community'?" Maddy asked.

"You're right. I guess we keep at it and hope inspiration strikes." Zane sounded a bit frustrated and Maddy could not help but smile.

"It's just a game remember?" she reminded him. "Something that is supposed to be fun!"

"Speak for yourself. I want a year's supply of something!" Zane said.

Chapter 15

Sitting in front of the TV, watching some Netflix and sipping a glass of wine, Maddy was looking to relax after one very long day. Hump Day was finally coming to an end. She started scrolling through the available shows, trying to decide which new series she wanted to start. She settled on a Harlan Coben one when her cell started playing 'Stayin' Alive'.

"Good evening PopPop. Did you two gentlemen figure out what's what with Jennifer yet?"

"Sweetheart, I'm putting you on speakerphone. I'm staying with George again tonight. He's extremely worried about Jennifer. I'll let him explain."

"Hello, Maddy?"

"Yes, George, it's me." Maddy felt the need to pour herself some more wine. She decided to keep the bottle within arm's reach.

"We drove to Jennifer's house, but she was out. We ran into the couple who does her housecleaning. They've been cleaning it since well before we divorced, so they know me enough to trust me."

"And what did they say? Have they seen her?"

147

"No, that's the thing. They come daily to clean and tidy things up. They haven't seen Jennifer for quite some time."

Maddy put her wine down and sat up. This started to sound off, even though she did not know George's ex-wife.

"They can't remember, but it's been a few pay periods. They know because she usually e-transfers them, but she's been leaving cash instead. This time, she left them extra for the following pay period and told them they didn't need to come until she messaged them because she was going away for a while."

"Is that out of character for her, leaving like that without speaking to them in person?" Maddy asked.

"Yes, yes, it is. And they said her bed had not been slept in for over a week. The last time they saw her, she was with her gentleman friend. She has a gentleman friend!" George was even more upset by that last bit of information. "Why would she tease me like that?"

"George, did they say that he was a 'gentleman friend' or a gentleman 'friend friend'?"

"What's the difference?" Rudy asked.

"A friend is just a friend," she explained. "But a 'friend friend...'" She took a long sip of wine.

"Is more than just a friend," Rudy finished her sentence.

"Oh, I get it," George's voice relaxed a little. "Do you think her friend is with her now, Maddy?"

"I don't know, but I think you need to go to the police tomorrow morning and file a missing person's report if you don't hear back from her before then."

"Why not go now?" George asked.

"Because she hasn't been missing long enough," replied Rudy.

"That's correct PopPop, or really missing as far as the police will be concerned. I also think that you should call her friends and family if you still have their numbers. Check whether they have heard from her or not. This could help with the missing person report."

"Thank you, Maddy, I will. Rudy, could you please grab my phone book from the top desk drawer over there? We need to get started."

"George, one last thing."

"Yes?"

"Is Jennifer on social media?"

"I don't understand?"

"Facebook, Instagram, and such."

"I believe she has Facebook, Instagram, and that Tiki Tiki thing."

"He means TikTok," Rudy corrected.

"Oh, yes, that's it. The TikTok. Why do you ask?"

"I will go online and look around to see if she has been active as of late." She could not sit by and watch her grandfather's oldest friend, and her grandfather for that matter, try to figure all this out by themselves. Maddy might be upset about both attacks on her, but it was not George's fault. And it looked increasingly like it wasn't Jennifer's either.

"Good idea, sweetheart. Thank you so much! We better let you go so George here can get started on those phone calls."

"Good night PopPop. I'll be in touch tomorrow morning."

Maddy ended the call, turned the TV off, and switched her computer on. She took a last long sip of wine and put the cork back on the bottle. She shuffled over to her kitchen table and took a seat. Relaxation was over. It was time to focus on Jennifer and see if she was active on social media. Hopefully, it would not be another late night.

Chapter 16

"Look, Constable Kawasaki." Rudy was squinting to see the name on the officer's tag. "We're here to file a missing person report. I don't get what's so hard to understand about this?"

"First of all, it's Constable Kowalchuk. Secondly, I will ask you again. Are you related to the presumed missing person?"

"He isn't, but I am." George took a step closer to where Rudy was standing. "And she isn't supposedly missing, she IS missing!"

"And you are?" Constable Kowalchuk asked politely. He was trying not to lose his cool with these two older gentlemen.

"I'm her husband."

"Alright, this I can work with." Constable Kowalchuk seemed relieved. He didn't want another person making a scene. He had too many complaints made against him this month and wanted to avoid another write-up. "What is your wife's name?"

"Jennifer Buteau," George replied, pulling out from his wallet a photograph of Jennifer to show him.

"I will need a picture I.D. please."

"I don't have Jennifer's I.D." George was getting anxious. "She probably has it on her!"

"No sir, I need YOUR picture I.D." Constable Kowalchuk was struggling now. "A driver's license, a government I.D., a passport, any of these will do."

"Oh, I'm sorry. Here." He pulled his driver's license out of his wallet and handed it to him along with Jennifer's photo.

"Okay, Mr. George Biskoff, I assume your wife kept her given name then?"

"She changed it back to her maiden name after our divorce," George explained.

"Divorce? Are you submitting this report on behalf of her children then?"

"No, sadly we didn't have any children."

"Is there a relative who can file the report?" He looked up from the I.D. to George.

"She doesn't have any relatives here. I don't believe that she has any anywhere in the country even. I don't see what difference this makes. She's missing!"

"George, Jennifer has no living relative here?" Rudy looked surprised.

"None, they're all dead," he replied, then turned back to the constable. "She's an only child. I think she might have a cousin in France somewhere."

"We don't need a relative, but a relative can usually answer more questions than an ex-husband." Constable Kowalchuk was now using a condescending tone. "When did you realize that Ms. Buteau was missing?"

"I've been trying to reach her for a few days now. Her cleaning staff said they hadn't seen her for a couple of weeks "

"They said they last saw her with a male acquaintance," Rudy added. "We're concerned that maybe this guy hurt her."

"Hold on a minute." Constable Kowalchuk closed his eyes and took a deep breath. "Are you telling me that she was with a boyfriend the last time she was seen? Did you not think she could be with him, trying to avoid her ex-husband?" He turned away from his computer.

"She wouldn't do that to me!" George was becoming agitated. "And he's a friend, not a 'friend friend' boyfriend! I know the difference now."

"Please sir, do not raise your voice at me. It will not help your case."

Rudy pulled George aside and whispered, "Let me try and see if I can get anywhere with this chump." George nodded his agreement.

"Constable Kowalchuk, it's unlikely she has left with this man without telling her staff. That's what has us even more concerned for her safety."

"Yes, and she didn't call about the ransom money either!" George blurted out.

"Ransom money? Is there anything else you gentlemen would like to tell me about?"

"No, no, constable." Rudy quickly tried to distract from George's faux pas. "We're talking about game money, like Monopoly or Life."

"Well, let me tell you that filing a false missing person's report is not a game." Now it was Constable Kowalchuk's turn to start getting agitated. "It's a crime."

"But she's really missing!" George cried out.

"George, you need to calm down a bit, or else the nice constable here will ask us to leave," Rudy tried to talk sense into his upset friend.

"Constable, Jennifer has not been seen or heard from for several days now. Her last text didn't even sound like it was coming from her," Rudy was hoping that talking nicely and in a less aggressive tone might get them more results than George's quickly mounting desperate one. "Is there anything we need to do to be able to file this report? Please tell us what and we will do it."

"Did you check with all her friends?" Constable Kowalchuk asked them.

"Not all of them, we couldn't reach everyone last night," George replied.

"How about hospitals? Did you check if she was in any hospitals?"

Both shook their heads negatively.

"Does she have any favorite spa or out-of-town getaway spot?"

"Yes," said George.

"Did you call those places?"

"No, we didn't," Rudy answered.

"You need to start with all those options first." Constable Kowalchuk took the missing person form away from them and put it in a binder under the desk.

"Once you've done that you can return here and file a report. But you better be convincing. Right now, you sound like a jealous ex-husband. That's not going to get you anywhere. Have a nice day gentlemen. Next, please?" Constable Kowalchuk was done with them.

"But..." George was not ready to give up yet.

"No buts, sir. Please move along or someone will escort you out."

"George, let's go," Rudy tugged him by the sleeve. "You won't be helping matters if we get a police escort out."

Once outside, they decided they needed to gather more evidence to find Jennifer or at least something that would convince the police to start looking for her. They walked into a café, each ordered an espresso and Nanaimo Bar, and then sat down to formulate a plan of action.

"I thought you said that Maddy recommended we come downtown to the main police station. That her friend would help us. This was such a waste of time!"

Rudy could see how desperate George had become. "Maddy said to ask for her friend Kyle. That constable was one stubborn son of a gun. It's not Maddy's fault that he refused to call Kyle unless we told him what we wanted."

"Yes, stupid rules. As if we looked like criminals out to get Kyle or something."

The waiter arrived with their order. They sipped their coffee and ate pastries.

"We should have made up a story and not told that Kowalchuk everything." George wiped chocolate crumbs off the table.

"How were we supposed to know he'd be running interference, eh?" Rudy shook his head. "He was just doing his job, George."

"I know, I know," George sighed. "Now what?"

"Let's give my granddaughter a call. Maybe she can meet us here and help us figure this mess out." Rudy took out his phone and speed-dialed her number.

"Maddy? It's me, would you mind coming down to meet us? We're in that little café across Winston Churchill Square."

"Hi PopPop, I sure can. But first, tell me how it went at the police station?"

"It didn't. Some sanctimonious schmuck of a constable wouldn't let us see your friend."

"Let me guess. Was his name Kowalchuk by any chance?"

"OY VEY! YOU BOTH HAD a fun morning, didn't you?" Maddy said after hearing about their visit to the police station.

"Did you have better luck with her social media?" asked PopPop.

"Nope, not much. I looked at all her accounts, and she had tons of them. When you find Jennifer, George, you'd better have her change all her platform settings to 'Private'. But seriously, it was much too easy to see everything she'd been up to."

"She's a very trusting person," George admitted. "Sweet and forgiving. Jennifer never thought anyone would intentionally want to hurt her."

"Well, she told the world about her art collection. Even posted pictures of all the paintings, sculptures, and the Spencer Ducks."

"Oh no, please tell me that you're exaggerating, Maddy." Rudy looked so taken aback. "Please..."

"I wish I could tell you that, but unfortunately, she did."

"And this would mean that anybody who understood art would have known what she had and where she lived, wouldn't it?" asked George.

"Pretty much," Maddy confirmed his fears. "It's not like she had her address on there, but a total stranger could message her and make up some lie to meet her at her home if they wanted to."

"Or try to dupe her into selling some pieces to them," added Rudy.

"This really could complicate things. But there's no way of knowing if this happened or not. Jennifer hasn't posted on any of her accounts in at least a week and a half," Maddy shared some of what she had found out with them.

"This confirms it," George said. "She told me how she was constantly online, posting about this or that event, sharing jokes and such. Even if she was out of the country. Something is wrong."

"Maddy, what can we do?" asked Rudy. "We can't return to the police; they won't do anything yet."

"Look, how about I go home and call Kyle? I'll explain the whole situation to him," she said, looking at both men. "In the meantime, you two make those calls Kowalchuk told you to make. He is right about checking around. You never know."

"That sounds like a plan." George nodded in agreement. "I need to keep busy, or I'll lose my mind. Thank you for all your help. I owe you so much."

"Please don't mention it again. You mean so much to PopPop here. Any friend of this old guy is a friend of mine."

"Hey! Who are you calling old?"

"I CAN UNDERSTAND WHY George would be worried," Kyle said. Maddy had updated him on the missing Jennifer situation, and he sounded concerned.

"It sounds, in my professional opinion, that something is off. Can you help us, Kyle?"

"Your professional opinion? Would that be the professional opinion of an auction attendee or a re-seller?"

"Point taken."

"Regarding filing a missing person's report, my hands are tied," he said. "George and Rudy will have to check with all the hospitals, and such, first. Give me Jennifer's home address and I'll drive by later today to take a look around her property. I might find a clue or something. Weirder things have happened when searching for someone."

"Okay, thanks. I'll ask George and text it to you."

"I'll give you a list of other places they should contact when they've finished all their calls. They'll ask them for this information at the station. Once they have it, tell them to go down and file the missing person report after four this afternoon. Kowalchuk will be done with his shift then; with all the info they'll have at that point, it shouldn't be an issue with whoever's on duty at the desk."

"Sounds good. Hold on a sec, I need to get a pen and paper." Maddy grabbed what she needed from her kitchen drawer and went to sit at her dining room table. "Alright, shoot."

"Cute, never say shoot to a man with a gun, Maddy."

"You're so funny, Kyle. Look at you, dad jokes, and you aren't even a dad."

"It's in the DNA." He chuckled. "Ready?"

"Yeah."

"They will need a description of what she looks like, her age, and if she has any birthmarks or features that stand out. Also, what was the state of her mental health? Is she on any medications, does she do drugs, or hang out with gangs, or prostitutes?"

"I'm pretty sure the answer to the last two will probably be 'No.'"

"You'd be surprised at how often people have answered 'No' to these questions and were, sadly, proven wrong. For George's sake, I hope not, but it's those connections that end up getting people into major trouble. And by major trouble, I mean killed."

"Well, aren't you the eternal optimist?"

"I don't mean to be a pessimist, it's just that in my profession, you see a lot of bad stuff."

"I don't envy your job, Kyle. I do appreciate you doing me this favor. I owe you one."

"No worries. How's Ashley doing, by the way?"

'And there it was,' Maddy thought. The question that had been on his mind from the very beginning. 'Guess that was his way of telling me what kind of favor he will eventually ask for.'

"Ash is doing fine. Like you, she's seeing someone."

"What? I thought she didn't want a serious relationship. I don't understand why?"

"Whoa, slow down cowboy." Maddy was grinning. 'Here you have it,' Maddy thought. 'The proof that he was still hung up on Ashley.'

"She hasn't changed her mind about not getting serious. They're just having fun. She wants to play it safe if you get my drift?" Maddy said.

"Oh. I get it. I wish you hadn't explained it that way. I prefer not visualizing her having fun with another man."

"Well, I don't know how else to say it without being graphic about it, Kyle." Maddy thought this was fun.

"Please don't." Kyle sounded dejected. "Anyhow, I'll text you later this evening once I check out Jennifer's place."

"Sounds good. Thanks again."

Maddy looked at her cell and put it down. She thought that perhaps this particular conversation needn't be shared with Ashley.

Chapter 17

"Did your friend Kyle find any clues at all about my Jennie's whereabouts?" George asked. Maddy could see him pacing back and forth behind Rudy on her computer screen during their online call. "Anything whatsoever?"

"I'm sorry George. He even combed around the property," Maddy replied. "He looked everywhere he legally could without a warrant to enter the house."

"People don't just disappear into thin air!" Rudy jumped in. "She has to be somewhere."

"I don't know what to tell you." Shoulders slumped, she relayed that no clues had turned up on George's ex-wife during Kyle's preliminary search. "How did it go at your end with the police at the station this afternoon?"

"Rudy and I stopped by around 4:30 as your friend Kyle suggested. They took all the information we had. Please thank him for me. I wouldn't have been able to answer some of these questions if we hadn't been prepared."

"So, the report has been officially filed?" asked Maddy.

"Yes, George filed it. The constable on duty didn't put up any hurdles or anything. She was very understanding."

"It was very straightforward," George added, pulling up a chair to sit by Rudy. "Unfortunately, there's not much they can do other than assign the file to a detective, who then will go around to ask questions whenever they can."

"The constable told George they were short-staffed," Rudy said.

"Yeah, Kyle has been complaining about that for months. He's had to put in loads of overtime." She could empathize with the families of missing loved ones, like George. The police could only fit in so much in 24 hours. There was an enormous number of cases and not enough detectives were available to deal with them. "Did Jennifer's friends have suggestions or say anything about a boyfriend?"

"No, not the ones we could reach," George replied. "We still couldn't get through to all of them. There are also some places she likes to go but we didn't have time to call or stop by." They had spent every minute they could before and after the police station getting telephone numbers, they did not have, for some of her other friends and looking up addresses. It had been a painstaking task with so many dead ends.

"Maddy, do you think you could help George?"

"In what way, PopPop?"

"Maybe you could help look for her? Talk to her friends and the businesses she likes to frequent. With his leg the way it is, it's a bit hard for him. As for me, I don't have the energy I used to."

"I guess I could call around and ask about her when I can." There were a few empty spots on her schedule over the next two days. Working from home gave her some flexibility.

"Thank you, Maddy. Thank you! Of course, I will pay you for your time." George seemed to cheer up knowing she would help him look for his 'Jennie'.

"Don't thank me yet. I can't promise I'll find anything. Please send me a list of names and numbers you haven't contacted yet and I'll take it from there."

"Okay, we will," Rudy said. "Love you, my sweet Madsy. Goodnight."

"I love you too, PopPop. Bye for now."

Maddy never tired of hearing him tell her he loved her. She had not realized how much she had missed hearing anyone say those words to her until he had started saying them. Her friends did tell her they loved her too, but it still did not feel the same.

She made herself a cup of tea, grabbed two London Fog cookies, and settled on the couch with her laptop to surf the net while waiting for an e-mail notification that George's list had arrived. She had her eye on an expensive-looking rug. She usually did not buy rugs, but that one looked unique. Unique in her business occasionally meant valuable.

Before she went to bed, she called Zane to check in and see if he had gotten anywhere with the latest clue. The puzzle occasionally had come to mind when she wasn't thinking about George and Jennifer, but she hadn't figured out anything concrete.

"I haven't had much luck either," Zane confessed. "I've been so busy getting some auction items I purchased weeks ago ready for a sale this weekend that it has been pushed aside."

"What kind of stuff are we talking about?"

"I ended up with some vintage vases, a stamp collection, and, lucky me, an old sewing machine."

"Those shouldn't be too hard to get rid of."

"The sewing machine is one of those old Singers. The ones inside a table. It's a piece of furniture," Zane explained.

"I know how much you hate furniture." Maddy laughed. "If you can't find a buyer, take it to an antique mall. There's a woman there who collects old sewing machines."

"Seriously? I don't even want to imagine what her place must look like."

"Neither do I. But, all that matters to me is that she takes them off my hands."

"No kidding. Alright, where did we leave off last time with the clues?" Zane asked.

"Okay, last time we spoke, we believed it was either a bakery, coffee shop, or brewery, right?" she confirmed.

"Yeah, but none of the places in St. Albert fit that name," Zane said. "And we still need to work out the whole 'drive and strive', and 'community and unity'."

"Well, the first part refers to the business's name. I'll do a Google search for names synonymous with drive and strive and see if that gets me anywhere."

They sat quietly, each tapping away at their laptops, concentrating on their screens.

"I'm afraid there aren't any words that are synonyms for both," Maddy said.

"Let's start with 'strive' and look each of them up along with 'St. Albert'. What's the first word?" Zane asked.

They had gone through a few words when finally, they had a breakthrough.

"What about 'Endeavour'?" Maddy suggested.

"Bingo! Endeavour Brewing is in St. Albert."

"Does it fit the other clues as well?" Maddy's voice rose in excitement. "Let's look at their website."

"Well, would you look at that! They have information on both their beers and their coffees, on their front page!" Zane blurted out.

"Let's not get too ahead of ourselves," Maddy said. "The 'name says it all - Endeavour' and shows its drive as 'reaching forward I strive.' That fits. What about the second part, about its mission to create community?"

"Hmmm... it says here that they're a community-orientated craft brewery, so I think that pretty much speaks to that aspect," Zane responded.

"Great! It looks like the answer to this last clue is Endeavour Brewing. That means our answers are so far, Canada Post, West Edmonton Mall Ice Palace, and Endeavour Brewing. C.W.E. That seems strange," Maddy mused.

"Don't worry about that just now. Let's get all the clues and then work through the actual answer," Maddy could almost hear the smile in Zane's voice.

"What's the next clue? she asked.

"This one is a bit different.

'I'm the original land

from the north to the southern head

My name takes a stand.

A European shop in the southwest

A grocer's bounty that is eastern in the west.

Ask anyone

We know we're the best.'"

"Oh wow, this will require more than just tea." Maddy laughed. "I'm not sure where to even begin."

"We don't have to tackle it tonight, one clue figured out is enough I think," Zane reassured her. "My brain is usually a bit fried by this hour of night anyway."

"You'd never know it. You did pretty good tonight!" Maddy replied.

"We're good together!" There was an awkward pause before Zane stuttered. "What I meant is we work good together... umm... we're a good team."

"Yeah, we are, aren't we?"

"Well, okay then, I better get going. Talk to you later," Zane said, then hung up before she had the chance to say goodbye.

She looked at her phone, then at her laptop, wondering what that was all about.

Chapter 18

"Thanks for the java, Rick, What a nice surprise." Maddy hadn't expected to start her day with Rick showing up at her door with a coffee from her favorite roastery.

"I was in the neighborhood, so I figured why not?" He was sitting on her armchair, leaning back with legs outstretched, sipping away on his cup.

"Aw, you remembered that it was my fave. You're such a sweetheart."

"It's hard to forget, Maddy. Every single time we stop at that storage facility off Kingsway Avenue you mention it."

"You drove by Sentinel?"

"Yeah, I picked up some auto parts near there. I'm helping one of Tasha's uncles with some car repairs."

"That's nice of you," Maddy said. Rick was always more than happy to help anyone who asked him.

"It's not the only reason though..." he started fiddling with his keys, twirling them round and round.

"Spill it." Maddy had a feeling there was more to this morning's visit. Rick was not in the habit of stopping by with coffee for her. Beer in the afternoon or evening? He would often do that. Coffee in the morning? He had never done that before. She patiently watched him twirl his keys a couple more times before he put them in his pocket. She would wait until he was ready to speak.

"I'm worried about my mom." He bit his lower lip and ran his hand through his hair.

"What do you mean? Is she sick or something?"

Leila was Maddy's second mom. She had been her only mom since her mother died so many years ago. An incredibly kind woman in her mid-sixties, she and her husband took her in when all hell broke loose in Maddy's home. They shared what little they had without so much as a whisper of complaint. She had finally found out what family was all about. The thought of anything happening to Mama Leila caused her to sit up and take notice, worry written on her face.

"Nah, she's as healthy as a horse," he smiled, "but please, don't tell her that I compared her to a horse."

"I promise, I won't," Maddy said, relieved.

"Good!" Rick laughed. "She's lonely. Ever since Dad passed away a couple of years ago, she's been spending a lot of time at our place, perhaps too much of it; cooking, cleaning, looking after the girls." Rick took out his keys and started twirling once more. He fidgeted on the couch until he found a more comfortable position.

"And that's bad how?" She wished she had someone taking care of all the cooking and cleaning. Her place was not dirty because she cleaned it every Saturday morning, but she could be sleeping in or shopping instead.

"Tasha... Mama... The girls..." He lifted his arms and shook his hands to the heavens.

"Oh gawd! Say no more." Maddy could only imagine the overdose of estrogen and tension in the Nasser household.

"Yeah, Tasha loves Mama, but she's had her fill of hummus and constant vacuuming. Especially since she's between jobs again."

"Still no updates on when the funeral home will re-open?" Tasha had been temporarily laid off from her job at a funeral home a couple of years ago because they had to demolish and re-build it from scratch.

"The latest update was some delay due to a back order or something with a specific type of wood they want to have for each themed room." He rolled his eyes. "Honestly, there's other great-looking lumber out there. That owner is so damn picky."

"That's too bad. You need to either help Tasha find a job or get your mom a hobby."

"And that's where you come in!" he smiled his sweetest, dimpled smile.

"Damn you! I knew it. What do you want? I can keep my ears open for a job, but I don't know people who hire staff. I only know people who want to work."

"No, Tasha can find a job if she wants to. It's my mom. Maybe you can use her help or something?"

"I barely have enough work to keep myself busy. And, as much as I would love to have her come and take care of me, it's probably a bad idea."

"It's definitely a bad idea. I know firsthand."

"Maybe I can fix her up with someone? A boyfriend would keep her busy. I can ask PopPop?"

"What? NO! Habibti, he's too old for her! What are you thinking?" He was not amused. "That's all I need. Not only would I have to worry about my teenage daughters dating, but you want me to worry about some sex-crazed senior sniffing around my mother?"

Maddy tried hard not to laugh but lost it. She flopped over on the couch, unable to breathe, imagining her grandfather as being a sex-crazed senior.

"You think that's funny? Let me tell you, that's my worst nightmare, right there."

"No, that's NOT what I meant. Don't even go there." That would be her worst nightmare too. "What I meant, is that I can ask PopPop about community groups and activities. He's always busy volunteering to keep himself busy."

"Okay, that's more like it. That, I can live with," he said with relief.

"Oh crap." His phone alarm buzzed. "Sorry, habibti, I have to run. A highfalutin customer is coming in before lunch. Can't be late for that."

"Ooh, 'highfalutin', look at you getting rich customers now."

"Yeah, a cousin of Tasha's gave him my name. If I impress him, he could send his friends over. That could mean more money!"

The twins were always in need of something or another, such as new clothes, bikes, and shoes, and he was also putting money into a college fund for them every month. Plus, Rick liked having big toys.

"Good luck habibi. You better go then. By the way, I could get used to you dropping off lattes more often." Maddy walked him to the door and gave him a kiss on the cheek. "Give my love to all the ladies in your house!"

Rick waved a hand over his shoulder as he walked down the hallway toward the elevator. She double locked the door and returned to her laptop. Maddy opened the email entitled 'Jennifer's Friends'. George had taken all evening to type out a list of friends, preferred shops, and favorite hangouts. She made a mental note to show George and Rudy how to scan documents with their phones or, better yet, take a picture and send it. That would have been faster. She began by bringing up various social media sites to see if any of Jennifer's friends had posted anything for her on them.

As soon as Maddy had pulled up all the social media accounts, it was obvious that they would not be helpful. Nothing had changed since the last time she had checked them. The woman had not posted to her accounts for at least two weeks, and nobody had reached out on any of them either. Maddy had a bad feeling about things.

"Well, no time like the present to figure this out," Maddy muttered as she slung her purse over her shoulder and tucked her phone into it. First, she would stop by the day spa on George's list. Then she would pop into Jennifer's nail shop. In her experience, people took her more seriously if she showed up to ask her questions in person.

A FEW HOURS LATER, sitting at Campio's bar, Maddy was waiting for her late lunch pizza order. She decided she could not postpone the inevitable and called her grandfather to tell him that her search for Jennifer had turned up nothing. She had spoken to some of Jennifer's friends, and left messages for others, but couldn't directly connect with most of them.

When the pizza arrived, she ended her call and stood up, readying herself to leave. Turning around with her head down, she bumped into Marcus Hammond and dropped her pizza box.

"This is becoming a pleasant habit, Maddy," Marcus said, catching the pizza box before it landed on the floor.

"Good catch!"

"Pardon?"

"The pizza, good catch before it fell out of the box."

"Oh, yes. I have good reflexes. I used to play baseball a lot." His eyes twinkled mischievously as he handed her the pizza box.

"Damn!" Maddy said. 'Those eyes of his could melt an iceberg,' she thought.

"Is everything alright?" He tilted his head and examined her from head to toe. "I didn't hurt you by any chance?"

'Did I say that out loud? I better be more careful with my inside/outside voices,' Maddy made a mental note.

"No, no. Everything is fine," she replied. "I was only thinking that it would be nice to see you without accidentally bumping or tripping into you," she replied. "What brings you downtown to Campio's? And here? I hadn't pegged you as a bar kind of guy."

"I was meeting a client, but he just canceled. This place is his favorite hangout. Looks like you like it too."

"They make the best Detroit-style pizza in town."

"Are you in a hurry? I'd love to have a drink or lunch if you're not busy?"

"Umm... I have my lunch already," she said pointing at the box.

"Oh, yes, I see. Another time perhaps?" He looked down, shuffling his feet.

'How could one man look so good while looking so disappointed?' Maddy thought, hoping she had not sounded rude.

"You could still buy me a drink if you don't mind me eating my pizza in front of you?"

"I wouldn't mind at all." The smile came back to his face. "Pizzas are best eaten while they are hot out of the oven. I'll even order one, to keep you company, of course."

The restaurant wasn't full, but he led her to the back, choosing a secluded booth. She offered him a slice of pizza. When the waiter arrived, they ordered two rootbeers and Marcus' pizza. Seeing they were eating out of the box, the waiter quickly returned with plates and cutlery. Maddy stretched the mozzarella cheese off the pizza between her fingers, trying hard to wind it up. Marcus reached out with his napkin and dabbed a splatter of tomato sauce off her chin.

He then asked her about the paintings she had found in the locker at the Triple-A. He seemed particularly interested in the Billy Forest one.

"The Forest painting is quite valuable indeed. No wonder it had been hidden in a locker. It would be recognized in half a minute by anyone who knows anything about art," he said, then took the second slice of his pizza that Maddy had placed on his plate.

"How did you know it was that painting that was stolen?" Maddy asked.

"You told me when you bumped into me at the storage facility," Marcus replied.

Maddy could not remember telling him. She was certain that PopPop had stopped her before she had said too much. She must have been mistaken

"Tell me more about the other paintings. Did you find any buyers for them?"

Maddy described the paintings. Most were sold but two were still in her possession. Marcus listened intently. He nodded every so often to show his interest or agreement. He asked what other items she tended to come across and which type of items she preferred. Maddy was thrilled to share her passion for her work with someone other than her friends. Marcus seemed extremely interested. She might have judged him too rashly the other day. Maybe, her grandfather had been wrong about him too. Here she was, enjoying herself, with a man, out on a date. Perhaps she should take a page out of Ashley's book. It was time for her to have fun.

"It sounds like you lead a fascinating life," Marcus remarked.

"I can't believe it could be any more fascinating than yours?"

"Yes, but I usually frequent art houses or gallery auctions. I am an art buyer. Clients hire me to find pieces they want to add to their collection or by an artist they admire. And then there are some who want to invest in works of art for their potential future monetary value."

Maddy wasn't sure if that was a slight or not, but she decided to give him the benefit of the doubt.

"What a coincidence! One of my best friends does the same thing," Maddy said. "She travels the world looking for artwork for her clients. She loves her job."

"What is her name? Perhaps I know her. Art buyers tend to travel in the same circles."

"Her name is Ashley Mueller," she answered, half expecting him to say he knew her well.

"Ashley... Mueller..." he repeated her name and thought about it briefly. "Oh yes! I believe I met her once or twice at one of the auction houses in British Columbia. Tall, blonde, athletic looking?"

"Sounds like my Ashley."

"I can't say I know her well, though. We were introduced once, years ago. In general, we run in different circles," he said. "I'm sure she is a lovely person."

"She is. And fun too. She's always willing to tag along on any of my wild escapades. Just the other day, she was beyond excited to help me with Spencer's Ducks..."

"Did you say, 'Spencer's Ducks'?" Marcus interrupted her mid-sentence. "As in Mitchell Spencer?"

"Yes, you know about them?"

"Only someone living under a rock for the last 30 years wouldn't know about them! Tell me everything about them. How many are there? I've heard that someone in Edmonton owns several. Would the owner be interested in selling them?" The questions tumbled from his mouth one after the other before Maddy could answer him.

"Slow down, Marcus." She laughed. "One question at a time!"

"Sorry, but the Spencer Ducks are a big deal. I'm surprised someone involved with storage auctions would have the chance to come across them." He took a swig from his beer as Maddy stared at him in disbelief.

"Pardon, what do you mean by that?"

"It isn't in your line of expertise, that's all I meant. They are big-league works of art. I'm surprised someone of Ashley's lower caliber of art dealing has even come across them." The waiter had appeared with his pizza and placed it on the table. Marcus laid a napkin on his lap and took a slice. Maddy noticed he did not even acknowledge the waiter's existence.

"Hmm..." Maddy looked at him and for the first time, noticed that the clear blue eyes she had been so in awe of now looked cold and arrogant.

"I would love to have a chance to make an offer on any ducks he might have," Marcus continued. "Could you arrange a meeting for me?"

"I'm almost 100 percent sure he isn't interested in selling them."

"People are always sure until they look at a big cheque," Marcus chuckled. "It's amazing how often people change their minds."

"I don't get the impression that money is an issue for him,"

"Money is an issue for everyone, even those with lots of money, trust me," Marcus said. "Those that have a lot of money want more just as much as the buffoon who has none."

Maddy gave him a half smile and picked up the last slice of her pizza. Growing increasingly uncomfortable, she wanted to make excuses to get out of there as soon as possible. Her eyes roamed the bar as he continued to talk about the Spencer Ducks. 'What was it with these art people and those damned rubber duckies? Granted, they were cute with each having their own little personality, cowboy, superhero, diva, and so on, but come on,' she wondered. 'Why get excited over something you can find in real rubber on any dollar store shelf?' Maddy might have been exaggerating a tad, but she was getting fed up with everyone losing their minds over these ducks.

"So, if you can tell him, please, I will make myself available to meet him whenever he wants, and please, give him my phone number. That should get things started."

"I don't feel comfortable approaching him with this when I know he isn't interested in selling," Maddy protested, resentful that he was not taking no for an answer.

"Oh, he won't mind." He waved his hand, as though shooing away an annoying black fly. "As a matter of fact, he will thank you when he finds out how much my clients would be willing to pay for them." Maddy sat quietly, realizing that arguing with him was a losing battle. She simply was not going to do as he asked. There was no way she was going to abuse her friendship with George and allow art buyers to hound him. Especially with everything he was going through. No matter how elevated in status Marcus felt about himself, he was a small time in her eyes.

IT WAS THREE IN THE afternoon when Maddy arrived home, having finally extracted herself from Marcus' university-level lecture on Spencer's Ducks and his badgering for a meeting with George. She would not let this full-of-himself guy change her resolve to have more fun. All she needed was to find other guys to date. 'But who?' she wondered. Maddy made a list of all the men she knew, then removed the unavailable ones and those she would not date no matter what, Kyle and Rick being two of them. Her cell rang, it was Marcus. 'What could he want so soon?' She wondered.

"Hi Maddy, I had a wonderful time over lunch today. Did you make it home all right?"

"Hey, Marcus. Yes, I'm home safe and sound, thank you but you didn't have to check in on me."

"It's the least I can do to ensure that a lovely lady arrives unscathed after a date with me."

"Alright. Well as you can see, all is okay at my end."

"Speaking of dates... would you like to have dinner with me one evening this week?"

"Umm, I have a pretty busy schedule for the next couple of weeks."

"Why don't you look at your calendar and text me when you have a free evening then? It would be nice to spend time with you again."

"Okay, I will if something opens up, no promises though." The likelihood of that happening was slim to none if Maddy had her way.

"I understand. I look forward to hearing from you soon. Might even bump into each other at an auction before that."

"Haha, maybe. Talk to you later."

Maddy ended the call, sat back in her dining room chair, and crossed Marcus' name off her 'Possible Men to Date' list. She had to figure out a way to be dissuasive while keeping him as a potential buyer. This could be tricky. She went back to her list. While hovering over Jon's name, her phone rang again.

"Hello?"

"Hello Maddy, how are you this lovely Friday afternoon?" Jon asked.

"I'm doing quite well, and you?" Maddy could not help but smile. This call certainly improved her mood.

"I'm fine, thank you. I would be even finer if you would give me the pleasure of dining with me this evening?"

'WOW!' Maddy thought. 'Two dates in one day.' Lady Luck was on her side today.

"I happen to be free tonight and would love to have dinner with you."

"Wonderful, please wear something dressy, I'm in a celebratory mood. How does the revolving restaurant at the Chateau Lacombe sound to you?"

"The Chateau? What are we celebrating?" The revolving restaurant overlooking downtown Edmonton was quite fancy.

"I just sold an expensive Lawren Harris painting for a client and earned a large commission. I wanted to celebrate and you're the first person that came to mind. You made quite an impression on me the other day."

"Oh, that's so nice of you. Lawren Harris, the name sounds familiar, but I can't place him. I don't know much about painters. That's what I have Ashley for." She laughed, thrilled that he wanted to celebrate with her.

"He's one of the Group of Seven."

"Ah yes, I've heard of them as a group. I don't feel so clueless now."

"You're anything but clueless. How does six thirty sound? I'll text you when I'm on my way."

"Six thirty is perfect. I'll be waiting for you in the lobby."

"Excellent. See you then."

Maddy was delighted. 'What better way to start the weekend,' she felt, 'than on a hot date with an attractive man?' Her delight slowly faded as she realized she had a phone call to make before getting too excited. She reached for her phone again.

"Hello Mads, what can I do for you, darling?" Ashley sounded like she was on the speakerphone.

"Hey, whatcha doin'?"

"I'm driving back from a client."

"So..."

"Yeessss?" Ashley asked.

"Umm..."

"Okay, now I'm nervous. What's on your mind girlfriend?"

"So... I decided to take a page out of your 'I want to have fun' book," Maddy finally blurted out.

"Which page? That makes a significant difference in how I'll react to this revelation. Do I need to pull over?"

"I don't think you need to pull over. I've decided to start dating just for the fun of it. I feel like I'm missing out," she said, adding, "I bumped into Marcus today."

"Like bumped bumped?"

"Yup, literally. I ran right into him and just about ended up wearing my pizza."

"Is this going to become a habit, and does he have anything to do with your taking a page out of my book?"

"Yes and no. I don't intend to make running into him a habit, but that's a story to share over wine. Having lunch with him has me hankering for male company. You never know, I might meet someone decent like Kyle."

"Maddy..."

"I'm not nagging you. I'm just saying that Kyle is the kind of nice guy I would like to meet. That's all. Nothing more, nothing less."

"As long as we have that clear. Now, I sense you didn't call me to chew the fat. What do you really want?"

"Okay, here goes nothing. What would you say if I went on a serious date with your friend Jon?"

"Didn't we already have this conversation a few days ago, darling? I told you that I'm not interested in him, remember?"

"Yes, but this is a serious date."

"How serious are we talking here?"

"He asked me out to the Chateau Lacombe for dinner tonight." Maddy heard Ashley whistle.

"The Chateau? This could lead to heavy-duty action afterward. Are you good with that?"

"I'm nervous but more than good with that."

"Yeah, you have an itch long overdue to be scratched, girl."

"That's putting it mildly."

"Well, if it's my blessing you're looking for, you have it. Go get lucky. But don't expect a serious relationship from this guy. He's a ladies' man."

"I'm fine with that. Remember, I'm taking a page from your book."

"That's what I'm afraid of."

SITTING AT A TABLE next to the window in the La Ronde restaurant at the top of Chateau Lacombe, Maddy looked out at the setting sun reflecting over the river valley.

"I love it up here. It's so beautiful," she wistfully said.

"It is lovely." Jon agreed. His eyes never left her face, causing Maddy to blush.

"So how long have you been in the reselling business?" Jon asked. "You appear to be pretty successful."

"It's been a few years. I'm making headway in the business, but I have a lot of plans for the future,"

"Like what?"

"I want to set up a street-level retail shop where people can come to me rather than me running around the city."

"That sounds like a good idea. Have you done any market research yet?"

"At this point, only preliminary, and I am fairly familiar with the market in Edmonton. I will be developing a full business plan when I get closer to being ready."

"Well, if you keep finding art in storage units that are worth something, it won't be long," Jon raised his glass of wine to toast her. She took a sip and smiled widely back at him.

"How are you doing with the rest of the paintings from your unit? I know the Forrest was stolen, but have you been able to find buyers for them?"

"I've found buyers for most of them and one or two are going out on consignment."

"Have any other units with artwork come your way since then?" Jon leaned back as the waiter appeared with their appetizers.

She could not help but notice that he smiled at their server and said thank you. He had been kind and polite to all the staff they had encountered. He was attentive to her and seemed to honestly care how she felt about the different subjects they had discussed. Jon was a true gentleman. She was liking him more and more.

"OH, MY LORD, THIS IS one of the most divine dinners I've had in a long time." Maddy was thankful to be wearing a dress this evening and not pants. At least in a dress, there was room for expansion.

"I admire a woman who thoroughly enjoys a meal the way it should be and does not worry herself about calories," Jon said as he took the last bite from their shared mango cheesecake. "You savored every delectable morsel. It was pure ecstasy to watch you."

Maddy melted at his description of her eating. The food was exquisite. She hoped he did not think she ate too much. The last thing she wanted was to appear to be a glutton.

"Don't get me wrong, I do count calories but not when I dine in a place like the Chateau. I mean, how can you?"

"Darling Maddy, I did not mean to insult you. Please tell me that I did not hurt your feelings. I simply find you so refreshing to be around."

"None taken." She loved his British accent and melted further. "Do you come here often?"

"I try to eat in this restaurant at least once per visit. I enjoy the food and the breathtaking view," he said, still not looking away from her.

"It is a beautiful view." Maddy agreed. She could not help but notice that he had spent most of their meal looking at her and not at the view.

It felt warm in the restaurant. It could be because of the Châteauneuf du Pape they had been drinking. She had indulged in three glasses after all.

"This was such a lovely evening. Thank you, Jon."

"It doesn't have to end, Maddy. If you're so inclined." His piercing eyes looked deeply into hers.

Not trusting her voice, Maddy nodded yes. Jon paid their bill, put his warm hand on the small of her back, and led her to the elevator. They drove to her place in silence. She felt her body trembling in anticipation. 'Calm down,' she told herself, glancing furtively at him as he maneuvered his sporty rental car down Jasper Avenue.

Jon dropped her off at her building's entrance and went to park his car. Up in her apartment, she looked around to make sure she had not missed tidying anything up when she left earlier. She debated opening a bottle of wine but thought better of it. She had drunk enough wine during dinner. Instead, she took out a bottle of Frangelico that she kept as a treat and two small crystal liqueur glasses.

Her phone rang; Jon was downstairs. She buzzed him up and grabbed a mint from her purse on her way to open the door. She looked through the peephole and, taking a deep breath, let him in.

"You look stunning in that dress," he said, leaning against the door frame. "Absolutely stunning."

"Won't you come in?" she said, barely above a whisper.

Jon stepped forward and closed the door behind them. Maddy started to walk toward the living room when he took her by the shoulders and gently turned her toward him. He lifted her chin slightly and gently brushed his lips against hers. Maddy's knees felt weak, as though they might buckle beneath her. Her heart started to beat faster.

"Please forgive me for my forwardness," he whispered, standing mere inches from her. "I have been wanting to kiss you all evening."

She was at a loss for words, her breath taken away by his closeness. Spying the bottle of Frangelico on the counter, she cleared her mind enough to offer him a drink.

"Would you like a liqueur?"

"That would be splendid, thank you."

She brought the bottle and glasses to the living room and placed them on the table in front of the couch. They sat down and he poured them each a couple of ounces. As they clinked glasses, he accidentally spilled some. She got up and went to get a napkin from the kitchen. When she returned, he had moved the throw pillows off the couch. He took the towel from her, dried off the golden drops, and placed the folded linen on the coffee table. He then handed her glass back. He lightly glided his fingers over her hand as he let go of it. Maddy felt shivers run from her fingers straight to her spine. They took a few sips. She could feel him undressing her with his eyes. 'Oh, boy,' she thought, 'this is going to happen.'

He leaned toward Maddy, placed his hand behind her neck, and kissed her. More passionately this time, making her toes curl and her spine arch. His hand slowly moved down, unzipping her dress as it sensually caressed her back. Maddy moaned softly. His hand slid her dress off her shoulders, and with a single finger, he traced the curve of her breast. Their kiss became more intense. And then he stopped, stood up, and walked to the front door.

"I'm sorry Maddy. I can't do this," he said.

"What? Why? What do you mean you can't do this?" Maddy scrambled to pull her dress back on, fumbling with the zipper.

"I like you, but I think we need to wait."

"Umm... Why?" She half walked, half stumbled to the door, still trying to do up her zipper. He stood with his back to her, facing the small entryway dresser and mirror, unable to face her.

She could see her reflection in the mirror. She did not like what was looking back at her. It was a desperate woman. Maddy had no clue what she should do.

"Darling, I worry that if we go too fast, we'll lose some of the fun and spark we have. Once we sleep together, we can't go back. Let's take our time and enjoy the exquisite pain of longing. Let's take it slow, alright?" He turned around and took her chin in his hand once again. Why on earth did that move her so?

"Okay, I guess?" Maddy took a step back; she did not want to see herself in the mirror anymore.

"Let's plan to have coffee soon. Get to know each other better and see where this could lead?" He gently let go of her chin. "I'm in town for another week or so, depending on how quickly my business in Edmonton is done."

"And then what?"

How could they take it slow, Maddy wondered, if he was not around? A long-distance relationship was not what she had in mind when she decided to have fun.

"Then, maybe, you can come and visit me? I can find more clients here and fly in more often."

"I don't know about that, Jon. I think I need something else. No, I know that I need something else."

"Why don't you sleep on it? We can talk more tomorrow, alright?" He kissed her on the forehead, opened the door, shoved both hands in his pockets, and walked out, leaving her standing with her mouth agape.

"What on earth just happened?" she asked her reflection. "The hell with the Frangelico, I need Scotch."

She took out the bottle of Glenfiddich she kept stashed behind her only plant, grabbed a tumbler, and sat at the table. Staring out the window, she took a drink and listened to a Canada Goose honk goodnight.

"Guess it's just me and the geese."

MADDY COULD HEAR A strange noise somewhere in the distance. She groaned and opened her eyes to find herself still lying on her living room couch.

She sat up and rubbed her eyes. The bottle of Scotch and Frangelico sat next to each other. They were still full, but her tumbler of Scotch and liqueur glass were both empty. She could remember lying down because she felt dizzy. She must have fallen asleep. Maddy looked at the time on her phone. It was ten in the evening, and she had missed two calls. Only an hour had passed since Jon had left.

Maddy did not understand what had happened. She was left wondering if she was so out of touch that she could have possibly done something to turn him off just as things started to develop. Reviewing the evening with Jon, she could not think of anything that could have caused him to run for the hills.

'What grown man says let's take it slow when it's a sure thing?' she asked herself. She was too old to play these types of games. Ashley did say he was a 'love them and leave them' sort of guy. But Maddy had hoped it would go further than a petting session before he would leave her. What a crazy day; twice hopeful and twice disappointed. She needed to revisit her decision to 'have some fun'. It most certainly was not going the way she had anticipated.

Chapter 19

M addy had been on the road for over an hour when she saw the exit for Mulhurst. She was grateful the Saturday morning traffic had not been too bad. It would not be much longer until she arrived at her destination.

Earlier this morning, she had received a text message from Jennifer's friend Katie saying she had just remembered Jennifer mentioning something about wanting to go to the Inn at Pigeon Lake for a week-long spa getaway. Katie had passed on the invitation to go along and put it out of her mind. It could be that Jennifer had gone there with another friend or even on her own. Maddy certainly hoped so. A spa retreat would explain why she was not answering her phone or taking texts. But that still did not explain the attack on Maddy at Government House. She intended to get answers, especially regarding the attack.

A pair of Canada Geese flew overhead and made her smile. The family of geese on her rooftop had been happy to see her this morning when she dropped off a large plastic bowl of dried cracked corn, wild bird seed, and a bit of fresh kale. 'Who would have thought they liked kale?' she laughed. That was one for the trivia books. Maddy had learned so much about their behavior and needs. She planned to refill the bowl every two days or so. 'They can't only depend on me, they need to find some food on their own too', she thought as she pulled into the parking lot the inn shared with nearby businesses.

She spotted the cute café she liked going to whenever she came here with Ashley and Tasha for a girl's weekend. After dealing with the Jennifer business, she planned to stop there for lunch before heading home. It would be a well-deserved reward.

"WHAT DO YOU MEAN, SHE'S not here?" Maddy asked. "Is she not staying at the Inn, or is she not in her room at the moment?"

"I'm sorry, but we cannot give out any information about our guests' whereabouts on the property," the front desk clerk informed her.

"I'm her sister. It's a family emergency and we can't reach her," Maddy looked at the clerk's name tag. " Please Serena, can't you give me any information? Please."

"I'm sorry, Miss." Serena looked back at the computer screen. "Maybe I can take a message? I could enter it here and she will get a text asking her to stop at the desk if you would like?"

"I guess... "

"Oh, well this is odd."

"What's odd?"

"Your sister never checked in."

"She hasn't checked in at all over the last week?" Maddy leaned closer, trying to look at the computer screen. "But you said she wasn't in. I'm confused."

"She's in our system as a paid guest. See?" Serena turned the screen toward her. "Her room was booked and fully paid for a one-week stay. That explains why she didn't answer when I called her room. She never showed up!"

"Fully paid?" That made no sense to Maddy.

"Yes. There's even a note here saying that we tried to contact her twice by email and twice by phone, but the guest never replied. Serena pointed at the note section.

"I hope your sister's all right. Sorry that I couldn't be of any more help."

"Me too. Thank you anyway."

Maddy left the inn so distracted that she walked by the candy shop with not even a glance into its tempting front window as she made her way to the café. She took a seat by the window and stared into the distance. She only snapped out of it when it came time to place her order.

After glancing at the familiar menu, she ordered wild mushroom crostini, fries, and ginger beer. She called George and updated him on what she had found out. He would contact the police station to fill them in.

This could change the priority level, and the police might want to contact the inn themselves to confirm her findings. This latest situation had left her perplexed. That was an expensive no-show for someone who seemed very much interested in getting money. Jennifer loved money, and Maddy did not think she would throw it away, not like that. She wondered what could make her walk away from a much-desired spa getaway. Perhaps, she thought, the question should have been 'Who', and not 'What' kept her away. And why not cancel? Unless she could not cancel. Maybe she, or someone else wanted to give the appearance of her being away for a week. Maddy had so many unanswered questions.

'That's strange,' she thought as she looked at her cellphone. A call was coming in from an unknown number.

"Hello?"

"Hello, is this Maddy?" asked a familiar voice. "It's Marcus."

"Oh, hello Marcus," Maddy replied, wondering what on earth he wanted from her. She was not pleased to have her thoughts interrupted. "How did you get my cell number?"

"That odd little man who runs Triple-A storage gave it to me. I may have told him a little white lie to get it," he said. "I had such a great time over pizza with you the other day, and I was wondering if you might want to go out for drinks this afternoon?"

"That's sweet of you, but I'm out of town this afternoon..."

"This evening then? I could pick you up?"

"NO!" She had not meant for it to come out this way, but let it slip out before she could stop herself. Maddy did not want to fall victim to another man whose intentions did not appear to be the same as hers, especially one who thought too highly of himself. "What I meant is, no thank you. I'm not sure when I'll be home, and I will likely be tired by then."

"Oh, that's too bad. Next week, perhaps? I would love to talk more about the Spencer Ducks you found and any other works of art you might have encountered. Plus, I think you're quite lovely. Your green eyes mesmerize me. It would be wonderful to get to know each other better."

"Umm, I don't know Marcus. I have a pretty busy week," she said.

'Talk about artwork? So that he could condescend to her again?' Maddy thought. 'No, thank you very much.'

"Perhaps some other time then? I won't give up until you say yes."

"Right now, it's hard for me to pin anything down. I'm in the middle of something and it's taking up most of my time outside of work..."

"Maybe I can help?"

"No, that's kind of you, thank you, but it's not necessary. My friend Zane is helping me." She hated using Zane this way.

"Zane?"

"You may have seen him around during some of the auctions. He has spiky hair and a tattoo sleeve. We're rather close."

"Oh, I see. Well, whenever you are free, please call me at this number."

"Alright, I'll be seeing you around the auctions. Talk to you later."

Maddy put her phone away and looked out the café's window. 'What was going on here? Marcus seemed very determined to go out with her,' she thought, reflecting on their conversation, 'He must have wanted something more than to talk about art, but what? The paintings she had left were not worth much. He must want an in with George. Damn it! She should never have mentioned those ducks. Her grandfather had been right about him.'

She thought she had better text Zane and let him know what she had just done. There was nothing worse, in her opinion, than getting caught in a lie, even an innocent one. Hopefully, he would not mind. She sent him a much too detailed text but felt it necessary, it would be better that way.

'Let me get this straight,' Zane texted back. 'We're really close? How close is really close? Wink Wink. Plus, I'm helping you with something and you don't want to give this Marcus guy any false hopes?'

'Pretty much,' she texted back.

'Got it. LOL! You owe me BIG time now.'

'Name it, anytime.'

'Words you will regret. ;-)'

'Ha! Ha! Thanks, chat later.'

She was smiling at her phone when a shadow fell across her table. Anticipating her food, she happily looked up but it was not the server.

"Maddy? I can't believe my luck! I have been wanting to call you."

"Jon? What are you doing here?"

"I was told there was a wonderful antique shop in the village. I thought I would take a Saturday to drive out to the countryside and investigate. One of my clients is quite taken with Canadian antiques," Jon replied. "Might I join you?"

"It's not a good time, nor a good idea, right now." Maddy needed to concentrate on this Jennifer mystery, not on a good-looking man who wanted a serious relationship.

"Please, Maddy. I won't take much of your time, I promise."

"Alright, just for a few minutes." He was making it hard for her to say no.

"I'm surprised to see you here. What brings you out this way? Were you shopping for antiques too?"

"No, I'm here on a personal matter. An elderly friend has been trying to reach someone who might be here. I thought I would check it out for him." She was not going to give him any more details. Keeping this conversation as short as possible was her goal.

"Oh, that's nice of you. Are you going home soon? Perhaps we can have dinner tonight?"

"No, I'm sorry, I plan on staying here for a few hours. I have stuff to do." There was no way Maddy wanted to have dinner with him. She was still smarting from their last encounter.

"Maddy, I'm sorry things didn't go the way you might have wanted them to last night." He reached for her hand. "I know that if we had jumped into something, it wouldn't be as rewarding as if we waited a little longer. I don't want to rush this relationship. You're different from all the other women I know."

"Look, Jon, I'm not interested in any long-term relationships, believe it or not. I'm not in that kind of place yet. Emotionally, that is."

Over a year ago she had ended a dysfunctional relationship with a needy guy named Chad. Jon appeared needy but in a different way. She could not quite put her finger on it but the signs were all there, warning her to stay away.

"I guess I had hoped it could be more than a single night of fun," Jon said. "But I understand. You're a marvelous lady, Maddy. Could we remain friends? I'd love to reach out to you business-wise. You have a good eye, and I could always use someone on the lookout for works of art for me at this end of the world."

"Absolutely, Jon." She smiled. "It would be my pleasure to keep in touch on art and such."

He took her hand and lightly kissed it before getting up and leaving. Maddy watched him walk out the café's door and sighed.

"Damn, he's delicious looking," she sighed.

Her luck with men needed to improve. Maddy wanted a fun, casual, friends-with-benefits type of relationship. She really liked Jon. If he had been living in the city, maybe she would have changed her mind about having a more serious relationship. A cross-country affair would be the opposite of what she was looking for. Jon was so nice. She liked him a lot. Her new resolve to have fun was not as easy as Ashley had made it look. Maybe that is why Ashley was playing it safe with Garry. There is nothing worse in Maddy's opinion than being involved with someone not on the same wavelength as you.

'Should I be looking for a long-term relationship?' she asked herself. 'Dang it! This is too complicated.' Celibacy was starting to look like a viable option.

Having had enough of male distractions for one day, she decided to drive down to the lakeshore and go for a walk. Maybe it would help her to come up with some new possibilities regarding Jennifer's disappearance. She needed to gather her thoughts and sort out what she had uncovered.

After fifteen minutes of trying to find a parking spot on the village's busy lake drive, she drove two blocks from the boardwalk and lucked out. She grabbed her water bottle, crossed the street, and walked until she found an unoccupied bench looking out across the lake. The events of the last two weeks spun in her mind like a roulette table. Every time it stopped on a thought, she took it apart and analyzed each piece.

Maddy tried to put everything back together. No matter how hard she tried, nothing made sense, not logically, that is.

First, if Jennifer only wanted the money for the rubber duckies, then she could have asked. George would have paid a fair price for them. He had already said that. So, it was also about enjoying the game for her too. But why suddenly stop?

Second, if she had stopped due to a new boyfriend, her friends would have known about it, and her social media posts would have had his picture all over them.

Third, there was also Maddy's apartment to think about, she reminded herself. It had been broken into once, and she had also been followed and twice accosted. Could all four events involving her have been related to George's art pieces? But she had not known about George when the first break-in occurred.

Fourth, if someone had indeed hurt Jennifer and stolen the art, why not sell it on the black market instead of running the risk of getting caught while doing exchanges? And why go after Maddy and not George? Or why not offer Jennifer lots of money for them? Where could Jennifer be? Why make it look like she went on a spa getaway? Did she still love George? Was that why someone interfered? What about the last duck? Was the Billy Forrest painting worth attacking someone for?

An hour later, Maddy had given up. She concluded there was more to this missing Jennifer mystery than she, her grandfather, and George could figure out together. It was time to let the police take over.

It was still early enough in the afternoon to stop at a few specialty shops along the way home. There were great little delis, bakeries, and a brewery on the drive back. A light charcuterie board supper on the rooftop would be the perfect way to end the day and take her mind off things. She felt terrible for George and his ex-wife, wherever she might be. Maddy had done everything she could, and if she were to be honest, this whole situation had nothing to do with her. It was a favor for PopPop. She had gone far beyond her definition of what 'doing a favor' was. She had gathered more than enough information to help the police find Jennifer. There were enough other things on her plate to manage these days.

At her last foodie shop stop, she texted Zane to ask him to join her. She did owe him a meal after all, and it would be a good opportunity to work on that puzzle. Yes, a nice rooftop dinner would help distract her from Jennifer, George, and those damned ducks.

JUGGLING HER PARCELS, she fumbled with her keys and the door locks. She was relieved that the bolt lock had not jammed as usual. Once inside her apartment, she placed her bags on the floor and locked the door behind her.

'It's so good to be home and know that you have a relaxing evening ahead,' she thought as she put away the food and beer. She needed more of these, no more doing favors for everyone who asked. Especially when the weather was nice and warm once again. Maddy disliked winter. It would be unbearable if it were not for NHL hockey, fireplaces, and skating. She entered the living room and pulled a picnic basket and blanket out from one of her chests. While closing the lid, she heard a loud noise coming from her bedroom. She looked up and saw movement through the open door. It wasn't coming from an open window this time as she had made sure to shut all of them before leaving for the lake this morning.

Maddy wondered what she should do. She had to walk by the bedroom to get to the front door. Whoever was inside her room knew she had heard them; the noise had been too loud. Her trusty bat in the front closet was out of reach. What else did she have nearby that she could use for self-defense? She spotted a vase sitting on the side table and quietly grabbed it. Holding it high over her head she tiptoed toward her bedroom. Slowly entering the room, she glanced around, but nothing and no one was there. 'The door!' she thought. They were probably standing behind it, or they were in her closet. She quickly pulled the door away from the wall and swung the vase toward that space. It went through empty air and hit the wall with a thud, shooting pain right through her arm.

"Oh, Ouch! Ouch! Ouch!" she cried out, realizing too late that she had cried out loud from the pain. Feeling a looming presence behind, she turned around and was engulfed by something heavy.

Everything went black.

MADDY HAD NO IDEA WHERE she was or what time it might be when she came to. All she was aware of was the stinging pain in her left shoulder and a burning sensation in the opposite arm.

"Un-freakin'-believable!" she swore under her breath. "Where the hell am I?"

She tried to get out from under whatever was covering her. She realized that some rope was probably wrapped around her body and held her arms down. She started to panic, then kicked, and yelled over and over. No luck. All that thrashing around had only made her shoulder hurt more. At least she had loosened one hand and could now grab her cell phone from her jeans' back pocket. She flipped it around and turned her flashlight app on. She was covered with what looked like a blue blanket. Yes, it was her blanket. She recognized the dark Merlot wine stain from when she had spilled some on her bed.

"Okay, Maddy, think." She leaned her head against what felt like a wall and turned her flashlight off, as there was no sense in wasting the battery. Bending her knees, she held the phone against them through the blanket, angled it, and held it with her pinky to stop it from falling over. Using her thumb, she entered her password.

"Hallelujah, it works!" Maddy speed-dialed Ashley.

"Hey Maddy, how was your outing to Pigeon Lake?"

"Ashley, listen carefully," Maddy whispered. "I don't know where I am. I've been kidnapped. I can't text because I'm tied up. There's not much battery life left. Can you track my phone?"

"Talus Balls! Maddy, are you hurt?" Ashley whispered back. "No, don't answer, keep as quiet as possible. I'll track you and come right away."

"Call Cops, please," she replied, trying to minimize any possibility of being heard.

"I will. Hang up and save your battery." Ashley said. Holding back her tears she added, "I love you."

Maddy did as she was told. A single tear rolled down her cheek. She lifted her free hand and wiped it away, still holding her phone with the other. That's when she realized her other hand was free. She must have loosened whatever had her tied up when she bent her knees. She pushed her phone through the opening of her shirt and into her bra, then inched her way up the wall until she stood straight.

She scooped up the bottom of the blanket with both hands. She tried to lift it over her head. That did not work. She let everything drop, and that seemed to loosen the rope. Maddy twisted and turned until she felt it fall around her feet. She lifted one foot at a time and the blanket came up too. She was finally free!

Standing still, in total darkness, she noticed something tiny glowing in front of her. It was a sticker that said, 'If you can read this, you're not dreaming.' Maddy realized this was the sticker she had purchased herself as a joke. She was in her bathroom! She ran her hands along the walls until she found the light switch and flipped it on. Temporarily blinded, she sat on the toilet seat holding her hands over her eyes and sighed. At least, she knew where she was, and that was a good thing. Able to focus again, she went to the door and tried to open it. The handle turned a bit, but something wasn't allowing it to turn all the way.

She texted Ashley, 'I'm home, locked in bathroom. Can't get out. Don't know if I'm alone in the apartment.'

Ashley texted back, 'I know, I'm downstairs waiting for Kyle and Rick. Sit tight.'

It was the longest ten minutes of Maddy's life.

Finally, she heard Ashley hollering her name and the sound of something being dragged across the floor away from the bathroom door. When the door opened toward her, Maddy was met with three very concerned-looking friends trying to enter the bathroom at the same time. Ashley won out and squeezed her friend in a tight hug.

"Are you okay? Please, tell me that you're, okay?"

"I am now that you're all here."

THEY STARTED BARRAGING Maddy with questions at the same time. She looked from one to the other, uncertain who to answer first.

Kyle quieted everyone down and took over.

"First, are you hurt?"

"My shoulder hurts and my other arm burns."

"Do you know why?"

"I remember swinging a vase behind the door and hitting the wall. The pain shot through my arm and up to my shoulder. I don't know why the other arm burns."

"Can you roll up your sleeve so we can take a look, please?" Maddy rolled it up and Kyle moved closer to her to look at her arm. "Your arm has a red area the size of an apple. It looks like you were injected with something and had a reaction," he pulled out his phone. "I'm going to call an ambulance; you need to get this checked out."

"No, please don't, I feel fine. I'm sure it will pass."

"Maddy, habibti, Kyle is right," Rick said, bending over to look at the redness. "You need to get this looked at. If it's an allergic reaction, it could get worse."

"I don't want to go to the hospital in an ambulance because of something small. It doesn't make sense to waste their time when someone worse off might need it."

"Mads, how about I drive you to the hospital?" Ashley asked. Then you could spend the night at my place. How does that sound?"

"That works for me," Maddy said. "Thanks, Ash, I'm not comfortable staying the night here anyway. Not until we figure out how someone got into my apartment."

"Maddy? I brought wine," a male voice called from the front door. "Are you home? The door's open, do you want me to come in?"

"Oh shoot! I forgot about Zane." She called out to him to come in. Zane walked into her apartment and assessed the scene in front of him.

"I feel like I walked into something serious here," he said. "Are you alright, Maddy? Do you need help?"

"It's okay, Zane. These are my friends, Ashley, Rick, and Kyle," she replied. The three smiled and nodded in his direction. "Kyle is a detective. I was knocked out and locked in my bathroom. They're here to help. I should have called you and canceled. I'm so sorry."

"What? Please, don't apologize. You had good reason to forget about tonight."

"I was just about to take her to the hospital to have her checked out," Ashley said.

"Good, I hope it's not another concussion," Zane said. "One a year isn't a goal to aim for, you know?"

"You're one trouble magnet, Maddy," Kyle said. "I'm going to call and get an investigative unit here to check for prints and possible evidence because, this time, you were hurt."

"This time?" Zane looked from Kyle to Maddy.

"She didn't tell you?" Rick looked at her. "Someone broke into her place last week and messed it up."

"I think they were probably looking for one of the paintings I got at the auction. I'd forgotten to lock my door, and they just walked in while I was out," she explained.

"And how did they get in this time?" Zane asked. "You didn't forget to lock your door a second time, did you?"

"No, I remember locking it. I don't know how they got in."

"Maddy, are your spare keys still on top of that dresser at the front door?" Ashley asked.

"Yes, I always leave them there."

Ashley went to look in the bowl where she kept them. They were missing.

"Damn! Now I have to change the locks on top of everything."

"Hey, that's how I can help you," Zane offered. "I know a locksmith. Let me call and have him come right over, okay?"

"That's a good idea, Zane, the sooner, the better," Kyle said. "Ashley, please take her to the hospital. I'll stay until the unit arrives and get them started. Rick, can you lock up after they and the locksmith are done?"

"Yeah, no problem," Rick said. "Let me call Tasha and update her. I'll even fix up your room when the cops are done so you can return to a tidy place."

"I can help you, Rick, if you want?" Zane said. "This way you're not here too late."

"I appreciate that, man," Rick said.

"Okay ladies, go to the hospital," Kyle instructed them. "Once I've updated the unit, I'll meet you there with a colleague to take your statement."

"Thank you, Kyle," Maddy said as she slowly stood up from the couch. "Thanks to all of you. I'm really lucky to have you guys around. I think tomorrow I'll be making arrangements to set up a security system too."

"That's not a bad idea," Zane said as he helped her to the door. "Please let me know if I can do anything else to help. I need you to be in good shape to help me solve that puzzle."

Rick gave Ashley a look. She shrugged her shoulders.

"Let's get you looked after missy," she said as she took over from Zane and walked Maddy out of the apartment.

"Oh, guys," Maddy called back as she was led down the hallway. "There's beer in the fridge and some nice charcuterie. Help yourselves."

"I'll grab two beers and a pop for our friend Kyle here while we wait," Rick said as he walked toward the fridge. "Know anything about charcuterie, Zane?"

"I can lay out one mean board."

"Go crazy, bro."

IT DIDN'T TAKE LONG for the unit to look for fingerprints. There were none. Neither were any found on the bathroom door nor the one at her suite's entrance. The locks had not been tampered with. It appeared a key had been used, most likely the set that had gone missing. Rick guessed that they had probably been taken during the last break-in. He and Zane tidied up the disaster area in Maddy's bedroom while waiting for an update from Ashley. The rest of the apartment seemed to be in decent shape. Nothing looked disturbed. Zane had tossed the infamous blanket into the laundry after the investigative unit had left. They were now waiting for it to dry.

"If I get my hands on the bastard that did this to her, I swear, it'll be ugly," Rick was fuming.

"Has she always attracted trouble like Kyle said?"

"Always. Not this type though, but some kind. And I've known her for a very long time. It's not like she is looking for it. It just finds her," Rick explained. "Doesn't matter what she does or doesn't do. It. Finds. Her."

"That's unfortunate. She seems nice to me. Why would anyone want to hurt her?"

"She IS nice. I say it's the evil eye. I'm going to get my mom to burn some incense in here."

"To get rid of evil spirits?"

"Yeah, you know about that?"

"Yeah, my best friend is Turkish. His mom made me put one of those blue glass eyes up on my door to ward off bad thoughts toward me and evil spirits. She burned so much incense you would have thought Easter mass was being celebrated."

"That's good. I should get her one of those too," Rick said, grabbing a beer. "Want another beer, Zane?"

"Sure, might as well."

"I'll save two for Maddy. She'd be pretty ticked off if we drank them all."

"Yeah, you better. I'd rather not be at the receiving end of a ticked-off Maddy."

"You and me both," Rick laughed. "What the hell is this?" He peeled off a Post-it note from the second beer bottle and walked it over to Zane.

"What does it say?"

'Give me the money or the duck gets it!'

Chapter 20

"Hey Azibo, Maddy here. Sorry to bother you on a Sunday but it's kind of an emergency."

"Good morning Maddy. You're not a bother at all. What kind of emergency are we talking about?"

"My apartment was broken into again yesterday and I was attacked. I think they might have used my extra set of keys. I need one of your security systems."

"Attacked? Are you alright?"

"Yes, a bit sore but I feel better today."

"Glad you're feeling better, but this isn't good. Did you let the condo management company know, or do you want me to?"

"I told them last night. They canceled the main door key fob. I also had the bolt lock changed to a keyless one."

"That's good. I can come by tomorrow morning and go over the options with you."

"Would you mind coming today, please? I stayed with a friend yesterday, but I need to come home tonight. I just don't feel safe being there without a security system in place."

"Let me see what I can do. I'm sure I have something in stock that can work for now at least. I can come but I'll need one of my staff to be there too. Can I call you back to confirm?"

"Thank you so much Azibo. My friend Rick will let you in if that's okay. You can show him how the system works, and he'll explain it to me."

"Sure, sure. Text me your email and I'll send you a few options. We can discuss them when I call you back. Can you also send me the locksmith's information, please? I need to find out what they installed to see what I have that's compatible."

"You bet. And thanks again. I owe you."

"Bake me a marble loaf like the one you brought to the building's spring gathering last year and we can call it even."

"Absolutely!"

Maddy ended the call and checked another item off her list. She had had a busy morning. The doctor in the emergency room last night gave her a heavy-duty antihistamine injection and recommended that she drink a lot of water to flush out the toxins from her system. She believed that Maddy had been injected with an analgesic, one she was allergic to. She was lucky she did not have an anaphylactic reaction. Her having to follow the doctor's instructions to a T meant that she needed to stay at Ashley's place, and close to the bathroom.

"Hey, Ash!"

"Yes? Do you need anything?"

"Just the address of the bakery you buy that marble cake from, please."

MADDY SPENT THE AFTERNOON napping on and off. Between whatever she had been injected with and the hospital's antihistamine, she had been very sleepy. The sluggish feeling had finally dissipated by dinner time. She and Ashley had taken advantage of this time together to gossip and catch up. That is when she remembered that she had not shared what happened on her weird date with Jon nor the run-in with him at Pigeon Lake.

"I don't know what to tell you, girlfriend," Ashley was incredulous as her friend shared what went down, and what did not. "It sounds a bit bizarre. He wants to make things more exciting by holding off on sex? That's a new one. I mean holding off during sex is one thing..."

"That's enough detail, Ashley." Maddy laughed. "I don't know but I am not interested in a serious relationship."

"Now you're sounding like me," Ashley remarked. "Do you want some ice wine for dessert?" Ashley lifted a tall slender bottle and waved it in Maddy's direction.

"Don't tempt me, woman." Pushing herself away from the dinner table, she rested her hands on top of her stomach. "I'm so full, I can't even find room for ice wine. I also don't think I should have any alcohol for a few days after yesterday."

"I'm so disappointed in you Maddy. You're letting me down." Ashley smiled as she put the bottle back in her wine rack. "But that's the wise thing to do. We can save this for another day."

"What I could find some room for is some peppermint tea. Now that would help my digestion while I wait for Rick to come and get me."

"What are you and Rick up to tonight?"

"He's going to go over the new security system that my neighbor, Azibo, installed today. But before he does that, he's driving me over to George's to have a chat with him about everything that has been happening with his ex-wife. I want to sit him down and impress upon him how dangerous this has become. People are attacking me in the park, breaking into my apartment, and leaving threatening notes. The poking around we've done has stirred a hornet's nest and is making someone extremely nervous. We need to be careful. Hopefully, if I lay it out for him, especially after this last attack, he'll take it seriously."

"Well, good luck with that. George strikes me as a man who's used to getting his way, and he's set on finding his ex."

"Can't argue with your take on that," Maddy said as Ashley handed her a large mug of tea. "That's why I'm taking Rick and showing up in person. We need to convince him to let the police handle things going forward."

The two friends sat in the living room chatting until nine when Maddy's phone dinged. Rick had arrived and was waiting for her downstairs.

"Thanks for dinner my friend, and for letting me stay over," Maddy said as she hugged Ashley and headed for the door. "Wish me luck!"

"Good luck. You'll be needing it!"

Chapter 21

Driving to George's residence, Rick and Maddy reviewed how they wanted to handle the situation with him. He was, like Ashley said, pretty determined to find Jennifer. They had to convince him to sit back and let the detectives conduct their investigation at their pace, no matter how slow he might think it was going.

"Showing up unannounced is chancy, but he just had hip surgery so he should be home at this time of night," Maddy said. "I didn't want to give him too much of a heads-up and have him start planning a defense. He's a determined man and I know he'll want to continue looking for Jennifer by himself. He's not a man used to sitting and waiting for things to happen," she explained further. "It's important he understands that I'm not a detective or even a private investigator and this is getting out of hand. It's more than what any of us should be messing with."

"Well, I'm relieved to hear you say that," Rick replied. "Dealing with crazy lunatics seems to be something you tend to gravitate to."

"Not true. Crazy lunatics seem to gravitate toward me," she huffed. "I don't go out looking for them. It's not like I have a sign on my forehead that says 'Wanted: Crazy Lunatics' or anything of the sort."

"Mmhmm... If you say so."

"I do say so...Turn around! Turn around!" Maddy shouted, pointing out the front windshield, and then turning around to look over her shoulder.

"What?" Rick twisted around trying to see what she was pointing at.

"Just turn around!" Maddy smacked him on his shoulder. He checked for traffic and then wrenched the steering wheel. Maddy's body swung to the right, her aching shoulder hitting the passenger door with a thud, making her grimace and grab the handle hanging from the top side of the car.

"Where are we going?" Rick yelled out in confusion as he straightened the steering wheel.

"George was driving in this direction! Why is he out so late? He's still recovering from hip surgery!" Maddy's eyes scanned the road ahead, trying to catch sight of his vehicle again.

"There! It's that one, the white car."

"Are you sure we should be doing this Maddy? It seems rather intrusive. If he wants to go grab a bag of chips at the corner store, he doesn't owe us an explanation," Rick said, rubbing his neck.

Maddy grabbed her phone and punched in George's phone number.

"George? Where are you going?" she said loudly into the phone. "You should be at home resting."

She listened intently, then said, "I know you're going somewhere because Rick and I are behind you. We were headed to your place to talk to you, and you drove by." She then fell silent again. "What's going on George, how could our visiting you ruin everything?"

"What's going on?" Rick mouthed to Maddy while gesturing wildly. "Do I keep following?"

Maddy waved to him to continue.

"What does that even mean? No... George do not put me on hold... George!" Maddy growled in frustration. "Something is happening, and he says we are ruining it by showing up. Whatever he has gotten himself involved in, I don't like it. Not one bit. He sounds completely panicked."

Just then, Maddy's phone made a loud double beep. Her connection with George had been lost.

"Oh great," she said. "He hung up on us."

"Maybe we should stop trying to catch up to him. If he says we shouldn't be following him, maybe, we need to listen to him," Rick said. "We don't know what's happening and it's not our place to intrude."

"Yes, we should keep following him! He's an old man with a bummed leg. And he's my grandfather's oldest friend. This all feels very wrong. My guts say so."

"Well, if your guts say so," Rick said glancing at her.

"Don't even go there, mister, not if you know what's good for you. Plus," Maddy added, "George made it my business to intrude when he got me involved in this whole rubber duckie mess."

They sat in silence for a moment before Rick, unable to help himself, mumbled under his breath. "They aren't rubber duckies."

Her death glare shut him up.

ULTIMATELY, RICK CONVINCED Maddy that it was best to go back to wait for him at his house. They drove to the mansion, Rick paying attention to the road and Maddy chewing a cuticle. When they arrived, they were shocked to realize that George was not far behind them.

"He must have turned around almost at the same time we did," Maddy commented as she twisted around in her seat to look behind her and watch George getting out of his car. He may have just had hip surgery and was moving slowly and carefully, but Rick and Maddy were not fooled by his deliberate movements. They had seen the look on his face. He was a brilliant shade of pink; his lips were pursed, and his jaw was clenched.

"Uh oh," Rick said. The two of them got out of the car and walked tentatively toward George.

"What kind of cockamamie piece of stupid-ass move was that? What a numbskull thing to do! What were you thinking?" George ranted. Both watched him go from pink to red right before their very eyes.

"Whoa, whoa, calm down!" Maddy raised her hands in front of her, half in surrender and half in a soothing motion. "We don't know what's wrong. What's happening?"

"They have my Jennifer!"

"Who does?" Maddy asked.

"The person who phoned me!" His voice was laced with frustration. "You ruined everything!"

Maddy led him over to the small bench lining the walkway.

"Sit down and take a deep breath," she spoke to him in a low, calm voice. "Then tell us what happened, from the start."

George sat down heavily, as though his legs were giving out from beneath him. He took a couple of deep breaths, removed his hat, and rubbed the sweat off his face.

"About an hour ago, I received a phone call. The man on the other end said they had Jennifer, and I could have her back if I brought the money I owed them for the other ducks. Then, and only then, they would return Jennifer and the last remaining Spencer Duck."

"Okay, and?" Maddy encouraged him to continue.

"He said I had to come alone, without anyone else. Now you've gone and ruined it!" George's voice kept rising, panic began to creep back into it. "He said specifically not to bring you, Maddy!"

"Me? Why? How does he know me?"

"I don't know. He called you that auction chick."

"How did they know we were behind you?" Rick interjected.

George looked at him up and down.

"And who the hell are you?" he asked.

"Oh, sorry this is my good friend Rick. He helps me with lots of things," Maddy quickly explained. "Do you know how they spotted me? I was in the passenger seat of another person's vehicle."

"I don't know but I got a call, and he was mad. He said I hadn't listened to their demands and hung up!"

Rick sat beside them and the three stayed still for a moment. Then Maddy started admonishing George.

"You should know better than to head out on your own. You need some kind of backup, or you'll get yourself hurt!"

"What was I supposed to do? Ignore him? Leave my poor Jennie to the wolves?" Anguish was evident in George's question. "I couldn't just sit and do nothing! What do I do now?"

"I think we need to call the police with this information. Now that you've heard from the kidnappers and we know for sure there's been foul play, they should be willing to give the case a higher priority," Maddy said definitively, slapping her hands on her knees and standing up.

Chapter 22

Maddy and Rick sat on a leather bench in the hallway, sipping on the iced tea Bradley had provided them while George gave his statement to the police. Detectives Morin and Seb arrived shortly after Maddy had called Kyle to explain the situation. She felt a huge sense of relief now that the police were fully involved and the decision-making in Jennifer's kidnapping had been taken out of George's hands. This whole situation had been too much excitement and stress for her.

The door to George's study opened and the two detectives exited after shaking George's hand. They thanked him for his statement and Detective Seb told him someone would return later tonight. Recognizing Maddy from a previous case, Detective Morin nodded in her direction as they walked by her and Rick.

"You know this guy?" Rick asked her.

"Yeah, he's one of the detectives that worked on Juliette's kidnapping case. The nicer of the two," she replied.

"You're getting to know a whole lotta cops these days, aren't you?"

Maddy elbowed him in the ribs.

"Come in you two," George stepped aside to let Maddy and Rick enter.

"The police are going to tap my landline in case I hear back from the kidnapper," he explained. "They took my cell phone and will try to trace the number that called me earlier but are skeptical. They believe the call probably came from a burner phone, but it's worth a try." He sat in one of the overstuffed chairs, wincing as he tried to find a comfortable position.

"Is that why the detective said someone would be by later? They're going to tap your phone tonight?" Rick asked.

"Yes, and to return my cell phone. They'll tap it as well," George responded. "I can only hope it isn't too late for my Jennifer."

Maddy felt a twinge of guilt seeing George so dejected and unhappy. She wondered if he would have been able to save Jennifer had they not foiled the kidnapper's plan. No, she would not allow herself to go down that path. Nothing good would have come from an old man entering such a dangerous situation alone.

"You did your best George. Let's leave it to the professionals now." She patted his hand and gave it a slight squeeze. "Get some rest and let your body heal a bit more. The police are seriously on it."

Chapter 23

"Talk to me Mads." Rick looked over at his friend sitting quietly in the passenger seat beside him. They had left George's home and were driving back to her apartment.

"Not much to say, is there? I'm trying not to feel like I messed up, but I feel so bad for George. I feel guilty and like I need to do more to help but there's nothing I can or should be doing right now."

"I know this is hard for you. You're a get-it-done kind of person and it's hard to sit back and let someone else take care of a problem, but you need to let this go, for your own sake. You've done all you can, and then some. The police have lots to work with which they wouldn't have if it hadn't been for you. Look, you know it, don't you? They're short-staffed. The detectives wouldn't have had the time to go around and talk to all her friends or go to Pigeon Lake. They can only follow leads. You gave them that."

"Hmmm..." Maddy responded. Rick could not help but notice that she hadn't agreed with him. He wondered if she had even heard him.

BACK AT THE APARTMENT, Maddy flopped onto her couch and sighed. Rick walked to the kitchen and opened the fridge.

"Want to eat something?" Rick asked, staring into her refrigerator.

"Might as well, nothing better to do," she replied, kicking her shoes off.

"Aw, c'mon Mads."

Maddy sat there, shoulders hunched staring into the distance.

"There's not much to eat in your fridge. I'm afraid Zane and I ate most of your cold cuts. There's a bit left. We finished your bread though."

"That's okay."

Rick started to open cupboards, hoping to find something to go with the cold cuts.

"What are you looking for?" Maddy asked.

"Crackers or anything we can put the meats on. Something to snack alongside."

"I have some cookies from Sugar & Spiced in the cookie jar on the counter."

"Hmm..."

"Want some chips?"

"Chips?"

"Yes, chips. There's a bag in the cupboard. The one above the fridge."

"Since when do you keep chips in your place?"

"I had an existential crisis and needed junk food. That's why it's in that cupboard. Makes it harder to reach." Maddy explained.

"Chips it is then. You need help getting rid of them. They're bad for your cholesterol."

"I don't have a cholesterol problem."

"Exactly. We need to keep it that way."

"Rick, always the hero."

"What can I say?"

"Not much."

"Ha!" Rick dumped the chips in a bowl and placed it on the coffee table with the leftover cold cuts. "This isn't going to be as fancy as what Zane had laid out for us. That guy sure knows his way around charcuterie."

"I wouldn't know. I was at a hospital getting shot up with epinephrine.

"I'm glad it wasn't worse, habibti," Rick said as he took a seat next to her. Maddy looked so dejected. He had to think of something to change her mood.

"Speaking of your buddy Zane, how's that puzzle you guys are doing coming along?" he asked.

"It's okay. We've solved a few of the clues but I haven't looked at the latest one yet," she answered, sounding tired and resigned.

"Well, let's see what it is, and we'll work on it. Maybe that'll get your mind off George and his problems," Rick waited while she pulled out her phone to find the clue.

"I'm the original land
from the north to the southern head
My name takes a stand.

A European shop in the southwest
a grocer's bounty that is eastern in the west.
Ask anyone
We know we're the best."

"The first part makes it sound like it's something Indigenous, 'the original land,'" Rick observed.

Maddy leaned over and looked at the clue again.

"That makes sense, so that tells me we're looking for an area or a location, especially considering the constant reference in the second part to directions."

Rick knew Maddy needed something else to occupy her mind, and solving this puzzle worked perfectly. She reached for her laptop and began to type in searches. The first thing she entered was 'Indigenous territory, Edmonton' and was taken to a website called 'Explore Edmonton'. The site explained that the actual name of Edmonton was Amiskwacîwâskahikan.

"Maybe we should start with the second part," Maddy suggested. "Let's begin with the word 'Grocer.'"

Rick leaned over to show her the results of one of his searches. He had found a page on the City of Edmonton's website that outlined the Indigenous names of the different election wards of Edmonton.

"Now we just need to solve the second part and place it in the correct area," Rick said with a grin. He was beginning to enjoy himself. "I'm stuck in search results of hundreds of grocery stores; it could be any of them. Let's concentrate on a small area at a time and narrow it down to the northern part of Edmonton. I suspect 'from north to the southern head' might be the Yellowhead Freeway."

"Sheesh, there's a lot of moving parts with this clue," Maddy said.

She did another search but this time for North Edmonton. She discarded the big chain supermarkets that could be found on every corner and marked the remaining stores off on her Google map, then set her laptop down. She looked at the clues on her phone one more time.

"We need to solve more than just this one clue. They're all going to need to work together. I think we need to come up with options for each part of the clue first, then look at them all together. I have a handful in north Edmonton flagged on the map. Now let's work on narrowing down the location."

"Okay, I'll work on 'My name takes a stand'," Rick read the clue out loud. He was quiet as he studied the City of Edmonton's website. "I don't see anything that could mean taking a stand."

Maddy leaned back in her seat, twisting and untwisting a strand of her hair while Rick entered another word to search.

"You seem to enjoy spending time with Zane these days," Rick said while going over the results that were popping up on his screen.

"Yeah, surprisingly. I didn't think this puzzle would be fun to do. It turned out that we get along. He's cool," Maddy replied.

"You guys spending a lot of time together?"

"Not really. We're both busy with work and stuff. Why do you ask?"

"No reason."

"No reason? You seem curious about him."

"Nope, just making conversation while waiting for stuff to load. Hoping something makes sense with those clues," Rick replied. "Man, some of this is brutal. But I can't find anything that fits."

"The history we were never taught in school is pretty brutal," Maddy agreed.

"Hey, one of the areas is Tastawiyiniwak," Rick said.

"Wow, that's a mouthful! Try saying that ten times," Maddy said with a smile. "I do like the sound of it though, 'Tass-taw-win-ee-wok', sure sounds nicer than plain old 'Westmount.'"

"I think this could be something," Rick said excitedly. "It's a Cree word that means the in-between people. It refers to the LGBTQ2S+ community and its importance in the Indigenous culture. That could be considered taking a stand, couldn't it?"

"Definitely could. What part of Edmonton is it?"

"Well, look at that! It's in the north!" Rick recited the area's boundaries as Maddy wrote them down. Looking at the map of the city first, she then flipped back to the list of grocers.

"T & T Supermarket, Glengarry Food Store... Wait! T&T is an Asian grocery store!" Maddy sat on the edge of her seat. "That could be the 'Northern one that is Eastern in the west'!"

"Huh?"

"It's in North Edmonton," she explained. "It's eastern food but located in the western part of Tastawiyiniwak! So that fits!"

"Wow, you're good at this." Rick smiled as he high fived her.

"Or maybe we're just a good team," Maddy replied, beaming back at him.

"That too," Rick agreed.

"So, the only thing we need to confirm that we have the correct answer is to find a European shop. At least now we know it should be close to the southwest part of the ward. But European?"

Just then, Rick's phone dinged with an incoming text.

"I'm going to have to get going soon. Tasha needs some help with stuff around the house," he explained after reading his message.

"No worries, you run along. I'll give Zane a call and see if he thinks we got this one right," Maddy reassured Rick. "Give my love to Tasha and the girls."

"Why don't you come with me?" Rick asked

"I appreciate the offer, but I need some alone time."

"No problem. If you change your mind, I'm sure Tasha would love to see you," Rick said as he walked to her front door.

"Thanks!" She waved goodbye as he left, picked up the dirty plates from the coffee table, and placed them in the sink. She then took a soda from the fridge and sat back on the couch as her cell phone dinged with a message.

'Got time to chat about clues?'

Rather than text Zane back, she decided to phone him.

"Hi!" he answered.

"Hi to you too! Funny you should reach out now because I might have solved our latest clue."

"Would it by any chance work with a European shop that goes by the name of London Drugs?" Zane asked.

"What?"

"I was thinking that could be the European shop, and maybe the eastern in the west was a type of food or ethnicity."

Maddy pulled her laptop in front of her and quickly searched London Drugs.

"You are brilliant Zane!" she said, laughing.

"And you didn't know that already?"

"Cute."

"That, I am."

"Anyway, back to the clue. Edmonton's Tastawiyiniwak ward is the original land." Maddy quickly explained how she and Rick came up with their answer. "It also has a T&T Supermarket on the west side of the ward and a London Drugs in the Southwest."

"Excellent! So, the fourth answer is Tasta... winnie..." Zane fumbled over the name.

"Tass-taw-win-ee-wok" Maddy repeated slowly.

"Okay, I'll look up the spelling," Zane laughed at himself. "That turned out to be a piece of cake."

"For you maybe! It took us quite a while, thank you very much! So, what's the next clue?" Maddy was feeling lucky.

"Here you go Ms. Smarty pants."

'The largest in the West,

My honor goes to the Queen.

I'm definitely the place to see and be seen.'

"Oh, that's easy!" laughed Maddy. "The Royal Alberta Museum."

There was stunned silence at the other end of the phone.

"How?" Zane sounded doubtful.

"I spent a couple of summers volunteering at the museum and happen to know it's the largest museum in the west and the rest is obvious," she explained.

"Obvious, of course," Zane said. "How could I be so obtuse?"

Maddy was pleased with herself and was glad Rick had suggested she work on the clues; doing so had taken her mind off George. She looked at her watch wondering if the police had tapped all of George's phones yet. 'No,' she told herself. 'Stop it right now.' She didn't want to think about Jennifer and if the kidnapper would call again.

"So do you want to try another one?" Zane asked.

"I have a couple of calls to make right away, but why don't you leave the clues with me so I can roll them over in my head when I have some more free time?"

'1867 the topic was created

But it took 113 years to become official.'

"That's it?" Maddy asked.

"Yup, that's the entire clue. Of course, the topic must be Canada. We didn't become officially independent until 113 years later."

"No, we didn't," Maddy laughed. "Let me think about it. We can chat about it soon, okay?"

"Sounds good!"

Right after ending her conversation with Zane, she decided to call George to find out if the police had returned.

Bradley answered and informed her that George was lying down. Maddy was glad to hear he was getting some rest after all the stress he had gone through and told Bradley not to disturb him. She asked Bradley about the police, and he told her they had been there to work on the phones.

Unsure what to do with herself now that she knew what was happening with George, she wandered around her apartment, aimlessly, going to the window to look out, then retracing her steps back to the kitchen to open the refrigerator. Maybe she had been wrong about wanting to spend time alone. But what did she want to do? Then it hit her, she knew exactly what would help her conquer this restless mood. But first, she had to go feed her geese up on the rooftop. Poor things! She had been so busy with the whole kidnapping and then the puzzle that she hadn't had time to go check on them. They probably were wondering what had happened to her. Maddy hoped they wouldn't be too upset. Maybe they would forgive her if she brought them an extra-large portion of feed this time? Then she would get working on her plan.

Chapter 24

Her kitchen smelled amazing. Maddy had spent all last night and most of today preparing a homemade fried chicken dinner with all the works for her friends. It had kept her mind off everything. She did not cook often, but when she did, she did one heck of a job.

Maddy quietly hummed an upbeat tune as she picked at a moist piece of chicken on her plate. Listening to her friends teasing each other around her kitchen table, she chuckled at their good-natured ribbing. Evenings like these filled her soul, and she knew it did the same for her friends.

"Great idea Maddy," Ashley said as she raised a chicken wing in salute. The rest of the gang murmured their agreement between chews. "Your homemade Southern-style buttermilk fried chicken beats any restaurant's, and that slaw is so yummy!"

"Thank you, daawling," Maddy said with a Southern drawl. "I had a hankering for good chicken, but I also needed to chat with y'all."

"I knew it, here we go. There's always a catch to free chicken," Tasha said, tossing a chicken drumstick on her plate in mock disgust.

"Ha. Ha. I need to talk this whole George and Jennifer thing out with you guys. I'm feeling powerless, and I can't help but think we should be able to help him in some way but for the life of me, I can't figure out how," Maddy explained. "But, please, don't stop eating dinner. We can chat while you dig into that chicken. I made lots thinking the twins would be coming too."

"They're with Mama Leila," Tasha said. "She was more than thrilled to have something to do. We can bring leftovers home for them though. I'm sure they would be pretty upset if they found out they had missed out on your chicken."

Maddy looked across the table at Rick and raised an eyebrow. He shook his head imperceptibly, warning her not to ask any further.

"Didn't you say you were done with this whole, what did you call it? Oh yes, that 'Duckin Ducky Affair.'" Ashley pointed out.

"I know I said that, and I meant it when I said it. But I don't know if I feel the same way now. This whole Spencer Duck thing has me tied up in knots. One minute I want to wash my hands of it, then the next I feel guilty, and I need back in."

"Guilt is never a good place to be motivated by bella," Tasha admonished her. "It will only lead you down dark paths that you didn't want to go to in the first place."

"Perhaps."

"Well, it can't hurt to talk it through Maddy," Rick said. "Maybe we talk it out and realize there's nothing we can do, then it will definitely be out of your hands."

"Okay, so what do we know so far?" Ashley took the lead by ticking off each fact on her fingers. "One, things were going along fine until suddenly she was done with the one duck at a time thing. Two, someone tried to bonk Maddy on the head at the exchange point."

"Three, Maddy got away with the money and all but one duck," Tasha jumped in. "Four, Jennifer goes missing and no one can find her until George gets a call from the kidnappers."

"What about the painting?" Ashley asked and the table fell silent.

"What do you mean?" Maddy finally asked.

"Doesn't it seem like a bit of a coincidence that you find the stolen painting and return it to George just as he's trying to get various art pieces returned by Jennifer?"

"I never really thought about that," Maddy frowned, her mind at work. "But how would that play into Jennifer and the ducks?"

"I don't know but it just struck me as coincidental and in things like this, I find coincidences suspect," Ashley said.

The group sat pondering Ashley's words. Rick was the first to speak up, saying that at this point, they should not disregard anything.

"Let's keep it in the back of our minds for now," he suggested.

"I don't see what you can do to help George or Jennifer," Tasha said. "Just be there for support and make sure he doesn't do anything foolish."

Maddy pushed herself away from the table and patted her belly. "I suppose you're right," she said as she reluctantly agreed with Tasha.

Silence fell over the table. They continued with their dinner. Tasha nibbled on more fries and Ashley picked out the last bit of chicken off the drumstick on her plate. They were all sated and content.

Rick stood up and took his plate to the kitchen counter, returning with Maddy's bottle of Frangelico and five glasses. He poured the liqueur and passed the glasses around.

"It's a ducking shame we can't help more."

"Rick!" Three napkins came flying at him.

"What?" Maddy can say it, but I can't? That's discrimination. I protest!"

THEY WERE ALL PITCHING in with the dinner clean-up when Maddy received a call from her grandfather.

"Hi PopPop, anything new?"

"Hi, Maddy, I just wanted to update you on George. He got his phones tapped so if the kidnappers call again, the police will be on it," he began. Maddy interrupted him and told him she was switching him over to speakerphone so everyone could hear him.

"Yes, I know, I spoke with Bradley last night."

"Did he tell you about the painting?"

"What painting?"

"George heard from an art gallery owner last night. Someone showed up at their gallery wanting to sell them an Inuit painting. His staff wouldn't buy it but agreed to keep it on consignment. They were pretty sure it belonged to George's collection. George is well known in the art community, so they called the gallery owner, who then went in to look at it and agreed with them. He decided to call George to check if he had sold or given his painting to anyone," PopPop said. "It turned out to be a piece that Jennifer had received as part of her divorce settlement."

"Oh boy! Did he let the detective on the case know?" Maddy asked.

"He did call them but, with his phone being tapped, they already knew. The police are trying to run down the contact information he gave the gallery owner, but they suspect he used a bogus name and phone number."

"Another painting showing up? I'm telling you, there's no such thing as a coincidence." Ashley shook her head.

"Well, keep us posted if anything else develops, okay PopPop?" Maddy asked.

"I will. The police are going to see if they can pull a picture of the person off the surveillance camera," PopPop added before saying goodbye and hanging up.

"What do you know?" Rick said as he leaned in his chair, balancing himself on the back of two legs while chewing on a toothpick. "Do yew tink we 'ave an adder cloo?"

Tasha stared at him with laser-like eyes, and he slowly set the chair legs back on the floor.

"I don't know, Inspector Clouseau, but that accent of yours sucks big time," Ashley told him rolling her eyes.

"Boy, tough crowd tonight!"

Maddy's phone rang again. She frowned and looked at her phone's display, then smiled when she saw who it was.

"Hi Zane, what's up?"

"Hey Maddy, I figured out the last clue!"

"That's fantastic! What is the answer?"

"'O' Canada!' The national anthem's topic is Canada, and it was created in 1867 and in 1980 it became the official anthem," he said all in one breath.

"Perfect! So, what do we have for clues?"

"Canada Post, West Edmonton Ice Palace, Endeavours Brewing, Tastawiyiniwak, Royal Albert Museum, and 'O' Canada!' We only have one more clue to solve and then we should be able to figure out the whole thing."

"What is the final clue?" Maddy moved over to her couch and settled down on it.

'I'm known for my cigar
and a rough demeanor too.
Some say in the war
I was a star.
In a square
you will find me there.'

"Hmm..."

"It sounds like it's referring to an actual person," Zane said.

"It does. Why don't I run it past my friends and see if they have any idea what it could be?"

Just then, Ashley said something to Rick that caused him to laugh loudly.

"I'm sorry, is this a bad time?" Zane asked. "It sounds like you have company."

"My friends are over. I should probably go but I will ask them if they have any ideas on the clue," Maddy said. "I'll get back to you later or sooner if we figure anything out."

They said goodbye and Maddy put her phone down. Looking up, she found all her friends' eyes on her, brows raised.

"Why are you staring at me?" Maddy asked, looking confused. "What's wrong?"

"Nothing's wrong darling," Ashley said. "We're just curious, that's all."

"About what?"

"About you and Zane. First, he shows up when you're broken into and now, he calls to chat?" Ashley raised her eyebrows and tilted her head in Maddy's direction.

"Yeah, we're working on this puzzle thingy. He solved one of the clues and wanted to let me know. I was hoping you guys could give us a hand with the last one." Maddy decided to ignore Ashley and kept talking. "Do you guys want to hear the clue or not?"

"Sure hon, let us have it," Tasha said, coming to her rescue.

Maddy repeated the clue Zane had shared with her.

"So, a guy who smokes a cigar, is rough around the edges, and was a star in the war," Tasha said.

"Are you sure about you and Zane?" Rick asked, ignoring his wife.

"That's right Tasha, and yes I'm sure Rick. Zane and I are just friends," Maddy confirmed to both.

"Does he know that?" Rick asked.

"Of course, he knows that!" Maddy's nose was getting out of joint.

"I hope so. You shouldn't be leading that man on, he seems like a good guy," Rick continued. "Nothing worse than not knowing you're in the friend zone."

"You sound like you're speaking from experience Rick," Ashley poked him in the shoulder and laughed.

"Never you mind, Ash," he replied.

"Well, as much as I would love to stay and debate whether Maddy has a love life or not, we need to get back home," Tasha declared. "The twins are probably driving Mama Leila crazy by now."

"Aww, already? I could use your help figuring out the next clue," Maddy said.

"Why don't you hang around and help Maddy," Tasha told her husband and then turned to Ashley. "Do you mind giving me a ride home, Ash?"

"Sure, no problem, it'll give me a chance to talk to you about some contract work that's coming up in my office. It might be of some interest to you."

"Really? That sounds perfect. You can come in and see the girls too. I'm sure they would love that."

The two of them gathered their things and said goodbye to Maddy and Rick, encouraging them to have fun figuring out the clues as they left.

"Okay Rick, enough chatter about Zane. How about we focus on this clue, shall we? You were a major help last time. Let's see if you can repeat your brain prowess once again. Who smoked cigars during a war?"

"Churchill."

"Churchill?"

"Yeah, you know, the guy who looked like a silhouette of Alfred Hitchcock?"

The blank look Maddy gave Rick was enough to make him throw up his arms in resignation.

"Winston Churchill, you know? Google him! Sheesh, public education."

"I know who Churchill is, but I don't think I've ever seen a silhouette of Alfred Hitchcock."

"Sure, you have," Rick insisted. "At the end of his movies, there's that silhouette of him smoking a cigar!"

"Okay, I'll take your word for it Rick," Maddy widened her eyes at him. "If it is Churchill then the last part makes it easy, 'In a square, you will find me there', it's Sir Winston Churchill Square, downtown."

"Yup, you're welcome." Rick opened the fridge and poured himself a glass of water. He brought over a glass for her and the jug.

Maddy was about to make a teasing comment about his level of help in solving the clue when her phone dinged with a new text. She looked at her phone and jumped up.

"Holy Duck!" she shouted.

Rick stood up and looked over her shoulder so he could see. He read the text she had just received.

"Come to the abandoned gas station near the temple on Manning Freeway NOW if you want Jennifer alive! Bring the money or else we will decapitate George's precious David

Spencer, and he will never see that woman again. This is the last chance I'm giving you. Come alone or don't bother coming at all. Be smarter than the old man."

Chapter 25

"What are we going to do?" Maddy shouted as she stood there, looking left and right around her apartment as though she would find the answer hidden somewhere. She sat down on the couch, then got up and sat on a chair, then stood up again. Rick watched her, at a loss for words, unsure what to do either.

"Do you think this is legit, Maddy?"

"Of course it's legit! Why would anyone text me that if it wasn't? We can't ignore this threat and put off doing anything like last time with Juliette and the funeral home. I can't wait and see this time, Rick, I just can't!"

"I don't know, I don't know," Rick ran his hands through his hair and began pacing.

"I don't know either, but we need to take it seriously and go. We don't have time to discuss this. The text said now!" Maddy headed for her apartment door. Rick followed close behind her, talking rapidly as they moved toward the elevator.

"Shouldn't we call the police?" asked Rick. "We said no more acting on impulse without telling them."

"This isn't on impulse! This is responsive. We'll text Kyle while on the way."

TASHA AND ASHLEY WERE halfway to the Nasser's home when Ashley's phone rang.

"Hi Kyle," she said after hitting the hands-free button on her steering wheel.

"Hi Ash, how are you doing?"

"I'm doing good Kyle. What's up?" She was curious as to the reason for his call. He had stopped his habit of just calling her up to chat.

"Are you with Maddy?"

"No, I'm in my car, why?"

"Do you know if George told Maddy about his stolen Inuit painting?"

"Yes, he did. I was there when she got the call."

"Okay, good. Well, we had a chance to interview the gallery owner who reported the stolen Inuit painting," Kyle explained. "He was able to get a screenshot from his security footage of the guy who brought it in. Could you please look at it? I know you're familiar with a lot of people in the local art world so I thought I'd see if you might recognize him. I also need to get hold of Maddy and have her look at it, in case it's someone she's encountered before."

"Sure, just fire it to me via text," she responded.

Ashley made a turn onto a side street. Pulling into a parking stall, she grabbed her phone and opened her texts.

"Oh my God, NO!"

"Ash, what is..." Kyle's call with Ashley ended without warning. The moment she recognized the man in the screenshot, she hung up on him and dialed Maddy's number.

"What is it Ashley, who is it?" Tasha asked. "Please, talk to me! You're making me very nervous."

"I will in a minute, I need to talk to Maddy, right away. Talus Balls! Answer your damn phone girl!" Ashley hung up. "I'm going to keep trying until she answers. Come on Maddy!"

Tasha was busy tapping away on her phone, texting Rick.
'Ashley needs to talk to Maddy NOW!'

"I texted Rick. Hopefully he sees it."

"She's still not answering!" Ashley slammed her cell on the dashboard. "They're together, right? What the hell are they doing and why aren't they answering us?"

"Who was in the picture Ash, who did you see?"

"It was a picture of..." Her phone buzzed, interrupting her midsentence. Kyle was calling her back.

"Ashley, what happened? Why did you hang up?" He was not impressed that she had hung up on him and hoped she was not going to do anything stupid like go after the guy in the picture.

"I recognized the person in the picture! I'm trying to reach Maddy."

"I have to go, Ash. It's Maddy. She's texting me. I'll call you back." It was his turn to abruptly end their conversation.

'Received threatening message from kidnapper. Going to save Jennifer. Send help to abandoned gas station near temple on Manning Fwy.'

"Damn!" Kyle immediately radioed for help, hoping he would get there in time. To what? He did not know.

Chapter 26

"I think Ashley is trying to get a hold of you," Rick said, looking down at his phone. "Tasha says you need to contact her now."

"I bet my phone is still on silent from dinner!" Maddy started rummaging around with one hand until Rick grabbed her purse, found her phone, and took it off silent mode.

"Is it hooked up to your car?" Rick asked.

"No, my hands-free has been glitchy so I disconnected it."

Her phone rang in Rick's hand. He answered it and put it on the speakerphone.

"Hello, Maddy."

"PopPop, did you get a message from the kidnappers?"

"No, we haven't heard a peep from anyone. I'm here with George. We thought maybe it would be worthwhile to put out a reward for information on Jennifer's whereabouts. What do you think?"

"I can't talk right now PopPop. Rick and I are on our way to that old gas station on Manning, by the temple. I got a text from one of the kidnappers. We're on our way to meet them there right now. Hopefully, a reward won't be needed."

"What? That derelict one? And you're going there by yourselves? You know better than that! You told George not to go it alone!" PopPop's voice was getting louder. "I don't like this. It's dangerous! Please, please Maddy, don't do this."

"I know PopPop. It's okay, we let Kyle know what's happening. It's just that we needed to move quickly. Look, I need to go now, I need to focus on my driving."

"Okay, Okay, but you be careful young lady, do you hear me?"

"I will PopPop,"

RUDY HUNG UP THE PHONE and looked across the room at George.

"Why did they contact her? She's MY Jennie! I thought the kidnappers didn't want her involved?" It had not been too hard for George to get the gist of the conversation. Rudy had been quite vocal.

"It was probably because they only wanted one person to go, and they knew you might be too hot under the collar right now. Or they knew you went to the cops," PopPop surmised. "So, what are we going to do about this?"

"I'll tell you what we're not going to do!"

"What?"

"Sit around like two senile old farts, that's what!"

"Damn right, we're not!"

George picked up his hat from the couch, plunked it on his head, and told Rudy to hurry up and follow him to the garage. He had no time to wait for his chauffeur to bring the car around. He was a man on a mission.

"We're not going to waste time with the Bentley. We're taking my Ferrari. I have an ex-wife to rescue!"

Chapter 27

"Chop off David Spencer's cute rubber duckie's head? I can't believe that someone would go to such lengths. I mean, I don't get why everyone is crazy about these duckies, but a decapitation threat?! And Jennifer! Why harm her?" Maddy was furious as she sat behind the wheel of her car. "What could she have done to deserve this?"

The kidnappers' threat of violence to George's ex-wife and his duck blinded her to everything else. She desperately wanted to pass all those stopped cars in front of her.

"Damn it! Why is there so much backed-up traffic at this time of day? This is nuts!" Maddy was getting increasingly frustrated at the bumper-to-bumper situation.

"They would move if they could. There must have been a bad accident, Maddy. People might be hurt," Rick anxiously replied. "The exit we need is next. There's no alternative route to get there from here, all we can do is wait. I know this isn't what you wanted to hear right now, but we're stuck here like everyone else." Rick was at a loss. They were in complete gridlock.

"Why can't they clear the shoulder or something?" Maddy hit the steering wheel with her fist. "There's room on the shoulder!" she yelled at no one in particular. "Are they all blind or something? The ambulances and firetrucks have come through already!" she gestured in front of them then banged her fist down three more times.

There had been a multi-car crash on the Yellowhead Freeway. At least twenty cars had collided, two cars had rolled over, and there appeared to be injuries. It was chaos. Ambulances and firetrucks had closed the eastbound lanes. It had taken almost half an hour to free up one lane to let the mile-long backed-up traffic slowly creep forward.

"Maddy, you're not the only one stressing here. I hate this feeling of being helpless too!" Rick was having a tough time hiding his frustration. He did not like being a passenger, not that it would have made any difference had he been the one behind the wheel. "Ya Allah, move it! Walking would have been faster! Yalla!!" He looked over at Maddy, saw her biting her cuticles, and realized he was not helping the situation.

"Okay, listen, what we need to do here is calm down and try staying level-headed. I know exactly where this gas station is. Tasha and I have driven by it every year when we go to this greenhouse she insists is the absolute best in the region. Unfortunately, there are no shortcuts from where we are. Once we get off this freeway, the traffic should clear up, it'll go faster." There was nothing else to add.

Rick and Maddy had left her apartment as soon as they had received the text. Once they had gotten Bugsy out of the underground garage, they sped toward the abandoned roadside gas station as fast as they could, only to find themselves slowed to a standstill a little over halfway there. The Yellowhead was crawling with police and emergency vehicles. They were quiet on the drive until then. Worry had occupied their thoughts. They had not wanted to say out loud what both had been thinking, that the kidnappers wouldn't be so callous as to commit such a horrific act for a few minutes of tardiness. But now, having been stuck on this parking lot of a freeway for so long, they worried that the unthinkable might happen.

"You don't think they would really hurt her, do you?" Rick was unable to shake the thought. As much as he knew he should be calming Maddy down, the worry over what they might find at their destination was all-consuming.

"One of them was going to bash my head in. I'm lucky to have gotten away." The memory of her barely escaping injury was not a pleasant one. "Who knows how far they're willing to go?"

"You seem to attract danger. I'm not sure I want to be friends with you anymore." Rick said, trying to create a bit of levity.

She gave him an angry look that stopped him from attempting this any further.

"Look!" Rick pointed to the cars in front of them. "They're finally allowing people who want to take the next exit to use the shoulder. See, you put it out there in the universe, and the universe listened. We should be able to get there in less than twenty minutes."

MADDY DID NOT BOTHER to turn off the engine before jumping out of Bugsy and racing straight to the abandoned gas station's padlocked door. There was no way of breaking the lock. Two steps behind her, Rick grabbed a brick he found lying on the ground and smashed the window to the left of the doorway. Taking off his sweatshirt, he rolled it around his hand and used it to clear off the broken glass. He cupped his hands together and gave her a boost so she could climb through the window.

Mere seconds had passed when he heard terrified screams.

"What's wrong? Did they decapitate the duck?" He wondered if they were too late.

"Yes... but... that's not the worst of it. Oh God!"

"What do you mean, it's not the worst of it?"

"There's a dead woman's body next to the head. There's blood everywhere."

"COME ON! CAN'T YOU drive any faster Rudy?" George had asked him to drive as his leg was still too weak to maneuver his manual sports car.

"George, there's lots of traffic. Can't you see that?" Rudy's hands were holding onto the steering wheel with a death grip. He'd never driven such a fast car before but was determined to speed beyond his comfort zone. He did not like the idea of his little Maddy dealing with an unknown criminal. Even if Rick was with her, it was still dangerous. He had an unbelievably bad feeling deep in his gut. "I'm going to drive on the shoulder as far as I can. Hopefully, someone will let me in, we'll give them the old 'Sorry I'm a confused senior' look."

"Do whatever is necessary. Just get to my Jennifer as fast as possible, please," George rolled down the window and stretched his neck out to try and see if the shoulder was free. "Okay, there's nobody on the shoulder. Go for it! I'll pay any fine you get so don't let that stop you."

"I don't want that kind of attention. Having the cops follow us with sirens blaring is a very bad idea. The kidnapper could end up hurting all of them, or worse!"

"Damn it, you're right. Okay, drive safely but pass as many cars as you can."

After ten minutes of driving on the shoulder, they noticed a break in the traffic ahead. Rudy signaled and waved nicely at a couple of older ladies. They waved back and let him cut in front of them.

"Thank God you still have that old charm of yours, Rudy!"

Chapter 28

"Oh God, I think I'm going to be sick," Maddy told Rick after he had climbed through the window and joined her. "We didn't make it in time!" Maddy turned away from the body and threw up. Jennifer's body lay on the cold cement floor. Beside her was David Spencer's missing duck, its head separated from its body.

"I don't think we were too late for Jennifer, Maddy..." Rick searched for the right words to describe what he was seeing. "She doesn't look too... umm... fresh..." His stomach turned at the sight of the dead woman. While he had never met her, he felt sadness overcome him as he realized that he was staring at the remains of a once active and loved woman.

Maddy pulled herself together and turned back toward the scene. She took a deep breath.

"Rick, we need to call Kyle again."

"Yeah, I guess we better."

"I wouldn't do that if I were you," they heard a voice say, followed by the sound of a gun clicking.

"THERE IT IS! THERE it is!" George exclaimed, pointing excitedly. "Here! Here! Pull in here!"

"I am, I am!" Rudy yelled back. He pulled into the front of the gas station and saw Maddy's car and the broken window. He slowly drove around to the back and threw his car into Park. Rudy did not want to be seen by the kidnappers. The two men tried to spring from the car but ended up having to turn sideways in their seats, placing their feet on the ground one leg at a time, then standing up cautiously.

"Oh man, my sciatica!" Rudy groaned.

"Try a brand-new hip," George retorted.

"It looks like they got in through one of the front windows," Rudy said. Let's make our way around to the front."

"Do you expect us to climb through a window? Have you lost your mind?"

"Keep your voice down, George. We don't want them to hear us," whispered Rudy. "We're not going to go through the window. We're going to look through it, get a feel for the situation. Then we'll figure out what to do."

"Well, that's a relief. Okay, follow me."

George led the way and pointed to the broken glass window. Rudy nodded. They walked over and stood quietly beneath it, listening to a murmur of agitated voices. While they could not make out any words, they could tell it wasn't a pleasant exchange as one voice shouted over the other two and began to speak insistently.

"I'm not liking how those voices sound, George," whispered Rudy.

"It was hard to tell what they were saying. I'm worried, Rudy, I didn't hear Jennifer's voice in there."

"She might be tied down and gagged. You can't speak if you have a gag on, right?'

"Yeah, you're probably right," George flexed what little muscles he had in his arms. "Okay, what's the plan now?"

Rudy turned to George and whispered in his ear. George nodded and the two men headed back toward the other side of the building.

Chapter 29

"Where is the money?" said the familiar voice as a man stepped out from behind a post.

"We don't have any money," Maddy said, squinting as she tried to make out the man's features in the dim light of the abandoned building. "Jon? How did you get involved in all this?"

"Shut up. You need to know everything, don't you? Well never mind that." He waved his gun at them. "Move over there, to the other side of the room."

"Is that Jon, Ashley's friend? The one who helped you with George's painting?" Rick whispered to Maddy.

"Yes, they've known each other for years," she said as they slowly moved toward the spot where he was pointing his gun.

"I said shut up! Now move it! I don't have all day." His jaw was clenched and the hand holding the gun was steady. His calmness did not bode well for them.

"Don't lie to me about the money," he snarled. "Why would anyone with half a brain come here if they didn't have it?" He took a step closer to them. "I want the truth, Maddy. Don't try lying to me."

261

"We came to try and save Jennifer," Rick said as he moved Maddy behind him. "We couldn't just leave a woman to die without doing anything about it. It appears that we were too late. Quite late from the looks of things."

"I wasn't talking to you, whoever you are," he waved the gun menacingly at Rick. "How did you plan on saving her without the money, Maddy? Please do tell. Did you think you could sweet talk me into just handing Jennifer and the duck over? That I would say 'Sure, here you are. I really didn't want the money after all'? Do you take me for a fool?" He took another step closer to them.

Maddy did not want to tell him that they were counting on the police to show up in time and save the day. Maddy tried to distract him, hoping the delay tactic would buy them time.

"I thought you liked me, Jon. Why would you want to hurt me if you wanted a relationship with me?"

"Are you that daft?" Jon laughed. "It was but a ruse to get to the ducks and to find out what was going on with the investigation!"

"But why kill Jennifer?" she asked.

"Why? WHY?" Jon looked at her in disgust. "You ARE that simple-minded, aren't you? She's been dead for some time. Can't you tell?"

"I knew it!" Rick said under his breath.

"I told YOU to shut up, didn't I?"

Maddy nudged him to be quiet.

"What happened, Jon?" She hoped to get him to talk more. It could not be much longer until the police arrived.

"Jennifer lied to me," he continued. "You modern women are all the same. She, just like you, only wanted to have fun. I was in desperate need of cash after a couple of unwise investments. The silly woman posted photographs of the artwork she owned, all over social media. Jennifer sounded lonely on so many of her posts. 'Easy target' I told myself. I did not imagine for one second that I would fall for her. But I did. Then that damned woman had to go and ruin everything. She said she liked me but did not love me. That she still had deep feelings for the old man and was only looking for someone to warm her bed. She told me that she loved playing those games with him more than spending time with me! I had enough of her and their games. I demanded that she choose ME OR SPENCER'S DUCKS. She chose those DUCKS and the OLD MAN over ME!" His voice took on an unnatural tone. "That's when I lost it. I don't know what came over me, but I needed to end this stupid charade once and for all. She would not stop yelling at me to get out. I had to make her stop. It wasn't intentional, you know. It was only meant to scare her. I grabbed her by the neck and started squeezing, slightly at first. She mocked me. Said I was a sissy of a man, with no strength in my hands. A SISSY! So, I squeezed tighter until her eyes showed fear in them. When she took her last breath, I realized that I had to get rid of the body." His eyes glazed over as he continued describing what followed.

Jon told them he had grabbed a drop cloth and plastic sheet from a room she was having painted, wrapped her body with both, and half dragged, half carried her to his car. Unfortunately, he had dropped her on the garage stairs and her head hit the concrete hard. That was all the dried blood on the sheet Maddy and Rick had seen around the body. He remembered this abandoned garage from a romantic drive he and Jennifer had taken in the countryside.

"It was serendipitous, don't you think?" he asked Maddy. "What better place to hide a body?"

"You can't be the one who attacked me on the golf course. You're much taller. And who locked me in my bathroom? Maddy asked, still trying her best to distract him. "You seemed so sincere about liking me. Why do you want to hurt me now or is it your partner that wants to do away with me?" In shock by what he had described to them, she had difficulty believing that this was the same man who had tried to sweep her off her feet. She was going to have some work to do with her therapist after learning why he had wanted to get closer to her. Not only was she disappointed at having fallen for Jon, but she was also terrified of what he might be capable of doing to them.

"I wish I had been the one on the golf course! And that buffoon is not my partner. You cannot find good help these days. That hired thug was supposed to get information on the painting's whereabouts. Instead, you stabbed him repeatedly. With keys at that! He came back to me and demanded danger pay. And for what? To tell me that you gave the painting to the police! You couldn't hold on to it just one more day, oh no. You wanted that reward you greedy little bitch. You lost me money that I desperately needed," Jon was rambling and had lost his cool. "That's when I knew I had to get involved with you somehow. Then you called out of the blue to ask me out for coffee. It should have been a cakewalk after that. How was I to know you were a floozy? I had zero interest in sleeping with the likes of you. That's when I decided to search your place myself. Forget about depending on someone else to do the job right. I planned everything to the last detail. The fake spa getaway was a no-brainer. But you had to mess that up too, didn't you? Imagine my surprise when you ended up in Pigeon Lake. You're too smart for your own good. After our little luncheon fiasco, I sped back to the city. I had everything I needed ready. I even had Midazolam to knock you out in case you returned to your apartment before I was done searching for the ducks and money. That stuff was ridiculously easy to find on Edmonton's black market."

"You lied? You weren't even a little bit attracted to me?" Maddy's head was spinning. She could not believe how naive she had been.

Rick looked at Maddy, wide-eyed. "That's what you got out of what he just said?"

"Did you really think that someone like me would be interested in someone like you? I can't even imagine why a smart lady like Ashley would want to spend time with you," Jon snidely said.

"Hold it right there you jerk!" Rick's hands clenched into fists by his side while Maddy grabbed his arm and tried to pull him back.

"She has more class in her little finger than you will ever have. Why say those things to her? You, nimrod!"

"You know, friend, I'm getting pretty tired of your interruptions. I think I shall dispose of you first. Actually, I'll do it right now. Then, I'll deal with Maddy dearest here, once

I ransom her for the money George owes me for the ducks." He was now looking straight at Rick, pointing the gun at his head. He cocked it and smirked.

"Jon, please don't!" Maddy could not believe what was happening. How could things have taken such a drastic turn? She looked around to see if she could find something to use as a weapon. There was nothing within reach. A feeling of panic overwhelmed her. Rick took another step forward in front of her. He was not going to go down easily. Tasha and the girls were waiting for him, and he had every intention of making it back home to them.

A loud creaking noise interrupted the unfolding scenario. A door behind and to the right of Jon was slowly opening. All three turned their eyes toward it.

"What the hell?" Jon scowled, moving cautiously toward the door. He held his gun out in front of him, readying himself to shoot at whoever was going to come through it. He was only two feet away when the door swung open, its corner violently catching Jon's nose. Blood spurted everywhere. He bent in half, grabbing his nose with his free hand.

Momentarily in shock, Maddy and Rick only managed to take two steps forward before Jon straightened up and turned on them, his gun still raised and steadily pointing in their direction.

"Geh bac, now. NOW!" Jon was angrily waving his gun, his nose gushing with blood. With his attention momentarily distracted away from the door, he did not notice a body swinging into the room at the end of a thick rope. Maddy and Rick, jaws agape, could not believe what they were seeing.

"Wat dat?"Jon stared at the moving apparition. Unnoticed, a second person hobbled through the door. That figure quickly tossed a burlap sack over Jon's head and kicked him behind the knees. The gun went off in the air, barely missing a still-swinging Rudy. With lightning speed, as Maddy had never seen Rick move, he ran forward, grabbing Jon by the wrist, and knocking the gun free. He then kicked the gun out of reach and tackled Jon to the shop floor.

"What the hell is going on here?" Maddy frantically shouted as she realized it was Rudy who was swinging back and forth, holding onto the rope for dear life. He seemed reluctant to let go, the rope was losing its momentum, and he was slowly sliding down. He tried to tighten his grip. Maddy tried to catch him but kept missing as he swung by out of reach.

"Police, put your hands up in the air!"

Maddy turned around, hands quickly going up, as did George's. Rick scrambled to his feet and reached for the sky too. Rudy, on the other hand, was not going to let go no matter what and continued to hang onto the rope, still swinging back and forth.

"Kyle, thank God, you finally made it! What took you so long? I was afraid you would never get here on time. He could have killed us all!" Maddy, relieved, lowered her arms as she saw his familiar face coming in behind an officer, who she recognized as one of the two constables who often worked on Kyle's team.

"Ma'am keep your hands UP!" Constable Sidhu shouted.

"Yes sir! I mean ma'am!" Her arms went immediately back up, no questions asked.

Kyle stood in the doorway looking at the scene before him; the dead body on the floor, a decapitated duck, Maddy, George, and Rick with their hands in the air, a person rolling on the floor with a burlap sack over their head, blood stains spreading rapidly through it, and Rudy, dangling by a rope. After he had taken in the sight before him, Kyle closed his eyes and momentarily shook his head.

"Maddy, what were you thinking, coming here on your own?" Kyle sighed.

"She wasn't alone, I came with her," Rick reminded him.

"Rick, you're not helping, my friend," Kyle replied.

"Umm..." PopPop interrupted, making a throaty sound as he swung by, hoping to get their attention.

The police realized the rope was attached to a sliding hook, and that Rudy was still swinging like a pendulum, in and out, through the door.

"Could someone please help me out?" he begged as he swung out of the room again.

"Would one of you constables please help this gentleman down from the rope, I don't think he can hang on much longer," Kyle said looking at Maddy's grandfather who was noticeably struggling. "And take that man into custody."

Pointing Constable Janvier toward Jon, Kyle added, "And make sure you read him his rights. I don't want him getting away over a formality!"

"The rest of you, come outside with me if you please."

OUTSIDE THE ABANDONED building, Kyle waited for the group to gather around him. Rudy was rubbing his sore, red hands. George was standing with his head bowed low, while Rick and Maddy stood quietly waiting.

"Guys, what happened here?" he gently asked.

Maddy, Rick, and Rudy began all at once to speak unintelligibly.

"Okay, okay, hold on!" Kyle held up his hands. "Please, one at a time! Maddy, you start."

"I received a text saying I had to come immediately to save Jennifer and the Spencer Duck. So, Rick and I jumped in my car and drove over here, as fast as we could. When we got here, we smashed out a window and climbed in," her words came rushing out all at once, for fear of missing anything. "Then Jon came in waving his gun and threatening us. Next thing you know the door opened, smacking Jon in the face. Then, PopPop swung through the room, like Tarzan of the Jungle, and George followed with the sack and tossed it over his head. Jon's head, not George's. Jon confessed everything to us! He was boasting about it all."

"Okay, thank you. And how did you two gentlemen end up here?" Kyle looked over at Rudy and George.

"I was talking with Maddy on the phone, and she told me what was happening," Rudy began. "Then George and I, we jumped in the car... Perhaps 'jumped' isn't the right word. We more like slowly climbed into the Ferrari, and came here to see how we could help, right George? Did I miss anything? George?"

Everyone looked around in surprise. George was no longer standing with them.

"Where'd he go?" Rudy asked, turning around, and searching for his friend.

"Oh, PopPop," Maddy said quietly, pointing toward George's car. He was sitting on the driver's side of the Ferrari, head bowed over the steering wheel, shoulders hunched, sobbing quietly.

A silence fell over the group as the adrenaline rush wore off and the gravity of the situation hit them.

"Oh, my friend!" Rudy said. "My dear, dear friend." He left the group and walked toward the car.

As they stood there, not knowing what to do, Constable Sidhu approached Kyle, to let him know that an ambulance had arrived but was waiting for the coroner to get there before they could take Jennifer's body away.

"We've called homicide sir; they should be here fairly quick" she reported to Kyle. "Do you need help getting statements?"

"No, I would rather they go down to the station to give their official statements. It's preferable than having them stand here with the deceased nearby." He looked at Maddy and Rick. "Can you two make sure George and Rudy get to the station or would you prefer that one of the constables here give them a ride?"

"No, it's alright, I'll drive them. Rick can follow in George's car."

"How are you two holding up?" he asked.

"I think I'm okay, but we're still in shock," Rick replied. "At least, I am. We need to process all of this."

"It's a bit surreal but I'll be fine," Maddy said. "I'm more worried about George."

"We'll have a social worker meet with him at the station," Kyle told her.

Constable Janvier, who had escorted Jon to the police car, gestured to Kyle to come over.

"Is there a problem?"

"Sir, the suspect is refusing to give me his name. He won't stop mumbling over and over the same thing. He's not making any sense whatsoever. We'll need to get psych to meet us at the station."

"Can you make out what he's saying?" Kyle asked.

"Something about an insane asylum and geriatric Home Alone lunatics."

Chapter 30

At the police station, Maddy finished writing her statement, signed it, initialed the bottom of the pages, and handed it to Detective Morin who was assisting Kyle in the investigation. Her emotions were raw; she was spent, both mentally and physically. The trip to the police station had been somber with George and Rudy barely uttering a word. Rick had followed them in George's car. Once at the station, he and Maddy had spoken in hushed voices, working through what had just happened to them. It was an odd feeling; Jennifer was now dead, for no other reason than Jennifer loving George more than Jon and Jon loving money more than Jennifer. They had not known her, but the senselessness of her death saddened them. Jon holding them at gunpoint had rattled them, and yet, two hours later, it seemed dreamlike, as if it had happened to other people. Everything had developed quickly, even though it had seemed like the events of the day had unfolded at a snail's pace. Had it not been for Rudy and George, things might have ended differently. But, they had not. For that, they were grateful.

While a social worker spoke with George, Maddy called Bradley. She asked him to come down to the station. He arrived surprisingly fast with the chauffeur in tow. The latter drove George and Rudy home in the Bentley while Bradley took care of the Ferrari. Rudy, not wanting to leave him alone after such a difficult loss, decided to spend a few more nights with his friend.

Tasha came right away once she found out what had happened. It had been hard to convince Mama Leila to stay behind but she relented. After all, someone had to stay with the twins. She and Rick had offered Maddy a ride but at that point, she had not yet given her statement and told them to go home to their girls.

She would Uber it home.

In the end, Kyle offered her a ride. He ignored her half-hearted protests.

"Maddy, my friend, you've had a helluva few weeks," Kyle said as he walked her to his car. "Do you want me to call Ashley? Maybe have her come over?"

"No, thank you. She texted me offering a ride, but I refused. I need time to process things by myself. I'm not in any danger now, right?"

"You're not. Are you sure about Ash?"

"Yes," she assured him. "Tell me, Kyle, is it weird not to feel anything after having seen a dead body?"

"What do you mean 'not feel anything'?

"Well, I feel somewhat detached. Like it all happened to someone else."

"Yeah, it's a way of coping." He stopped and opened his car door, helping her in and closing it behind her. He walked around the car and got in. "You know, Maddy, it's weird seeing dead people. It's also scary being held at gunpoint. I've experienced both more times than I'd like to have. You never get over it, but you learn to handle it. It's hard to explain."

"I guess if the person didn't mean anything to you, it's a bit different, right?

"Exactly, when it comes to dead people. But being held at gunpoint? It's rattling, then you push it away. You carry on. It's the only way I know how."

"The funny thing, Kyle, is that I was really, really scared back there, not for me, but for PopPop and Rick, and, in a way, George too. I wasn't worried about myself." Maddy looked down at her hands. "I knew that I was going to be okay. I also knew that you were on your way." She leaned over and gave him a light kiss on the cheek. "If I hadn't told you this before, I'm telling you now. I really appreciate your friendship."

"It looks like Ashley didn't take no for an answer," Kyle told Maddy, pointing towards her friend's car as it pulled into the parking lot.

Ashley didn't bother shutting the car door. She came running towards Maddy.

"I'm so so so sorry Mads. I feel terrible," she said, hugging Maddy.

"Why are you sorry?"

"It's my fault for bringing Jon into your life!"

"Ash, it wasn't your fault," Kyle said. "It was simply a coincidence."

"He was already deeply involved with Jennifer when you introduced him to me," Maddy added. "He would have inserted himself into my life one way or another to get the money."

"I can't help but feel responsible in some way."

"Well, you're not." Maddy hugged her back. "Since you're here, you might as well give me a ride home. You don't mind Kyle, do you?"

"Of course not," he replied. Kyle then turned to Ashley. "We will need you to come back. We have a few questions to ask since you know this guy."

"I will," Ashley replied.

"You know what, Maddy?" He asked while hugging her goodbye.

"What, Kyle?"

"I think you're going to be just fine."

"I think so too," Maddy said with a smile.

THE NEXT MORNING, SITTING on a plastic patio chair on her building's rooftop, Maddy slowly sipped her coffee, feeling the tension in her shoulder muscles begin to ease. She closed her eyes, letting the sun rays shine down on her face, as she reflected on how long it had been since she had time to do nothing but relax. She had survived another strange escapade. Her life certainly was not boring. She could do with boring right about now, though.

"Honk! Honk!"

Maddy opened her eyes to find the Canada Geese happily eating the food she had brought. She knew she did not need to constantly feed them; they should be more than capable of finding food for themselves now, but it made her feel all warm inside and somewhat helpful. Her condominium did not allow pets, and so these geese were the closest thing to one she could have. She wanted to have something or someone of her own to care for. The Canada Geese would have to fit the bill for now. It was a safer kind of relationship for her.

"Enjoying your treat?" she asked the gaggle. "I meant to bring you something yesterday, but I got caught up in a drama you wouldn't believe, even if I told you."

"Honk! Honk!"

"I appreciate your understanding," Maddy responded. "If I can teach you guys anything, it's to be very careful about getting involved in other people's business. I had no idea when I got into the buying and selling of storage units' contents that it would take me down this road. Imagine, Jon was trying to convince Jennifer to sell some of her art, but she didn't want to. That's when things began to get ugly. Very ugly and so, so sad."

Maddy took another sip of coffee and thought about what Kyle had told her on the phone this morning. Once Jon had arrived at the station, he appeared quite coherent. The detectives felt he was sane enough to question. She had found that difficult to believe. Kyle had also listened to Jon's taped confession. Once Jennifer was dead, Jon knew he had to get out fast but still did not have enough money. That was why he was trying to set up an exchange, at first with George, and then with Maddy. It was also why he took a chance and tried to sell one of the paintings to that art gallery. At that point, Jon realized that he had lost control of things.

"The whole situation is bad for everyone," Maddy continued telling the geese. "Poor George is just devastated. I'll get over it. I'm learning, let me tell you, that judging men is not one of my strong suits. My self-esteem is battered and bruised, and my feelings are a tad hurt. But George? George's the truly broken-hearted one. And to top it all off, PopPop told me the last Spencer Duck can't even be repaired. The bullet Jon shot in the air, the one I told you had barely missed my grandfather as he was swinging from a rope, well, it ricocheted off a metal paneled wall and hit the duck's decapitated head, totally pulverizing it to smithereens! There was nothing left to put together. That was one unlucky ducky, I tell you. Sorry, I didn't mean to offend you. It was fake. Okay, no, what I meant is, it wasn't a fake Spencer Duck, but a fake duckie. Not a live one like you cuties."

Maddy sat staring and cooing at the geese for a while longer before noticing that one of the goslings had a slight limp. She frowned and leaned closer to them. The geese looked at her curiously and continued to snack. The gosling was tottering around, trying to find a spot to slip in between the bigger geese so he could get food for himself. Eventually, he grew tired and gave up.

"You poor little thing. Don't you just hate it when people hog all the snacks?" She reached into the front pocket of her sweatshirt and pulled out a handful of cracked corn.

278

"Come here little guy, I have some just for you," She leaned forward in her chair, holding her hand out to him.

"Whoa! Whoa!" she yelled, as the family of geese noticed her outstretched arm and came charging toward her in excitement, honking madly. She jumped backward in her chair; it then flew out from underneath her. She quickly recovered and stumbled to her feet. They continued stampeding forward, wings flapping, necks outstretched, honking like their life depended on this handful of feed. She finally tossed the corn as far away from her as possible, sending the geese in another direction while she ran toward the fire escape.

"Dang gluttonous cobra chicken!"

Chapter 31

Over two weeks had passed since the kidnapping ordeal. Maddy had put off her daily chores and was now overdue to do her housecleaning. She did a light sweep, dusted countertops, and furniture, put her many dirty plates and glasses in the dishwasher, and then decided that she had done more than enough for the day. She had not spoken with Zane for a while. Curiosity over the puzzle was gnawing at her. Now that they had all the answers to the clues' questions, it was time to figure out the rest. She was in desperate need of a lifetime supply of something, anything.

Rather than phoning Zane, she picked up her phone to text him. Maddy wanted to make sure it was a good time to chat. She noticed her cell phone had been left on 'vibrate' and she had missed texts from Ashley and PopPop. She was finishing her reply to her grandfather when her cell dinged. It was a text from none other than Zane.

'Call me when you have time to chat puzzle - Z'

"Hi Zane," Maddy greeted. "Ready to figure this thing out?"

"I'm more than ready, but I wanted to be sure you were," Zane responded.

"Things have settled down. I need a distraction and the solution to this darn puzzle."

"That's a relief. You had me worried. I'm glad you're safe, Maddy. Now, let's distract you. I've been looking at the clues, but haven't gotten far," he said.

"Okay, so we have seven clues we answered, right?"

"That's correct. The answers we have come up with are Canada Post, West Edmonton Ice Palace, Endeavours Brewing, Tastawiyiniwak, Royal Albert Museum, O' Canada, and Sir Winston Churchill Square."

Maddy jotted down the answers on a piece of paper, listing them one below the other.

"The clue says that 'the answer will point the way to a year's supply', right?" she asked.

"Correct. I started with the obvious, that perhaps it might be an acronym, which gives us CWETROS and that makes no sense whatsoever," said Zane. "And I don't think it could be something about the latitude and longitude. There aren't enough letters to convert to numbers. These numbers would be 3, 23, 5, 20, 18, 15,19 which isn't enough for both."

"Hmm..." Maddy scratched her head with the end of her pencil, then reached for her laptop. "Let me throw those letters into Google followed by Edmonton," Maddy said. "Nope, nada. Even when I drop 'Edmonton', the search comes up empty."

"Okay, how about this? I need to run a couple of errands right now. Why don't we think about it some more and then meet at the coffee shop across from your place?" Zane suggested.

"Sure, I have a few hours before I meet Niko at Triple-A," Maddy agreed.

"Niko?"

"Yeah, Bob's son. From Bernards? He wants to look at a couple of large pieces of furniture I picked up this week at that auction in the west end," Maddy explained.

"Right, right. I'll see you in about half an hour, forty-five minutes, tops?" Zane asked.

"You betcha!"

MADDY ARRIVED AT THE coffee shop, laptop in hand, ready to finally unravel this mystery once, and for all. When Zane walked in, she was right in the middle of researching different methods for solving word clues and puzzles.

"My head hurts," she said, scribbling on a piece of paper and peering back at her laptop screen. "There has to be an easier way for cracking these things."

"On my way over, I got to thinking. I'm wondering if maybe we didn't quite solve all the clues right. The final one is 'the answer will point the way to a year's supply', that doesn't sound like it is overly complex to me. I mean, I would expect it to tell us outright."

"I suppose it's possible, but I was so sure of our answers,"

"Okay, well, let's take a look at them and see what we can come up with," Zane suggested.

"The Endeavours Brewing is pretty solid I think. Same with Tastawiyiniwak, O' Canada, and Sir Winston Churchill Square," Maddy said.

"I'm pretty confident in the Royal Alberta Museum as well," Zane added.

"So, we have Canada Post and West Edmonton Mall Ice Palace,"

"The clues were pretty solid for those though." Zane rested his chin on his right hand.

"But those are the two that make the least sense, at least as a combination of letters. C and W together is not likely," Maddy said.

"For the sake of argument, let's assume one is wrong, which one would it be?"

"W is less common than C, I think. We're left with C something 'ETROS'." Maddy searched on her laptop again. "Nothing obvious comes up, except it keeps trying to search for citrus. What if the answers are right but we got it just a wee bit wrong? Like, instead of Canada Post, it was 'post office' or 'mail depot', or something similar but different?"

"Oh my God!" Zane began to laugh.

"What?" Maddy, surprised, looked up from her laptop. "What is it?"

"What word does it look like if you change the C to a P for post office?" Zane asked. "P something 'ETROS'."

Maddy grabbed her pen and scratched down the letters. Her eyes widened.

"And it could be Ice Palace instead of West Edmonton Mall Ice Palace!" Maddy exclaimed with excitement. "A year's supply of... Pietro's?"

"I think it just might be!" Zane nodded, a wide smile spreading across his face.

"A year's supply of pizza," Maddy spoke in a hushed tone as though she were in the presence of something holy.

"Of Pietro's pizza to boot! Let's go and find out!" Zane drained his coffee in one shot and stood up. "I left a car-share auto outside. Hopefully, it's still there and I can drive us.

As they hurriedly drove toward their favorite pizza place, they talked excitedly about the possibility of eating pizza for the rest of the year.

"Do you think it would cover breakfast pizza?" Maddy asked.

"They carry breakfast pizza?"

Maddy looked at him and raised an eyebrow. "Isn't all pizza breakfast pizza?"

"Good point."

ZANE FOUND A PARKING spot not too far from Pietro's. Maddy could barely contain her giddiness. The moment Zane had the car in 'Park', she had her door open and was leaping out. While Maddy was wrenching open the door to the pizza place, Zane was taking his time to lock the car and walk over to the restaurant. When he finally stepped inside, Maddy was waiting impatiently for him.

"Hurry up! We did this together. You don't want me to cash it in without you, do you?"

"Cash what in?" he asked as he dug into his pocket and pulled out a piece of paper. "This here?" He waved it in front of her.

Maddy stared at him as she realized he had the paper with the answers in his hand.

"Oh, aren't you the funny one!"

They walked up to the counter and Zane asked the teenager at the till if they could speak to the manager.

"Pop!" the boy yelled over his shoulder while continuing to stare at them through bangs of dark, lank hair.

They stood there awkwardly, looking at the teen looking back at them with a bored look. After a minute, he reached into his pocket, pulled out a cell phone, and started scrolling. Maddy looked at Zane who shrugged his shoulders.

"Pop!" he yelled again without looking up from his phone. "There are people here who want to see you!"

An older man came lumbering around the corner, wiping his hands with a tomato sauce-stained rag.

"Whad'ya want, Dino? Why all the yelling?" he asked his son irritably.

The teenager lifted his chin and pointed at Maddy and Zane, eyes still on his phone.

"Hi!" Zane greeted him with a big smile and his hand outstretched.

The man ignored Zane's hand, instead, lifting his hands to show a handshake would not be forthcoming.

"How can I help you two?" he asked.

"We successfully completed the promotion you ran for a year's worth of free pizza."

"Huh? Whatcha talking about?"

"Don't you have a promotion with clues that spell out your place's name?"

He stared at Zane and Maddy for a long time before he realized what they were referring to.

"Are you talking about that thing about places in the city? The one that spells Pietro's?"

"That's the one!" Zane triumphantly produced the completed sheet.

The owner looked down at the sheet but did not reach for it.

"That was something a fancy PR company tried to sell us," he shook his head as he talked. "Didn't ever run with it. D'you know how much it would've cost us to give free pizza for a whole year? Plus, we would've had to pay those other places to use their names in the contest. Imagine the fees for that!" His belly shook from laughter. "We would have had to shut this place down. Hey Dino, remember that crazy puzzle contest they wanted us to run? These guys solved it!" He laughed even harder.

Dino ignored his father and kept tapping on his phone.

"What?" Maddy exclaimed. "But we worked so hard on it!"

The man shrugged and threw the rag to rest over his shoulder. "We never ran the promo; they showed it to us as an idea and we said no. How you ended up with a copy of this, I have no idea."

"No?" Maddy could not hide the disappointment from her face as she saw a long line of pizzas marching off into the sunset.

"Nope," he said. "Where'd you get that old thing from, anyway?"

"I found it in some stuff I bought," Zane said. "And we've been working on it for weeks."

"Sorry to hear that." He grabbed the rag off his shoulder, turned around, and walked away.

"You wanna order something?" the teen asked.

"I guess so." Maddy's expression was forlorn.

"Here, I'll get us one," Zane said. "We'll have a medium supreme please."

"With extra cheese?" Maddy asked.

"With extra cheese," Zane repeated.

He paid for the pizza, and they walked back to the car, feeling dejected.

"Where do you want to go and eat this pizza pie?" Zane asked.

"You paid for the pie; I'll cover the suds. Why don't you come over, I have some 'Once in Oaxaca' sours from Campio Brewing in the fridge."

"Oh, nice! I've been wanting to try it for a while now."

"We'll eat on the rooftop, that way you can meet my crazy family of Canada Geese."

"Did you say Canada Geese?"

MADDY TOOK A BITE OF pizza and let out a very loud, forlorn sigh.

"You look like you just found out your chocolate supply melted in the sun," Zane teased.

"No, you can always eat melted chocolate once it re-solidifies," Maddy said glumly.

"Don't be sad," Zane said. "All was not lost. We had fun solving the clues, didn't we?"

"Yeah," she sounded unconvinced.

"And we get to have some pizza," Zane continued.

"Uh-huh." She took another bite.

"And we have a new brewery to check out in St Albert," he continued, ticking off a finger as he itemized each positive thing. "And I learned a few pieces of trivia about the city..."

"Go on," Maddy reluctantly encouraged him.

"We exercised our brains; we spent time doing something fun with people... didn't your friends and grandfather help you?"

"Yeah, that was kinda fun," Maddy agreed.

"And I got to know you a little bit better so that's a bonus," he said. "Always good to know nice people in the business."

"Did you treat me to lunch because you felt sorry for me?" Maddy asked as she sipped her sour.

"Sorry for you? What do you mean? I feel sorry for both of us. Why else do I want to drown my sorrows with a slice of Supreme?"

"You're one funny guy, you know that, Zane? I like that. I'm glad we're becoming friends. The auction world can be cutthroat, it's good to know you've got someone on your side."

"Don't you go all sappy on me now, Mizz Maddy. Not sure I can manage this side of you," Zane teased. "Anyway, didn't you say you had a family of geese you wanted me to meet? Where are they?"

"I did! That's odd, they're gone. I knew they would eventually leave but they were here this morning." Maddy stood up to look around. "They left without even saying goodbye."

"Honk Honk."

"Hey Maddy, there's still one over there, behind the planter." Zane pointed out. "He looks injured."

"Oh no, they abandoned the little fellow." She walked toward him. "What do I do now? I can't keep him here; the board will want to get rid of him. Who knows what they might do to him!"

"Hey, don't worry," Zane said, coming to stand next to her. "I have a friend who works at a wild bird sanctuary. I'll call her and see what they can do to rescue this little gosling."

"You'd do that for me?"

"Sure, we're friends now, aren't we?" He winked. "But first, you must give this gosling a name."

"Oh, I already have."

"What is it?"

"Ryan, of course!"

ZANE'S FRIEND HAD COME right away to help rescue little Ryan. She promised he would be well taken care of at the sanctuary and that they could visit him anytime they wanted to. After saying a long goodbye to her feathered friend, Maddy thanked Zane again for lunch. He went home to work, while she went to meet with Niko.

Maddy jumped into Bugsy and headed to Triple-A. Niko was coming to pick up two Victorian end tables she had found in her latest storage auction purchase.

"Hey Maddy, how goes it?"

"Hey Rod, fancy meeting you here."

"Still the jokester, eh Maddy?" Rod had heard her pull into the storage parking lot and came out with Engelbert on a leash.

"Why's Bertie on a leash?"

"I felt sorry for the little guy, cooped up in his kennel on such a nice day. I figured that at least on a leash he was less likely to run and hump anyone's leg," he explained. "This gives me time to warn people to stay back."

"That makes sense," Maddy approved. "It's very thoughtful of you."

"I try to be a good cousin to Engelbert, you know?" He blushed. "Anyway, what ya up to today? I wasn't expecting you. There's no auction or anything."

"I sold two tables; the buyer is coming right over to pick them up."

"Well, let me help. I'll meet you at your locker with the larger trolley, eh?"

"Thanks, Rod, you're a real sweetie!"

Maddy walked over to her storage office and unlocked the roll-up door. She turned on the light and went to dust the tables to get them ready for Niko.

"You don't have to do that, Maddy," she heard Niko say from behind her.

"Hi there! That's no problem, I can't let you have them all dusty and whatnot."

"Nah, don't worry about it," he replied. "When I forwarded my dad the pictures, he said his new lady friend wanted to paint them pink."

"Pink? Paint them?" Maddy was taken aback. Bob had always been very particular about his antiques. She could not imagine him painting two Victorian pieces, let alone in pink. "Has your dad lost his mind somewhere in Hawaii?"

Niko laughed. "Ha! Not his mind, his heart. He fell for some lady there. A pretty flamboyant one I gathered from how he described her."

"He met someone and fell in love that quickly?" Maddy could not believe how easily love found everyone but her.

"He met her at Bingo on the Beach."

"Bingo on the Beach?" asked Rod who had arrived with the trolley and overheard the end part of their conversation. "Who's in Hawaii?"

"Niko's dad is," Maddy replied. "Rod, this is my friend Niko. He's part owner of Bernard's Antiques and Collectibles, downtown."

"Nice to meet ya, buddy." Rod waved in his direction as he maneuvered the trolley closer to the tables Maddy was standing by.

"Actually, my dad was in Hawaii," Niko corrected. "He and his lady friend came back late last night. He didn't fare well in the hot climate there. They're on their way here right now. Dad said that she was super excited and couldn't wait to see those tables. Go figure, he met someone as nuts about antiques as he is."

"Lucky man." Maddy laughed.

"And there they are! Hey Dad!" Niko said, looking around the side of Maddy's storage unit.

"Hi Niko," Bob replied as he entered the unit. "I'd like everyone to meet my new girlfriend..."

Rod's face turned sheet white, and he sat down on the trolley with a thud. Maddy turned away from the tables and looked at him, then looked toward the door to see what had turned talkative Rod into a sudden mute.

"Aunt Shirley?"

Did you love *Lucky Ducky*? Then you should read *Fowl Play*[1] by Carla Howatt and Monique MacDonald!

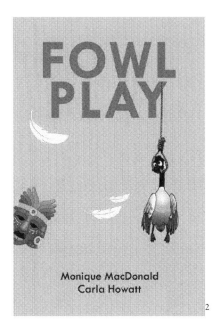

[2]

It's all fun and games until your goose gets cooked.

Maddy Whitman, the sharp-witted aficionado of the storage auction world, is on a rollercoaster ride through hilarious mishaps and heart-pounding twists in "Fowl Play". When she stumbles upon a peculiar Mexican mask in a storage unit she bought at an auction, she unwittingly sets off a chain of events that lead her straight into the heart of a gripping mystery. With danger lurking around every corner and a kidnapped woman's life on the line, Maddy must decode cryptic clues left by a cunning killer.

As tensions soar and the clock ticks, can she untangle the web of deception before it's too late? Packed with humor, suspense, and the irresistible charm of its female sleuth, "Fowl Play" is a must-read adventure that will leave you guessing until the very end.

Also by Monique MacDonald

Maddy Whitman Mystery
Fowl Play
Lucky Ducky

Also by Carla Howatt

Maddy Whitman Mystery
Fowl Play
Lucky Ducky

Standalone
For Crime's Sake
For Love's Sake
She: a cautionary tale
The Deception
Eve
Bearing Witness

Watch for more at
www.facebook.com/CarlaHowattAuthor

Manufactured by Amazon.ca
Bolton, ON

41595816R00180